JUST ENOUGH
LIGHT TO KILL

JUST ENOUGH LIGHT TO KILL

A.E. MAXWELL

Doubleday
NEW YORK LONDON TORONTO SYDNEY

DESIGNED BY PETER R. KRUZAN

Library of Congress Cataloging-in-Publication Data
Maxwell, Ann, 1944–
Just enough light to kill
I. Title
PS3563.A899J83   1988   813'.54   87-34333
ISBN 0-385-23713-8

BG

for

J

and for every other border agent
who has shoveled sand against the tide

JUST ENOUGH
LIGHT TO KILL

1

Everything started coming apart on Uncle Jake's birthday, or what would have been his birthday if somebody hadn't put two bullets through the back of his head with a .45-caliber Colt semiautomatic pistol. I don't draw black borders around his birthday on the calendar or anything like that; Jake lived and died pretty much the way he wanted to. But I do remember the day and the dirt road south of Puerto Peñasco because I was there on that dusty road with Jake. Actually, I was only about half-there. The other half was already headed for what my poor Montana mother—Jake's sister—used to call "a better place." The guy who shot Jake shot me first. I guess I looked like more of a threat since I was bigger and wasn't stoned. But if I was such a big threat, why didn't he waste a second round on me, the way he did on Jake?

Hell of a question to ask yourself when you're ass-deep in a hole the size of a grave.

I was half-done with the excavation for a new koi pond. The fish had grown too big for the old one. All eight of them had to swim in tight formation or their maneuverings looked like a watery version of Destruction Derby. Even when they managed the close-order drill, Lord Toranaga frayed his fins on the concrete. Every time I looked at him, I felt guilty. I should have been shoveling a lot sooner.

Digging the new pond had been put off all summer. The ground was too dry, too hard, I kept telling Fiora. No sense in using dynamite when the winter rains will do the job for you. When the rain finally came, it was too wet, of course, and I had to wait a week for the soil to dry out a bit. Then it would rain before I could start digging, so it was wait and dry out, and then the rain came again. You'd have thought I had Mother Nature on a retainer. All through December and January, the storms came through on a perfect seven-day cycle that kept my excuse fresh.

But finally, on Jake's birthday, the game lost its savor. Fiora was too busy trying to take over a local investment bank to notice what I was or wasn't digging. In fact, she was so busy she barely had time at dawn to remind me that my tux had been cleaned and pressed and would I please appear in it at 7 P.M. on Pacific Coast Highway in front of Savories Cafe. Then she kissed me in a half-assed, distracted way, patted my cheek and hopped out of bed before I could grab her.

When I woke again hours later, I was feeling surly as hell. I told myself it was a combination of Jake's day and having to wear a tux tonight. A brisk run along the beach didn't help to shake out my mental kinks. Neither did sitting on my butt. So I sharpened the spade, went up the little rise in back of the cottage and took out my frustrations on something inanimate.

An hour after I sliced out the first chunk of grass and clay, the raw wind off the water picked up, promising the arrival of another storm. The cold wind was what got me thinking about Jake and the border. The wind had been blowing that day, too. I had turned my shoulder against the stinging sand, only to realize an instant later that I'd made a mistake because I caught a glimpse of Refugio turning toward me with the .45 in his hand.

Oddly, I never heard the shot that hit me, although I did feel a hard blow on the back of my head. But I heard the two shots that were for Jake. In my mind I watched him move off slowly, disappearing into the bright light of the overhead sun, the wrong-century cowboy headed for the place he loved best, the shimmering, beckoning border between what has been and what will be. . . .

Jake always had loved crossing boundary lines. His favorite was the U.S.-Mexican border. I sometimes think he was a smuggler *because* he loved the border. It ran through his life like a black silk thread, stringing together all the bright possibilities from here to tomorrow. On this side of the border, everything is ordinary; on the other side is the Mexico of the soul—uncharted territory, blistering chili peppers and .45 slugs.

Why are they trying to kill us, Jake?

That was just one of the haunting questions that swirled around me like the cold February wind as I turned over spade after spade of dirt. I really should have remembered a few other things about the border when I switched to a round-edged shovel, looked up and saw the clouds scudding inland to pile up against the mountains like great white grave markers. I should have remembered, but I didn't. I plead guilty to oversight. After all, I thought I was just digging an ordinary hole in the ground.

Actually, Kwame Nkrumah and I were digging the hole together. Kwame is the princely black and tan Rhodesian Ridgeback that lives next door. Technically, Kwame belongs to Dr. J. Samuel Johnson, a black dentist who has one of the most lucrative orthodontics practices in Newport Beach. But Kwame is convinced that Joe Sam doesn't really understand or appreciate him. Kwame is right. Joe Sam hasn't a clue about real watchdogs, because he is one of the nicest people I've ever met. He hasn't a single enemy, despite the fact that he hurts people for a living.

I hurt people once in a while, too. It's just as unavoidable in my line of work as it is in Joe Sam's, only some of my patients try to hurt back. That's why Kwame hangs around with me. I don't shush him or tell him to go lie down when he starts making a spine-chilling noise deep in his chest and lifts the loose folds of his lips to reveal gleaming fangs. I also don't mind when Kwame just pals around with me, getting underfoot, watching everything I do as though it mattered. Let's face it; digging a grave-sized hole in a cold wind is a lonely way to pass the time.

As I dug, Kwame was in pal rather than guard dog mode. We were getting deeper into the little hill with each stroke of the shovel. About every third time I turned over a shovel load, Kwame would sniff, make a few passes with his toenails and watch intently. When nothing came out to play, he'd flop belly down on the fresh clay and wait for me to turn over something that wiggled. I'd look up from time to time to find him watching me with those clear, dark, calm eyes.

He had just finished his little ritual of scratch and flop when I became vaguely aware of a restless feeling. Kwame felt it, too. He got up, circled the bottom of the hole once and flopped back down. He was up again almost instantly. This time he went to the edge of the waist-deep hole and begged to be excused.

"Fine," I grunted. "Go home to your warm bed."

Kwame looked at me earnestly, then stretched up the side of the hole on his hind legs, and looked at me again.

The dirt was piled almost eye-high on that side, but he could have easily scrambled out any of the other sides, so I ignored him.

He whined very softly, deep in his throat.

Kwame's not the type to complain. I bent over and boosted him out. He could have made the welterweight class, with a pound or two to spare. He didn't pause to say thanks. He scrambled up the pile of dirt and stood stiff-legged. The hair on the back of his neck raised in a silent flag of warning. In case I had missed the message, he made the low, tectonic sound in his chest.

The hair on the back of my neck rose in reply. I slipped out of the hole in a single motion, but carefully stayed behind the pile of clay and stones that rose between me and whatever had lit Kwame's fuse.

At first it looked like just another day in paradise. The fifty turn-of-the-century cottages that made up Crystal Cove were as ramshackle and unthreatening as they had ever been. The open pastureland beyond was as calm and bucolic as ever. The whole scene presented a picture of rustic serenity that would have been hard to beat.

Kwame wasn't buying it. He growled again and held his ground, facing the highway. He was staring toward the turnout below an orange juice stand that had been built in 1931 and looked like it hadn't been painted since.

Easing around slightly, I got a look at what interested Kwame. One hundred fifty yards away, a blue car sat broadside to me. The car's nose was pointed down the coast toward Laguna.

There was something innocuous and nondescript about the car, as though it were a rental or part of somebody's corporate fleet. Beyond the fact that the driver sat alone in the front seat, I was too far away to see anything useful. The guy was probably just a tourist who had pulled over to watch the steel-gray Pacific on a choppy, windy winter day.

Except that this particular tourist seemed to be looking back up the coast toward Crystal Cove rather than out toward the restless ocean.

Even after a soft word from me, the African prince wouldn't budge. No longer growling, Kwame stood with his feet rooted in the clay, his neck ruff as spiked as a punker's Mohawk. I'm not one of those guys who asks for expert advice and then ignores it, so I eased back down into the hole and rolled out the other side, right into the cover of a bottlebrush hedge. Keeping the hedge between me and the highway, I duck-walked down the rise toward the cottage.

By sliding under the side porch, I managed to keep out of sight of the turnout until I could round the corner of the cottage and get in through the side door with a minimum of fuss. Fiora keeps a pair of Nikon zoom binoculars near the picture window, the better to count the oil tankers passing on the far side of Catalina Island. I grabbed the glasses and headed for the back bedroom, which faced the highway.

The curtains are always closed back there. I didn't want to disturb them; if the guy had been watching the house for any time at all, he would be waiting for just such a sign of life inside. That left only one way for me to get a clear view of the turnout. I went into the bathroom, lowered the toilet lid and stood on it to peer out through the narrow louvered window. The zoom lever on the binoculars was down at seven power. When I racked it up the scale, I almost fell backward into the sink. The increased magnification was so great I could damn near read the brand name on the hinge of the guy's binoculars.

He was looking right at me.

2

I don't know how long I stood there, with him staring through high-powered binoculars at my cottage and me staring back at him through the same. The primitive part of my brain—the part that raises neck hairs—kept suggesting that if I could see him so clearly, he sure as hell could see me. The sophisticated part of my brain knew that the shadowed interior of the cottage would shield me so long as I didn't do anything stupid, like wave.

The sophisticated part of my brain also calculated that one hundred thirty yards was an easy shot with a good rifle. I didn't have one handy, but I wasn't sure about him.

Finally the man in the blue car put down his glasses, fumbled in his lap and then lifted something to his ear. That told me he wasn't driving a rental, unless Hertz had started putting cellular phones in their midsize sedans. A few seconds later the phone in my living room rang. Somehow I wasn't surprised.

In the middle of the fourth ring, the Ansafone snapped on. I smiled and waited. I'm all in favor of answering machines. They relieve you of the guilt you inevitably feel when you're rude to some hapless commission salesman who's sitting in a boiler room in Costa Mesa, peddling Brazilian silver futures, generic five-point diamonds or the Los Angeles *Times*.

I listened to my recorded voice informing people that I wasn't available to come to the phone but if they had a message, they should wait for the beep and make it brief. The man in the car was listening too. I waited and watched through the glasses, fairly confident that we were hearing the same canned message. But fairly confident isn't good enough in an unfair world.

If you don't believe me, ask Uncle Jake.

When the beep came, I heard the faintly hollow sound you sometimes get from a cellular connection. Then I watched my visitor hang up. The clattering sound of his disconnect on the machine coincided exactly with what I saw through my glasses.

In my mind I ran through the angles and distances and elevations again. He might not have been able to see me up the hill and down in the hole. If he didn't see me, he must be wondering if anybody was home. Prowlers are a cautious lot. They like the extra protection of a last-minute phone call, just to make sure no one's around. No answer, no sweat.

I counted off the time he would need: thirty seconds to pull down into the Crystal Cove parking lot, ninety seconds to stroll nonchalantly up to the front door of my cottage, another few seconds for a precautionary knock, just to make sure that I didn't work nights and sleep days. Then, when he was sure he was alone, he'd go to work on the doorknob lock.

It would be Channellock pliers if he was a burglar and lock picks if he was something else. I was betting on the picks.

The phone rang again.

I lifted the glasses and looked. He was still there, but this time he didn't have a cellular phone in his hand.

After four rings the message came on again, then the beep and Fiora's voice.

"Fiddler?"

There was an uneasy, unhappy edge to Fiora's voice, the sort of unspoken message that usually brings me to the phone instantly. But this time I wasn't going to answer. Fiora disapproves of the parts of my life style that result in strangers watching my house with high-powered binoculars.

"Damn it, Fiddler. Answer me."

My former wife knows my habits pretty well. She's one of two people who can tell when I'm fronting the machine. The Ice Cream King is the other.

"All right, if that's the way you want it," she said in a bleak tone of voice, the one intended to make me feel like an unusually large outhouse rat. "I'm on the freeway, just heading down to deal with this Pacific Basin Fund mess."

She was referring to the $50 million investment bank in Newport Beach that she was hell-bent on acquiring, the one that had put her into full money-shuffling mode, keeping her so preoccupied she left a perfectly accommodating warm bed at dawn and didn't even notice that the koi pond game had ended.

"I just heard on the radio that Aaron Sharp has been killed. Not that he has died. That he has been *killed.*"

The interrupt button on the answering machine almost broke under my thumb. I snatched up the phone.

"I'm here."

"I thought so. I'm sorry to bring bad news."

"What happened?"

"Sharp was killed near Jacumba. Is that in Mexico?"

"Might as well be, but technically it's fifteen feet on this side of the line. Anything else?"

"It happened last night during a, quote, routine encounter with alien smugglers, unquote, according to the radio report."

"If Sharp died, it was hardly routine." I swallowed, trying to get rid of the bad taste in the back of my throat, and said under my breath, "Happy birthday, Jake, wherever you are."

"What?"

"Jake finally has somebody to chase him around whatever place it is people like he and Sharp end up. They'll have as much fun as they used to in Calexico."

I was speaking very softly because I still didn't know if I would have a sneak visit from the guy in the blue car, but Fiora heard me anyway. I knew how she was feeling right now. Ambivalent. Sharp had saved her life, and mine. She had been duly grateful, but she hadn't liked him much.

She hadn't cared a lot for Jake, either, for about the same reasons. Fiora would have turned the world inside out in order to make me feel better after Jake died, but that's where her mourning ended. She hasn't been particularly grateful to his memory either, even though Jake's ill-gotten gains financed her entry into the international fraternity of money shufflers.

I didn't hold Fiora's ambivalence against her. I felt the same way about her dead twin brother, Danny. I would have done anything to spare Fiora the pain of Danny's death; but I didn't mourn him. He had been as self-centered, greedy and shortsighted as a child. Even worse, he had turned his sister's love for him into a weapon that he used against her. I could forgive Danny a lot, but not that.

"Sharp took too much pleasure in killing that Russian," Fiora said finally.

"It was pure professional pride," I said, "like what an oncologist feels after successful surgery."

"Wonderful. May Sharp and Korchnoi and Jake chase one another all over hell with dull scalpels."

Epitaph for men Fiora hadn't liked very well. But then, she was almost certainly thinking of someone else. Poor Danny, just smart enough to know that he would never be in Fiora's league and just dumb enough to think that he could pull off one spectacular coup to show the world how badly it had underestimated him. But it hadn't. Danny ended up the way all dumb bunnies do. Prematurely dead.

A scratching at the side door saved me from having to say anything at all about hunting and dumb bunnies, death and Danny Flynn. The timing was about right for the man in the blue car, but the sound was wrong for lock picks—not metallic enough.

"I've got to go," I said very softly. "There's somebody at the door."

"What's wrong?"

"Nothing."

"Damn it, Fiddler! What's wrong?"

The woman knows me far too well. And what she doesn't know, she sometimes senses in her dreams.

"I'll see you at seven," I said, and hung up.

It was Kwame at the door. He had undergone another personality change. He looked at me hopefully, wriggling all over with goodwill. When he saw that he wasn't going to be let in, he walked away and flopped along the deck, where he could watch the turnout up on Pacific Coast Highway from time to time. But his ruff had calmed down and he was breathing slowly, like a steam locomotive at idle.

I knew before I looked around the corner that the blue car had gone. I crossed the lawn and looked down into the hollow at the parking lot. It was deserted, too. I shook my own ruff back into place and told myself it probably had been some real estate salesman looking for prospective beachfront listings.

Uh-huh. If I kept wishful thinking along those lines, I, too, could end up like Danny and Korchnoi and Sharp, prematurely dead.

After a little aimless pacing, I settled in a kitchen chair and looked out over the water, wondering who had finally sent Aaron Sharp to his maker. It couldn't have been an easy thing to do. Sharp had been the son of dust bowl Okies, an Imperial Valley U.S. Customs agent, and one of the most clever, ruthless men I've ever met. Long before Sharp screwed a gun in my ear, I knew him by reputation, thanks to Uncle Jake's double-edged compliments.

Jake was one of the more daring and inventive smugglers in several decades, but Sharp had managed to catch him dirty, as the saying goes. One night the border cop busted Jake on the north bank of the All-American Canal. Jake was driving an old Buick, its boxcar-sized trunk crammed full of kilo bricks of mota. High-grade marijuana. The bust went down a few yards inside the United States, but Sharp was no lawyer and he didn't give a damn about surveyor's stakes. He shoved Jake back across the line and proceeded to "interrogate" him in the Mexican style. No really rough stuff, just leather gloves, but Sharp knew how to make them pop.

There was nothing personal in the beating Jake received. Sharp just wanted what every cop wants, information. Jake's connection, to be specific. But Jake had an unusually high pain threshold, and Sharp got arm-tired before he finally admitted that you could beat Jake to death but you wouldn't get enough information out of him in the process to pay for the casket. Once that fact was established, everybody got along as well as could be expected under the circumstances. Jake did his ninety days, kept his mouth shut and held no particular grudges. As for Sharp, I think he got a kick out of Jake. Sharp used informants —they were his stock-in-trade—but he liked stand-up dudes better, and Jake was a stand-up dude.

I continued to hear stories about Sharp for years after Jake died. They were smuggler's tales, told and retold until they became part of border legend. But I never had the dubious pleasure of meeting Sharp until he prowled into Fiora's life on the trail of her useless twin brother, Danny. Sharp suspected—rightly, as it turned out—that Danny was a smuggler, but there was an uncomfortable little wrinkle to the case. Danny wasn't smuggling dope north to the United States; he was smuggling an integrated-circuit factory south to Mexico, and from there to the Soviet Union. Actually, Danny had been no more than a shill. The real genius behind the scam was a charming Russian chimera who used the name Volker.

It's doubtful that was his real name. His true name was probably Ivan or Vlad or Boris. By whatever name, Volker was fascinating. I've never met a man with a more magical smile. It shone equally on everyone, like the sun, except that the sun can't turn itself on and off at will. What the smile didn't accomplish, the voice did. He should have been on the stage. He was as clever, low-key and inviting as a good corporate ad. He managed to subvert Danny, seduce Fiora, and even get behind the wheel of the Cobra with my permission. Now, that's charm.

Volker killed Danny, kidnapped Fiora, smashed both my hands in a packing crate and told a KGB colonel named Korchnoi to execute Fiora and me with a twelve-gauge shotgun. Korchnoi was drawing his bead when Aaron Sharp dropped the Russian in his scuffed shoes, and I tried my best to gut Volker with a hideout knife.

Sharp's aim had been better than mine. He put two neat holes through the front of Korchnoi's head. Also through the back, only not so neat. I managed to cut Volker somewhere high on the inside of his arm. Despite the wound, he slipped away and vanished into the night, running fast and quiet, drawing on the kind of reserves of stamina and will that you wish only the guys on your side had. Sharp tracked Volker through the chaparral for about a mile. He said the Russian must have been at least a quart low before the blood trail disappeared.

Nobody I know of has heard anything about Volker since that night, unless maybe it's Innes, the gray eminence from the FBI who had been hanging around the edges of the action like a vulture at Lourdes. But if Innes has some information, God is the only one with a security clearance high enough to hear it.

So on damp, cold, windy days like this, when my hands ache like somebody's driving ice picks through them, I wonder how Volker's wound responds to the Moscow winters. Or did they send him to Siberia? I'm not a vindictive man by nature, but I hope Volker hurts until the day he dies. Maybe pain would dim the lethal brilliance of his charm.

To no one's surprise, Sharp came out of that mess without a scratch. He was one of those fabulous coldhearted technicians who becomes a legend in the major leagues of cops and robbers—a shooter who never misses and never gets shot. That was why I wondered whether Fiora had heard the radio right. Sharp might kill routinely, but he didn't die.

The legs of the kitchen chair returned to the floor with a thump. I made a cup of coffee in the heavy china mug I use as a hand warmer on days like this and sat down in the living room near the phone. Sharp and I hadn't been close friends, but we had been close just the same, the way Volker and I had been close . . . an uneasy awareness of the other person as a reflection of the possibilities of your own soul.

That thought was a good deal less comforting than the warm china mug, but I reached for the phone anyway. Whether I loved Sharp, hated him or felt nothing at all, I owed him. I punched in the number of the Customs office at the port of entry in Calexico. When a Latina with a thick accent answered, I asked for Dana Lighter. He had been Sharp's partner. He would know what had happened if anyone did.

"He is not here," the Latina said, drawing the vowels out and softening them. "He has gone south."

"Is he working?"

"Oh yes," she said, turning the *y* into a *j*. "Everyone is working very hard right now."

I got a mental image of every Customs special agent on the western border twisting every informant he had ever had or ever hoped to have, trying to turn up some sign of the smuggler who had shown the bad judgment to kill a gringo cop. The term "kicking ass and taking names" was invented on the border.

"Is there anybody around who can fill me in on what happened to Aaron Sharp?"

"Are you a member of the media?"

A paper rattled, telling me that she was probably looking at a press release with the barest facts of Sharp's death. I didn't need that. I needed to know what the cops were telling each other.

"No, I may have some information on Sharp's death."

"Hold on, please."

A second later someone else picked up the line.

"This is Special Agent Suarez." There was no accent, just a faint softness to his voice, like a tenor choirboy. "May I help you with something?"

Muy formal, all business and no friendly chitchat.

"My name's Frantz. I've spent the last half hour trying to get some information on the Sharp killing." I purposely let it sound like I was holding Suarez himself responsible for the inconvenience.

"Uh, what agency did you say you were with?"

Cops are such inbred folks. If you ain't one of them, you ain't shit. If you are, everything is roses.

"LAPD, ad narc," I lied. Chances were slim that Suarez would gamble the cost of a long-distance call to check me out.

"You got a phone number where I can call you back?"

Once in a while you get a bureaucrat.

"Oh, for chrissake . . ." I muttered. "Yeah, it's 555-6651."

Five-five-five was the right prefix, and I figured Suarez was no more likely to know the extension in the Administrative Narcotics squad office than I was.

"That's area code 213," I added, like a city cop needling a country cousin.

"No shit," Suarez retorted. "What did you need?"

"I don't believe what I heard on the radio. Tell me how it really went down."

"You knew Aaron?"

"Well enough to know that if he'd been that easy to kill, he'd have been dead long ago."

"Ain't it the truth," Suarez said. "But what you see is what you get, until somebody comes up with a better story. Aaron and Lighter were out by Jacumba, sitting on a load of weed just the other side of the line. Snitch had told them it was supposed to come across about two in the morning. Sometime after midnight, here comes a bunch of illegals—about twenty, according to Dana. He and Aaron were just going to let them go on by. What the hell's another twenty Mexicans in California, right? Besides, Aaron was after dope, not Mexicans. Then somehow it all went from sugar to shit. Dana's still not sure what happened, but suddenly Aaron is taking the illegals down, and the next thing Dana knows, one of the wets opens up with a goddam piece. Three rounds, real fast, *bang-bang-bang.* Aaron caught two of them in the face."

"Two out of three in the dark. Hell of a shot, for a Mexican," I said, giving Suarez a hard time the way cops do with one another.

"Chinga tu madre, pendejo."

It was said without vigor, so I took it the same way. Besides, my mother was dead.

"The group split back across the line right away," Suarez continued, switching to English. "Dana tried to chase the shooter, but I guess he's getting old. Or cautious. Anyway, the Mexicans got south of the line before he could stop them."

"All of them?"

"Every last one," Suarez said in disgust.

"Why would illegals shoot their way out? Used to be that you guys would give them a free plate of beans and a ride back to the border."

"Jesus, man, you think cheap labor is the only thing crossing the line?" he demanded. "Whoever killed Aaron might have been muling coke or smack. He might have had a felony warrant outstanding on this side of the line, or he might have been some terrorist shit-listed by everybody from Interpol to the CIA." Suarez made a disgusted sound and then conceded, "Aw hell, he might even have been some poor scared indio hill boy that thought Aaron was a border bandit going to kill him and rape his woman."

"What kind of gun?"

"Nine-millimeter semiautomatic."

"Some poor indio," I muttered.

"Yeah," grunted Suarez. "A nine mike-mike is more a traficante's weapon than a poor hill boy's, or even an alien smuggler's. In the end it didn't matter. Bullets are bullets and Aaron was shit out of luck. Dana said there was enough light to see that no one was packing weed, so it looks like they were just camped on the wrong group. Wrong time, wrong place, wrong all the way. You know how it goes."

"Yeah. Sometimes you can't win for losing."

Suarez mumbled something in Spanish that could have been a prayer or a curse, then he sighed. "Everybody else is south of the line right now, trying to turn up something more useful than cockroaches. Border Patrol is working on it, too. Alien smuggling is their thing, not ours. Maybe they know a *coyote* who favors nine mike-mikes."

I could hear a wooden chair creak, as though Suarez had leaned back into it. Then came the crinkle of paper, the metallic click of a Zippo and the muted sound of a deep exhalation.

"Sharp ever get around to quitting cigarettes?" I asked.

There was a low chuckle. "Nope. Always said he wouldn't die of lung cancer."

"He was right."

"Funeral is Saturday," Suarez said, taking another long drag on the cigarette.

"Thanks." I started to hang up.

"Wait a minute! Linda told me you had some information."

"I was wrong."

Very gently I replaced the receiver and went back to staring at the slate-gray sea.

3

The U.S.-Mexican border exists only on paper. You can't point to a black line running through the rust-colored rocks along the Tecate Divide and say, *There it is. That's the line that divides us from them.* Except for about three miles of chewed-up chain link along the banks of the Tijuana River, the boundary isn't even fenced.

Not that it matters. Borders aren't made by fences. They happen in the mind. National borders are every bit as intangible as the line between good and evil, right and wrong, truth and lie. That doesn't mean borders aren't real. They exist, just as those other lines exist. Borders run through everything, even though they are sometimes as invisible as the fault lines beneath California's restless ground.

Like any good border cop, Sharp had operated on both sides of the line . . . of all the lines. He got away with it for years because he always knew exactly where any given border was at any given moment, especially when he was on the side of the line where his U.S. Customs badge meant about as much as a handful of warm spit. When it came to survival, Sharp was as shrewd a son of a bitch as I've ever met.

So how did he get his head blown off by some northbound homeboy with a nine-millimeter pistol in his jeans?

The ocean frothed and churned in shades of gray, waves going nowhere, always breaking against the same shore. Like my thoughts. I let a few more waves come and go, but nothing new surfaced. Maybe I'd think better at the bottom of a hole with a spade in my hand. At least I wouldn't feel so damned useless.

I clamped down on my own restlessness, knowing that it wasn't just Sharp's death that was sending prickles of unease down my back. It had been too long since I had done much more than breathe in and out and watch waves break. Most of the time I didn't mind, because Fiora was sleeping beside me again. It had taken her months to get over finding me shot up in Napa Valley. I was afraid if I got involved in something violent now, I'd be sleeping alone again. I didn't want that. I've been with Fiora and I've been without her, and with her is much better.

On the other hand, a man can only sit and watch so many waves come apart. I didn't know what my limit was. I did suspect that I was reaching it.

A few minutes down in the hole told me that I had surpassed my sitting limit. I couldn't get my shoulders loose, much less my legs. The winter sun had lost what little warmth it possessed. The wind had teeth. The more I dug, the stiffer and colder I got.

Kwame felt the same way. He hung around, but he wouldn't get down in the hole with me. He seemed uncomfortable unless he was on top of the pile, right where I was trying to throw the new dirt. No matter how often I suggested that he move his lazy ass out of the way, Kwame always doubled right back to the high ground. There he would stand guard with the patience of the trained predator he was.

After a while Kwame succeeded in making me jumpy. I gave the shovel half an hour more and then quit, no longer caring whether it rained in the hole or not. The koi had survived this long without an Olympic pool; they'd make it until summer if it came to that.

I went back to the house and took a long, hot shower. That got rid of the clay under my fingernails but did little for the stiffness in my neck, a physical reflection of my tension. I felt like I was right on the edge of a cliff and backed into a corner at the same time. But I still wasn't paying enough attention to my primitive instincts. I blamed my mood on Sharp's death, the real estate broker's visit and the charity soiree that was awaiting me as soon as I made myself respectable.

Frankly, I'd rather dig graves.

Soirees are not my thing. Neither are fetes, galas, plain old fundraisers, you name it. Everybody likes friends, good food, decent wine and exhilarating music, but a benefit concert sponsored by the Newport Shores Yacht Club offers none of the above. Normally Fiora is of pretty much the same opinion, but two key members of the board of Pacific Basin Fund were also members of the Newport Shores Yacht Club, so Fiora regarded the ten grand she had paid for two front-row, center seats as an investment in goodwill during her takeover bid.

Newport Shores is the oldest and most prestigious of the half dozen yacht clubs on Lower Newport Bay. It was founded in 1947, about two centuries after the oldest and most prestigious yacht clubs on the East Coast, so Newport Shores needed a lot of stuffiness to make up for its parvenu status. The members try very hard to be socially correct. As a result, there are some epic tight-asses in the club who have been given highly visible posts. It's the halo effect at work: being close to these just-so folks is supposed to make the rest of us feel better about our grubby selves.

Most of this local royalty consists of New Age remittance men and women, second and third sons and daughters of Eastern Establishment families with fat trust funds and little ambition. These well-schooled swells do what they can to keep the socialite tradition alive in the Western hinterlands with deb balls and costume benefits and other fancy fun and games. But the remittance men and women are little more than Gold Coast figureheads. The real work is done by a cadre of women who have the time and the inclination to carry off the pose. They are mostly the wives of success, the women who married the class president in high school and then supported him by working as a secretary while he got an advanced degree and started some business that nobody had ever heard of but had a product that turned out to be just what everyone had needed.

A lot of women in that position find themselves on the short end of a major divorce settlement when hubby becomes a multimillionaire. The lucky women get to hand in their steno books and become club wives who devise ways to spend their money and their newfound leisure planning for and participating in parties of all names and purposes. And if taking up the burden of noblesse oblige leaves the women too busy to fly to France for seasonal fashion shows, the wives simply pick out their Paris originals at Amen Wardy in Fashion Island or Yves Saint Laurent in South Coast Plaza. That saves enough time for the women to practice the openmouthed, vivacious laughs cherished by local society page photo editors.

Unfortunately, husbands of these club wives have neither the proper socialite impulses nor the time to cultivate them. Most of the men who show up at these Gold Coast benefit concerts stand around drinking too much white wine or too many vodka martinis, double, and wishing the London Philharmonia would play a tune they recognized.

It's not that the men are total dunces. They aren't. I know some of them very well. At work they may be cutthroat trial attorneys, incredibly innovative software engineers or high-voltage land developer types. They may own the biggest Mercedes dealership in five states or 57 percent of an OTC-traded company that manufactures motor homes or heart valves. Individually, their balance sheets might make the New Age remittance types look like Horatio Alger before lightning struck.

Unfortunately, these dedicated entrepreneurs still haven't learned how to look comfortable in a tuxedo, even when the tux is tailor-made. Their discomfort ruins my evening. But there was no help for it. I had promised Fiora.

It was almost seven when I apologized to the Cobra, pulled the TII out of the garage and locked the door behind me. The TII is the go-fast version of the boxy little BMW 2002 coupe that defined the term "sports sedan" in the early 1970s. The major difference between the 2002 and the TII is a mechanical fuel-injection system that punched the TII's horsepower from 105 to 135. It ain't a Turbo Carrera, which is the entire point. The TII is a straightforward, decently aged two-person car that gets around with a minimum of fuss and a maximum of efficiency.

Fiora bought this one for me last Christmas—with technical advice from the Ice Cream King—after I finally bowed to the realization that the Cobra had become too much of a good thing for everyday use. By definition of the California Department of Motor Vehicles, a 1966 Shelby Cobra is a piece of genuine automotive history. As such, it became just too tempting a target for every custom-car thief on the West Coast. Parking the Cobra on the street these days is like leaving your beautiful, slightly ditzy girlfriend alone in a singles bar. She doesn't know the difference between one driver and another; she'll go off with anybody who can get her started.

The TII is a decent compromise. It's spritely enough to keep you awake, but it's not so hot that every kid with a lock puller is going to take a cut at it. I've even let the dark purple Malaga finish oxidize a bit. It's called urban camouflage. The only problem the TII gives me is finding the high-octane leaded fuel the car needs to operate efficiently. Aviation gas works fine, although I get some funny looks when I pull in behind a Cessna 406 to fill up.

As I closed the padlock on the garage door, Kwame came ambling over to say good-bye. I rumpled his ears and told him to watch the place. He gave me a wave of his stumpy tail. There was no trace of his earlier skittishness. I wish I could say the same for me. I had debated a full ten seconds before I had opened the drawer, pulled the Detonics and its holster out, and put them on.

For a concert yet. That was an all-time high in paranoia for me.

Fiora had taken her party clothes with her that morning and had changed God knows where. She was standing on the sidewalk in front of Savories, looking faintly distracted and stopping traffic with her black velvet, diamonds, black mink and honey-blonde hair. I pulled up and tapped the horn in a special three-beat sequence.

The sound seemed to startle her, as though she had been a long way away in her mind. There were faint lines between her eyebrows and around her full mouth. I didn't have to touch her to know that beneath that polished feminine surface there was a dynamo running full bore, RPMs pushing right up into the red zone. She must have had a hell of a day.

I leaned over and popped open the door.

"Hey, sugar-pie," I called out, giving Fiora's legs an overdone but appreciative leer. "Unless you're a vice cop, you've just rented that lovely ass for the night."

Fiora looked surprised, then she walked across the sidewalk toward me, flicking her hips like a streetwalker.

"Sure you can afford me, honey? A night with me can be pretty expensive."

It was meant to be a joke, but something in Fiora's smile broke my heart. The closer she got, the better I could see her eyes. They were almost pure green, no gold or amber left at all. Whatever was eating on her was deep and very, very real, even if it was no more tangible than national borders or last night's bad dream.

"You can bill me later," I said, drawing Fiora into the car and into my arms.

The kiss she gave me was hard and hot and humming. After five seconds, so was I.

"To hell with the Center for the Performing Arts. Let's go home and make out," I said, biting her neck with just enough force to make her purr.

"Don't tempt me." She turned slowly against me, letting me feel the softness of her breasts.

"Okay. I'll let you tempt me. Where's the zipper on this damn thing?"

"We're in a 'No Parking' zone."

"Good. Parking wasn't what I had in mind." I found the zipper.

"Fiddler," she yelped, grabbing my hand. "I'll get arrested for indecent exposure!"

"Not a chance. Nothing you expose could be considered indecent."

Fiora went very still and looked at me intently. "Are you trying to tell me something?"

"Nothing new. I love you."

Sometimes when Fiora smiles, she can light up a room. It was like that now. She kissed me gently.

"You're good for me," she whispered.

After a few more moments I reluctantly returned the zipper to its upright and on-guard position.

"Home?" I asked.

Fiora hesitated for at least a three-beat pause. She doesn't usually take that long to make up her mind about anything. Her eyes were closed and she had a taut, pale look to her, as though she were trying to add columns of numbers that kept turning into smoke before she could reach the bottom line. That's the dream she often has when she senses a business deal going sideways on her.

I understand when she has that kind of dream. From time to time I still dream I'm playing the violin, but no matter how hard I try, none of the notes turn out right. Frustration dreams, echoes of daylight obstructions of the kind that led me to throw my violin beneath the wheels of a passing Corvette before I was old enough to understand that something could be very good without being perfect.

I hoped that a frustration dream was the only kind Fiora was having. Not the other kind. Waking dreams of the sort that had told her Jake was dead and I was shot before I knew it myself, dreams of a dying Danny before his blood had been spilled, the worst kind of bad dreams. When it comes to people she loves, Fiora is cursed with the ability to sense what's over the horizon. Not names and dates, times and places. Nothing that helpful. Just a gut awareness of danger creeping closer and closer to someone you love. You live with a scream wedged in your throat; but screaming doesn't help, and anyway, no sound comes.

Dreams like that can drive you crazy.

"Center for the Performing Arts," Fiora said finally, speaking quickly, rushing her words as though to make any choice was better than to dangle voiceless between choices for one second longer.

4

It was just as well that the worst of the rush-hour traffic had already passed. I was driving on autopilot, my instincts nudging me right along with the Detonics in the small of my back. It was irritating. I told myself that I was overreacting to Sharp's death, Fiora's sad smile, my own restlessness and the damned soiree waiting at the end of the ride. That didn't work, so I tried to drive out from under the cloud by turning onto MacArthur and ripping through the lower gears. It wasn't the Cobra, but the TII had enough acceleration to snap your head back.

"You want to talk about it?" Fiora asked.

I shot her a look. "I was about to ask you the same thing."

There was silence for a few moments while Fiora glanced over at Newport Center, which is a high-rise enclave on the knoll overlooking Balboa Island. According to Fiora and the late Teddy Portman, in those dozen buildings are housed the fast-growing financial institutions that will someday displace the East Coast as the money-shuffling center of the universe.

"It's that damned place," she said, nodding toward the thirty-story smoked-glass tower that housed the offices of Pacific Basin Fund. "I'm beginning to wonder if I should go through with this deal."

"I thought you were in love with PBF's balance sheets."

"Oh, the balance sheets still look good. Teddy knew precisely what he was doing, and he had the brass balls to back up his intellect. But since his death, everybody else in the organization has developed Alzheimer's disease. Dickie-bird almost molted this afternoon, right there in the boardroom, when I asked him a couple of simple questions about where he thought the fund should be heading in the near and long term."

Dickie-bird was Richard Toye, the heir apparent of PBF. Fiora had little use for him. But then, she had little use for anyone who lacked the courage of his convictions.

"Don't be too hard on Poor Richard," I suggested. "He's just a Yuppie stock trader. Besides, you intimidate lots of guys when you start in on your version of a 'couple of simple questions.' You get all alive and alert, your eyes get intense, your mind kicks in the afterburner, and lots of guys feel their scrotums start to shrivel."

"I'm not sure Dickie-bird has a scrotum," she muttered. Then she sighed and ran her fingers through her hair in a distracted sort of way. As she had one of those tousled shoulder-length hairdos to begin with, her fingers didn't leave much impression. "Dammit, Richard's been to business school since women got the vote. An intelligent female shouldn't intimidate him."

"It has nothing to do with a man's age or experience. It has only to do with the poor devil's faith in his own scrotum."

"For God's sake, he's the heir apparent! He'll probably be president, no matter how hard I fight. Mrs. Portman intends to vote Teddy's stock in Richard's behalf." Fiora shrugged. "I'll probably vote for him myself. He knows it, too. And that's what irritates me about his dumb show this afternoon. I was only asking where Pacific Basin Fund was in the five-year plan that Teddy laid out two years ago. I wasn't on the board back then, but I know the plan exists. Teddy told me about it, and it made a lot of sense, much more sense than this codswallop Dickie-bird is dishing out right now."

"Codswallop?" I asked, laughing.

Fiora gave me a smile and an up-from-under look that made me wish we were headed home.

"Like it? After I said 'bullshit' to Richard for the tenth time in as many minutes, I decided we needed a new communications vocabulary. 'Codswallop' is now defined as 'safe ventures.' You know, the kind that do most of their work on captive projects."

I searched my memory for the other conversations we had had about the Pacific Basin Fund. Most of the time I just look interested when Fiora comes home full of her day's work. I nod my head and make appropriate noises until she runs down, but little of it sticks in my brain. Lately, though, I'd been making a real effort to understand what the hell Fiora finds so fascinating about her work. That means I have to do more than keep my eyes open while she talks.

After a moment of ransacking the memory banks, I had what Benny would call a "hit." I remembered that "captive projects" was the term for work funded by government research grants or some other low-risk, low-gain venture. That memory brought a lot of others in its wake, tangled sheets and the flow of moonlight on Fiora's bare skin as she amply rewarded me for my attentiveness on the subject of money shuffling.

"Sometimes I think TRW and Watkins-Johnson Electronics are Richard's idea of entrepreneurial ventures," she continued.

"Aren't they?" I asked, dragging my mind back to the present.

"Hardly. They're locked onto the government tit but good. Both companies draw ninety percent of their profits from fat DOD contracts. Star Wars and the like."

"What's wrong with that? Even under hostile political administrations, defense contracts have less downside risk than AT&T."

"You really *were* listening that night, weren't you?" Fiora said, giving me a startled, approving look. "Well, projects like Star Wars are all right up to a point, but their profit margin is rigidly controlled. They're like a damned public utility. There's little risk of striking out, but there's also no chance of hitting a home run."

I nodded, understanding all that Fiora didn't say. It was the chance of a home run that made Fiora's eyes snap and her skin take on that special adrenaline shine. Don't get me wrong. She's not into making money. She's into keeping score, and money is the only scorecard that is universally endorsed in America. If we kept score in pinto beans or cornflakes, she'd get excited about shuffling them, too.

"What I'm really afraid of is that Dickie-bird and his yellow-feathered flock are going to ruin PBF," Fiora continued. "Teddy didn't build that fund on the government tit, and that's sure as hell not the way I want to see it go."

"No guts, no air medal."

She smiled. "What's that, one of Benny's aphorisms?"

"No. 'The faint heart ne'er fucked the fair maiden' is how Benny puts it."

"Teddy would have loved that," Fiora said, laughing. "Sexless though he was, he'd have loved it."

Sexless, perhaps, but not without the right equipment. Pacific Basin Fund was a venture capital firm that laid out seed money to promising technological projects all along the Pacific Rim from Irvine to Taipei to Tokyo to Kuala Lumpur. The fund had been the brainchild, the only child, of a young Caltech physics major named A. Theodore Portman. He believed that the economic and cultural past lay with Europe and the East Coast; the future lay with the West Coast and the Pacific Rim countries. He had piles of charts and graphs to prove his point. More important, he had those hard-to-find appurtenances, balls. He put his money where his mouth was.

Fiora believed that Teddy was one of the few real geniuses humankind had produced lately. By supplying venture capital to Pacific Rim countries, he amassed thirty or forty million bucks before he was thirty-five. Given an average life span, Teddy would have ended up in the billion-dollar club. But Teddy loved baked brie and other things that close the arteries. He was three hundred pounds and growing when his heart threw a piston one afternoon on the way back from a business luncheon. He died at the wheel of his Mercedes 560SEC before the Orange County paramedics could get him started again.

Like so many young tycoons, Teddy had thought he was immortal. He had planned for every corporate contingency except his own death. He must have had some intimation, though, because about two weeks before he died, he invited Fiora onto the board of directors of PBF. Fiora already had seen enough through the years to convince her that the fund was an undiscovered gem. She had been quietly mapping out a takeover strategy in the weeks since Teddy had died. Corporate raiding wasn't her style, but she made an exception for Teddy's legacy. Like him, she believed that the future lay west, not east, of the San Andreas Fault.

I had a special interest in the Pacific Basin Fund that went beyond the fact that Fiora had invested a healthy chunk of my dough in it. The fund's headquarters were five minutes from Crystal Cove. After too many years without Fiora, I wanted her warm presence in my bed every night; but when she was working out of Century City, she made it back to the cottage only four days out of seven. I wanted to raise the average.

I made no secret of the way I felt. When Fiora turned up at the cottage a few months after she left me in Napa, I asked for no promises and made no demands. I simply took her to bed, held her until she stopped crying and then offered her full-time use of the cottage—and me—for the short or long term. Then I kissed her until no was the furthest word from her mind. We both slept late the following morning. As a matter of fact, she took the whole day off, which, for a workaholic like her, was quite impressive. The next day she was back in Century City, but she returned to the cottage in the evening as though she had been doing it for years.

Although Fiora never addressed my offer of permanent cohabitation rights, more and more of her clothes turned up in the cottage closet as the days went by. The dry cleaner got used to seeing me push size-six silkies over the counter, and I got used to cooking for two and learning ways to keep food warm for the inevitable days when a gasoline tanker or a produce truck overturned on the 405 and backed up traffic from Long Beach to Sylmar. Neither one of us mentioned the changes and accommodations in our mutual lives. We were like children, hoping if we acted as though we'd never been apart, we would be sure of always being together.

Funny, huh? But it had worked so far. We had been living together successfully, covering our divergent natures with the same blanket and managing to keep the tension under control by tacitly refusing to plan more than a week in advance. It had worked for several months, one day at a time, but Fiora's active role at Pacific Basin Fund implied a longer-term commitment.

For both of us. And we knew it.

"I liked Teddy, but he won't have died in vain if you manage to pull this deal off," I said as we passed Newport Center. "And in case I haven't told you, I think you're at least twice as capable as Teddy was."

Fiora moved her fingertip lightly from my shoulder to my hand. I tightened my grip on the steering wheel to keep from reaching for her.

"I'll never have the touch he did with technology," said Fiora, "but . . . thanks."

"You need Star Wars advice, you just bring the Ice Cream King and me in as consultants."

"Benny, maybe," she said, smiling and stretching. "Not you, love. They don't do Star Wars in nine-millimeter, and sometimes I think that's the only measurement you understand."

There was more sadness than rancor in Fiora's voice, which didn't make me feel one bit better. But rather than get in an argument about the constructive uses of applied violence, I downshifted and kept the revs high while we cut across the heart of the Outer City.

You have to see a place like Irvine at rush hour to realize what Fiora and Teddy were talking about when they projected the future of economic life on the Pacific Rim. The maze of modern construction that used to be called suburbia has become so much more than a collection of cookie-cutter bedroom communities. A left turn took us through the manufacturing sprawl around John Wayne Airport and then down a long six-lane boulevard lined with branch banks whose home offices are in Hong Kong, Tokyo, Sydney and Vancouver. Another turn sent us through block after block of tilt-up slab buildings, the hottest high-tech manufacturing site outside of Silicon Valley. A right turn took us into the South Coast Plaza, the shopping center that does more business every day than downtown San Francisco does.

Bedroom suburbia? Hardly. But try telling that to people weaned on John Birch jokes.

Frankly, I liked the area better ten years ago, when there were more lima bean fields and fewer tinted-glass buildings. But Fiora likes it better today, with taller high rises and more frenetic energy of the sort that was expressed in the Center for the Performing Arts.

Orange County has always existed in the shadow of Los Angeles, which means that Orange County has always suffered an ugly-stepchild complex by comparison to its flashier, better-known older sister. That's why, when the civic leaders of Orange County got together a few years ago to build a monument to the arts and civic machismo, they decided to build the newest, most technologically up-to-date three-thousand-seat music hall in the United States. Never mind civic redundancy in the form of another extraordinary music hall, called the Los Angeles Music Center, twenty-five miles to the north. If Orange County was ever to amount to anything, it would have to do so by making its own independent statements of public culture.

Actually, the civic types did a decent job on the Arts Center. It's intended to rival the Sydney Opera House and the Kennedy Center. I won't speak for the architecture, but I can tell you that the acoustics are remarkably good. As for the outer package . . . the Arts Center is an odd building with red granite fascias and a smoked-glass front. There is a mammoth arch in the middle of the building that's all but filled with one of the most unnerving pieces of public art in captivity— an abstract aluminium sculpture that suggests a falcon made of anodized-metal Legos.

The bird is not without grace, as the art critics would say. I'm just not sure it will ever fly.

The rest of the Center for the Performing Arts is like that. It's striking, but it hasn't quite grown into itself. The Center is more than a music hall; it's a public statement by and about the community that anted up the $80 million to construct it. As a result, the Center is sometimes loud and often self-conscious. People overdress for performances. They clap enthusiastically, but at the wrong moments. They make more out of going to a concert than is really necessary.

On the other hand, I'm fully in sympathy with the impulse to celebrate music. The fact that I'd rather do it at one hundred miles per hour in the Cobra or with a glass of wine at moonrise simply means that I'm the primitive type. And who knows? Maybe someday all the aspiring swells in the world will clap between movements of the Brandenburg Concerto, following the tradition established in the latter twentieth century in that mecca of modern culture, Costa Mesa, California.

Fiora's ten grand hadn't been entirely wasted. It assured us of good seats and an invitation to an "intimate offstage gathering" before the performance. Intimate is a very elastic word. In this case it stretched to include three hundred aficionados. Rented tuxedoes on the men, glitter and black velvet and bare skin on the ladies. The refreshments were equally predictable. A free glass or two of okay champagne—French to prove that there's good taste in the provinces—and all the room-temperature hors d'oeuvres you could cram onto one plate.

The London Philharmonia felt compelled to front a heavy program that night, two Beethovens and a Mozart overture. It was going to be three hours before we got to a real meal, so while Fiora made nice with two of Pacific Basin Fund's middle managers, I went off to do my domestic duty by rustling up hors d'oeuvres. By the time I got back to Fiora with two champagnes in one hand and a plate of brie and cheddar and hot chorizo sausages in the other, her two middle managers had been run off by a very suave Richard Toye. If his scrotum was giving him any trouble, he wasn't showing it at the moment.

The executive vice president of Pacific Basin Fund was Eastern Establishment all the way. He had started out as a New York stock analyst, and even after five years in Lotus Land, he still carried himself with the perfect poise of a Wall Street refugee. We both wore custom-tailored tuxedoes. I don't know why he commissioned his; mine was specially made to cover the nine-millimeter pistol hidden in the small of my back. The differences between us didn't end there. Toye's smile had just the right touch of disdain and his eyes had just the proper way of looking over your shoulder, making sure he wasn't neglecting somebody really important while he was making nice with you.

Even if Toye hadn't been giving Fiora the runaround, he wouldn't have been my kind of guy. On the other hand, I was here to act as Mr. Fiora Flynn, family yuppie, genus West Coast, species *house-husband*. So I nodded and spoke politely.

"Hello, Richard," I said. I offered him a shot at the hors d'oeuvres I was carrying, because my mother had always told me to share with those who were less fortunate. "Care to join us for dinner?"

"Good evening," he said carefully, leaving me with the impression that he had been too polite to add "up to now" to his greeting.

He looked at the plate I was holding, took one of the two napkins, and selected the cracker I had smeared with pepper brie especially for Fiora. It irritated me, but I was going to be a good house-husband if it killed me. Then I caught Fiora's glance. She gave me a tiny nod.

I didn't need a road map. Sometimes I've found it useful in the past to turn Fiora loose on people who were giving me a hard time. And sometimes Fiora returns the favor.

I waited until Toye's mouth was filled with crushed pepper and creamy brie. "I understand you tried to pick a fight with my wife this afternoon," I said, offering the plate to Fiora. When I turned back to Toye, I was much closer to him. "Didn't they teach you better manners at Harvard?"

Toye stared at me like I had just reached over and honked his pecker. He swallowed several times as he tried to decide whether I was joking. He wasn't entirely stupid. He came to the correct conclusion.

"Cornell," Toye said, "not Harvard."

I shrugged, not giving a damn one way or another.

Toye's pale blue glance flickered over me like a snake's tongue looking for a place to sink the fangs. Then he thought better of it and turned to Fiora. "I wasn't aware that it was a fight. I hope I didn't offend you, Fiora. I certainly didn't intend to. It's just that, in the absence of Mr. Portman's financial genius, I believe the fund must proceed with more caution."

"Are you saying that Fiora and the rest of the board aren't smart enough to carry out Portman's instructions?"

Toye opened his mouth, but nothing came out.

Fiora stroked my arm. "Don't take it personally, Richard," she said carelessly, leaning against me while her delicate fingers hovered over the hors d'oeuvres. "Fiddler's just cranky because he spent all day digging a hole." She selected a cube of crumbly cheddar and bit it in half with her shiny, sharp front teeth.

"A ditchdigger, hmmm?" Toye said, keeping an eye on the crowd over Fiora's bright head. "Fascinating work."

"Actually, it was a grave," I said. "You never know when you're going to need one in my business."

"Your business?" Toye asked faintly.

"Digging graves. And filling them."

Toye discovered someone at the other end of the room, mumbled his excuses and fled. I looked down at Fiora. She's small even in four-inch heels, but any man who mistakes her for a bimbo boy-toy is soon bleeding from every available artery.

"Don't raise your left eyebrow at me," she said. "I would have done it myself, but I want Dickie-bird to believe he's important right up until the instant that I fire his tight Ivy League ass."

"Other than eat your brie, what did he do tonight?"

"He towered. I hate it when men do that."

"It's amazing that you put up with me," I said dryly.

Fiora gave me a very female kind of smile. At six two and twice her weight, there's no doubt that I tower over her. As if that weren't bad enough, my tendency to get involved in other people's troubles means that every pound I carry has to be on my side rather than gravity's.

"You don't tower. You protect. And put that damned eyebrow down! Drives me crazy that I can't make mine do that nearly as well."

"You can raise mine anytime."

She smiled. "And you can eat my brie."

I knew I wasn't going to get a better offer, so I surrendered.

5

The Beethovens were adequate, the Mozart was spirited and the double-doubles from In-n-Out Burger on Bristol Street were absolute gut bombs. Fiora, at size six, needed fries and a chocolate malt with hers. I had a warm beer that had spent enough time in the trunk to achieve lift-off the instant I popped the cap.

Because we were already so far inland, I took I-5 south to the Laguna Freeway and followed it into the wide end of the Laguna Canyon funnel. The two-lane blacktop—with an occasional suicide lane thrown in to keep you awake—was deserted. For five minutes we drove through a landscape that hadn't changed substantially since James Irvine II had put up a barbwire fence in 1874. The moon came out from behind a bank of clouds and bathed the cold black country-side with light, giving a silvery gloss to the ragged eucalyptus wind-breaks.

The moonlight and the cold wind made me think about Aaron Sharp, a subject I'd been trying to avoid all night. Fiora must have read my thoughts. Or my mind.

"Was it an accident?" she asked.

"Was what?"

"Codswallop," she said, yawning. "You know what I mean."

"Sharp didn't believe in 'safe ventures.' "

"So?"

"So maybe he pushed his luck too far. Or maybe somebody pushed it for him. I don't know."

She watched the dryland pasture and chaparral roll past her window as she let out her breath in a long, hard sigh.

"What the hell is the sigh for?" I asked.

Fiora drew her mink closer around her shoulders and looked at me.

"I know you," she said simply. "Even Mozart didn't get your attention tonight. Beneath your ruffled white shirt and polite smile, you spent all evening trying to figure out how Sharp died. You're not going to be satisfied until you find out. *That's* what the sigh was for."

I reviewed the evening in my mind. "I thought about Sharp twice in four hours. Maximum three minutes," I said, trying to keep a defensive tone out of my voice.

Fiora was silent for another half mile. Then she sighed again. "Okay, so I was the one who thought about him all night. You want to make something of it?" She stuck out her sharp Scots chin, daring me to take her on.

"I'm driving," I alibied.

"I hate a man who won't strike a woman. It demonstrates a potentially fatal weakness. Chivalry will get you killed someday."

"You think it was a woman who got Sharp?"

She shot me a bleak look. "Sharp never pulled his punch for any woman, and you know it as well as I do."

I didn't argue. It was true.

Laguna was deserted. Broadway was empty, like a bowling alley with no pins. We were alone except for the wind off the Pacific Ocean herding a light salt mist up the canyon. Five minutes after I turned onto the Coast Highway, we slipped into Crystal Cove.

"When is the funeral?" Fiora asked.

"Saturday."

I coasted down toward the garage with my lights out and the engine in neutral to avoid waking my neighbors. As I turned into the driveway, I had to brake to avoid hitting Kwame. He was lying in the middle of the dusty pavement, front paws stretched out in front of him. His eyes glowed like milk-colored marbles as they caught the moonlight. His stump of a tail beat twice in greeting, then he looked down at something between his paws. He was acting as though he had nailed something in the underbrush and was guarding or playing with it.

"Lazy monster," Fiora muttered, reaching into her purse for keys to open the lock on the garage.

My right hand clamped around her wrist, stopping her from opening the car door. With my left hand I reached overhead and moved the dome-light switch into the center position so the bulb wouldn't come on when the door was opened.

"I'll get the garage door," I said.

Fiora's eyes widened at what I hadn't said. She looked into the darkness with sudden apprehension.

"Nobody's close or Kwame would say so," I said. "I just want to see whatever he's been waiting to share with me."

Fiora handed me the Tekna flashlight from the glove box. I got out of the car quietly. Kwame stood over his treasure, wagging tentatively and looking from me to it. When I got close enough, he danced back and forth from one front paw to the other. He was obviously proud as hell of whatever it was, but he needed someone's permission before he ate it. It's a lesson good watchdogs have to learn early: if they eat the scraps they find in the brush, they'll die of strychnine poisoning the first time somebody really wants to get past them. So Kwame stood over the hunk of meat, drooling like an idiot child, visibly wrestling with the impulse to grab the goods and vanish before I could interfere.

I bent down and scooped up Kwame's prize. He hadn't been raiding trash cans. I've paid fifteen bucks, à la carte, for smaller pieces of sirloin. Beneath the veneer of driveway grit there were a dozen small slits in the meat. Somebody had poked a gelatin capsule into each one.

"Good boy, Kwame," I said, and meant every word.

He drooled and watched the sirloin and wagged his stubby tail. When I went to the car to open Fiora's door, he followed.

"Shut off the engine," I said softly. "I'll put the car away later."

Fiora bit her lip against the questions she wanted to ask, switched off the ignition and was standing next to me in less than five seconds.

Kwame paced us all the way to the house, his nose never more than a few inches from my right hand, the one that held the meat.

"Why not call the police?" Fiora asked as I unlocked the front door. She didn't even look at the Detonics in my left hand. "You always tell *me* to call the police."

"A Ridgeback is quicker than 911. *Kwame, alert.*"

The words were soft, but Kwame's whole body underwent a transformation. He became more compact, almost springy, and he bristled with alertness. He watched me with tangible intensity, completely forgetting the raw meat in my hand. Silently I opened the front door.

"Search."

Kwame went through the front door of the cottage like a deadly black ghost. We could hear his toenails softly snicking on the tile floor in the kitchen. There was silence for ten seconds while he padded around on the carpet and more silence while he vetted the back of the house. Then he reappeared and stood in the front doorway, wagging his stump, his eyes on the meat once more.

We went in and closed the door behind us.

"No light yet," I said when Fiora reached for the switch on the kitchen wall. I lit her path with the Tekna.

"I don't do bimbos," Fiora said, "unless it's by your very special request. Do I hear a pretty please with sugar on top?"

"The sirloin is loaded with bad medicine. Somebody tried to put Kwame down."

"Are they gone?"

"I don't know. They may be lying back in the shrubbery, waiting for him to die."

Fiora shuddered.

In the darkness the message indicator on the Ansafone blinked red, like a warning beacon. One blink, one recorded message while I was gone. I paid no attention. I was more concerned with making sure the blackout drapes in the bedroom were closed, just in case somebody was out behind the bottlebrush hedge with a twelve-gauge greeting card.

The tux jacket and my white shirt hit the floor. I pulled on a black sweatshirt. As always, there was a three-cell Kelite flashlight in my bedside drawer, and under the bed was a matte black Smith & Wesson shotgun with a folding stock and an eighteen-inch barrel. I gave Fiora the Detonics and the Kelite, keeping the Tekna and the shotgun for myself.

"You want me to shoot them or club them?" she asked dryly, hefting the two-pound spun-aluminium flashlight.

"Lady's choice. Keep Kwame with you. This time I'm going to find out who the clown is."

"This time?"

"Somebody was canvassing the neighborhood earlier. I thought he was just some realtor looking for listings."

I was glad the lights were off. That way I didn't have to see the sorrow and accusations in Fiora's eyes.

Clouds were scudding past the face of the nearly full moon when I slid the patio door open and stepped out into the shadow of the overhanging eaves. I waited until the moon was buried in clouds before I moved. When the landscape blurred into a single shade of black, I crossed the patio, vaulted the railing and dropped to the sloping flower bed just below the lip of the bluff. The leather soles of my black shoes slipped in the dirt, then scraped across a rock. I wished I had taken thirty seconds to change them, but it was too late now.

Just north of the cottage a dry ravine broke the line of the bluff. Fifty yards wide at its mouth, the ravine narrowed like a funnel as it cut inland, finally pinching out at the edge of the highway. Short of renting one of the other Crystal Cove cottages, lying up in the ravine was the only discreet way to watch my house. There were several spots where such a watcher might be. One was beneath a spreading acacia tree about thirty yards from the back of the cottage. That was a bit close, if the watcher was still worried about Kwame, but I couldn't turn my back on the tree until I'd checked it out.

The path slid in and out of moonlight, echoing the shifting veils of cloud across the face of the moon. Shadows melted and then regained definition when the moonlight returned. After five minutes of careful studying, I decided that the tree's angular shadows were too insubstantial to conceal a man.

During the next dark phase I eased forward again, moving as quietly as my leather shoes permitted. In the shadow of two head-high agaves, I studied the shaded patch beneath a live oak that hung over the lip of the ravine.

Shadows are like Rorschachs. Sometimes the mind makes more of them than it should. But there was something odd about the shadow beneath the oak, something that made the basement levels of my brain sit up and howl. I stared at the oak's amorphous shadow for several minutes, trying to decipher its message. Finally a hand moved in a brushing motion that allowed me to differentiate the shapes of two men lying close together on the cold ground, watching the cottage windows fifty yards away.

The agave plant rose beside me in spears of black and silver. I turned my head very slowly to look at the clouds the wind was moving in from the west. I wanted a long dark period in which to move, long enough for me to get behind the men. As I waited, the raw, brine-laden wind made me shiver with a combination of cold and anticipation.

When a cloud finally sucked up the moonlight, I stepped out onto the path and began to move. I had to keep one eye on the two men and one on the trail in front of me. That's why I didn't see the coyote until it was too late. The little brush wolf hadn't picked up my scent because I was downwind of him, but he was even more skittish than I was. When he suddenly found a large, dark figure moving toward him, he took off through the brush as if I had stepped on his tail. Whoever said wild animals are silent never spooked one in full dark.

The two men looked over their shoulders at the noise. I froze, but they couldn't miss me looming up out of the night, backlit by the returning moon. I dove for the ground just as the darkness was split by the muzzle flash of a pistol. It sounded like a standard-load .38.

Somehow I'd been expecting a nine-millimeter.

The guy was either a lousy shot or had pulled the trigger while he was still turning to face me. The slug tore through thick brush a good ten feet to my left. I belly-crawled forward a few feet to a knee-high piece of mudstone that lined the edge of the patch.

The shotgun isn't a great prone-cover weapon, even with a short barrel. The two men on the hill got off a shot apiece before I managed to bring the shotgun's muzzle to bear. My finger was squeezing down on the trigger when I realized that the cottage was directly behind the men. I couldn't fire without splattering double-aught buckshot through the bedroom windows.

Cursing silently, I waited for the men to move.

Their second volley was like a classroom demonstration on covering fire—calm, rhythmic, assuring the men and me that they were in control. Yet not one bullet came within twenty feet of my position. They were trying to keep me pinned down, not assassinate me. Fire and fall back, fire and fall back. Very precise, very professional, and very damned effective. I lay there behind my rock, waiting and hoping that their orderly little ballet would trip over a root and open a clear field of fire for me.

Finally there was a break in the measured rhythm, but not the break I'd been waiting for. The men were gone.

After counting to five, I crept forward carefully, just in case one of them doubled back. They must have stashed their car in the brush on the other side of the highway. Forty seconds after I lost sight of the muzzle flashes, an engine kicked over. It was some kind of husky V-8. Tires spewed gravel, then bit into tarmac with a receding wail. The engine wound tight, shifted and started winding again. By standing on tiptoe I caught a glimpse of a dark car fleeing toward Newport Beach, using the moon for headlights.

Two seconds later Kwame came barreling up the trail from the direction of the beach. Fiora wasn't far behind, pistol in one hand and switched-off flashlight in the other. I smiled. The lady hated violence, but she was far from stupid. She knew that shining a flashlight around a gunfight was a hell of a good way to get shot.

Kwame was so excited by the gunshots that he forgot his manners and jumped up, planting both his big paws on my chest and giving me a massive lick. Fiora was a good deal less enthusiastic in her greeting.

"They're gone," I said.

She said nothing.

I turned on the flashlight and did a quick damage assessment. The knees of my tux pants hadn't been made for belly-crawling. Other than that, there was no permanent damage. Fiora was still in her black velvet. She had managed to tear long runs in her pantyhose racing shoeless through the brush.

"You're losing your touch," she said coolly, glancing at my unfired shotgun.

Yes, everything was in working order, including her tongue.

I took the Kelite, turned away and began shining the light along the bank. The clay soil didn't take deep impressions, but there were clear marks left by two pairs of running shoes. I recognized the tread pattern from a pair of New Balance 670s. The other guy appeared to have been wearing Nikes. Hundred-dollar shoes, the both of them. Well-heeled prowlers. Men who chose their midnight athletic gear carefully.

Further searching showed that one of the two men had been a smoker. There were shreds of several field-stripped filter tips. There was also a spot where one of the men had carefully dug a shelf into the slope of the bank, as though he had needed a flat spot on which to rest something.

I poked around in the debris below the shelf. The tightly focused beam of the Kelite picked up a glint from a surface that was too clean to be a pebble. I put the object on my palm and shone the beam on it.

"Transistor?" Fiora asked.

"Yeah. Maybe they were robot gunmen dispatched from another planet."

She muttered something that I decided not to hear.

After I let Kwame nose around and catalog the men's scents, we went back to the house. A couple of leftover enchiladas compensated the Ridgeback for the loss of his sirloin snack. If he resented the swap, you couldn't tell it from the drool. The loaded bait went into a plastic bag. Somebody might be able to learn something of interest from the capsules. It wasn't likely with all the garbage sold on street corners these days, but still worth pursuing, considering it was the only thing I had.

The cold had begun to reach Fiora. She traded in her low-cut black velvet for a full-length pair of fuchsia sweats. I dumped the tux pants in the trash and dug out a pair of blue workout sweats. In one crystal balloon, I poured enough Armagnac for both of us. As I tipped back my head to take an impolite swig, the blinking light on the answering machine caught my eye again.

"Didn't you pick up the message?" I asked.

"Yes," Fiora said, taking the glass, drinking and shuddering. "God bless a few Frenchmen."

I waited, but she said nothing more about the message.

"Fiora?"

She jerked her hand toward the machine as though she wanted nothing to do with it. I hit the replay switch and listened to a strange, strangled voice, eerie and almost robotic, a voice run backward and forward through a distorter in order to disguise the speaker's identity. I listened once, rewound and then listened again. The message hadn't changed.

"Aaron Sharp's death wasn't an accident."

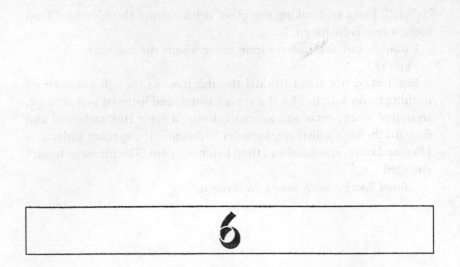

6

Somebody was jerking my chain.

I was in a hole in the ground with a choke collar around my neck. Some fool was yanking on it. I looked around and realized the other end of the chain was attached to Kwame's collar. Kwame was straining like hell to get away, chasing a piece of doctored sirloin that was inches from his muzzle, and each lunge tightened the choke collar on my neck.

I woke up to find Fiora's arm flung across my neck. I eased her hand down until it was lying across my stomach. She sighed and snuggled closer. I pulled the covers up to her chin and kicked them off of me. I stretched as much as I could without disturbing her and looked at the clock. Just before five. Normally I'd be good for several more hours of sleep, but it's not an everyday occurrence for me to have messages left on the machine telling me that a man I owed my life to has been murdered.

I closed my eyes and tried to sleep anyway. When that didn't work, I opened my eyes and thought about who might have wanted Sharp dead. The list was as long as his career. A hard-assed border cop doesn't get Christmas cards from his clients. So I tried thinking about who might be watching me for profit or revenge. That list wasn't as long as Sharp's, but I wasn't nearly as old as he had been, either.

Fiora moved restlessly and made tiny, disjointed noises. I pulled her closer and held her, running my hand slowly down her back, hoping her dream was simply a by-product of last night's encounter rather than a harbinger of the future. After a time her body relaxed and her breathing deepened. She stretched against me like a sleepy cat, offering her body to be stroked. I did just that, enjoying the sleek heat and softness of her.

By the time Fiora stirred and opened her eyes, bad dreams were not what was on her mind.

"I can't remember the last time you were awake before me," she murmured, pulling back slightly to look at my eyes even as she slid a slender leg between mine.

"It happens," I said, shrugging, although I couldn't remember the last time it had. But talking about it wouldn't change anything. I was awake.

Fiora slid one bare, elegant arm out from under the down comforter. If she noticed the cold air, she didn't show it. Her long fingers threaded through my hair.

"When are you leaving?" she whispered.

We hadn't talked about my plans. I was relieved that we wouldn't have to now. We would have argued, and the argument wouldn't have changed one damn thing. I owed Sharp, and he was dead.

"I need to put together a few things here," I said. "Then I'll drop by to see Benny for a minute. But I'll have to get moving if I'm going to beat the worst of the traffic."

Long, amber-colored eyelashes swept down, concealing Fiora's eyes for a moment. I could feel the wave of protest and resignation that went through her.

"So soon," she whispered.

When she opened her eyes, they were full of shadows and bad dreams that had come true. I wanted to tell her I loved her, but she knew that already, just as she knew that my loving her wouldn't change what had to be done. I wanted to tell her I was sorry, but she knew that, too, just as she knew that sorry didn't get it done.

Fiora's slender fingers traced my eyebrows and my nose, my cheekbones and the line of my mouth. Her hand slid around to the back of my neck, pulling me to her with an irresistible pressure. We had known each other too long to conceal our needs. We fit together easily, making love with our eyes wide open, watching one another, memorizing the experience, knowing that tomorrow wasn't guaranteed. At the last moment she closed her eyes and moaned with such intense pleasure that I would have stopped if I could have, just to prolong it for both of us. But I couldn't. It was too good, too hot, too deep.

We lay tangled together in the quilt, breathing like sprinters. I kissed the curves of her mouth and neck and breast, running my tongue down her smooth skin, loving her, wondering if she would be waiting when I got back, not daring to ask. Suddenly she took my hands and kissed the ragged scars where nails from a packing crate had slammed through flesh and bone. Then she quickly rolled away from me and started to get out of bed. I grabbed her wrist. She wouldn't look at me as I wiped tears from her cheeks.

"Fiora . . ."

"Two days. That's all I'm good for this time. If it can't be handled in two days, I'm going to quit worrying and dreaming if it kills me."

It would have been kinder to release Fiora from the two days of agony now, but I knew I didn't want her to quit worrying, because that might mean she would also quit loving. So I lied.

"I doubt that it will take two days."

I kissed the palm of her hand and released her. Her fingertips skimmed over my mustache in a familiar caress.

And then I was alone again. Can't live with her and can't live without her. She feels the same about me. A hell of a state, but it's the one we're stuck with.

While Fiora was showering, I packed, forcing myself to concentrate on what was ahead instead of what was behind. The desert would be cold. I stuffed in a pair of cotton long johns to go with a clean pair of jeans, wool shirts, a pair of slacks, boots and running shoes. Next came a tool kit of sorts, a hard-shell attaché case with full foam padding to cushion the Detonics, cleaning gear, Jake's Model 1911 and a few boxes of shells. I pulled the twelve-gauge from under the bed, stuffed it in a fleece-lined case and carried everything to the trunk of the TII.

Fiora was drying her hair when I got back. She knew what I'd been doing, but she said nothing. There was nothing to say. I was going. If she had known whether she would be here when I got back, she would have told me. Fiora was neither coy nor cruel.

"You want some breakfast?" I asked as I stripped out of my sweats and headed for the shower. "I'll do eggs in a minute."

She nodded, then walked over and turned on the little bedroom Sony to catch the opening quotes on FNN. Before I ducked into the shower I knew that stocks were up, bellies were down the limit and April cattle were steady.

Twenty minutes later I set scrambled eggs, toasted bagels and hot coffee on the table. Fiora came into the kitchen on very high heels, her business manner firmly in place. She was dressed in executive charcoal gray with a white silk blouse. With her makeup and hair flawless, she was impressive as hell for any hour, much less for dawn.

We ate quickly, watching the light begin to well up in a color-shifting radiance behind the coastal hills. The clouds of the previous night were gone. The sky was a clear, scoured blue, clean and uncomplicated. It would be a good day on the desert, the kind of day where the horizon was a hundred miles away in all directions and the shadows were sharp enough to shave with. I was ready for that. I'd spent a long time watching soft waves turn into softer foam thirty yards from my feet.

Fiora must have sensed my growing excitement. She stood up abruptly. "I've got an eight o'clock in Century City."

I still had half a bagel, but I laid it aside. "Coffee to go?"

She shook her head, wrapped her coat around her shoulders and picked up her leather briefcase. When I stood up she placed her hands on my shoulders and gently pushed me back into the chair.

"Finish your breakfast. I can walk to the car by myself."

"But you can't kiss yourself on the lips, can you?" I asked, rising again to kiss her gently. "Don't worry, love. I'll be back."

Her only answer was a shadowed glance.

"Where are you going to be tonight?" I asked. "I'll call you."

"Try the Beverly Glen Hotel. There's no point in commuting to an empty cottage."

When I kissed Fiora this time, her shoulders were stiff beneath my fingers and her lips were unresponsive. Suddenly she was like a desert horizon, a hundred miles away, shadows sharp enough to make you bleed.

"I have to go," I said, knowing it was futile but trying anyway.

"So do I." Fiora looked up at me. "I wish to God I didn't love you, Fiddler."

She quietly closed the kitchen door behind her and walked across the lawn without looking back. A few minutes later her BMW purred out of the garage and up the little hill toward Pacific Coast Highway.

I stood and listened for a long time, but only the sound of the surf came back to me.

I made it to Benny's house in record speed. The fact that most people were barely opening their bloodshot eyes at that hour helped keep the highway clear. At least I didn't have to worry about waking Benny. He wouldn't be asleep. He probably slept less than four hours a night. It had nothing to do with his paraplegia. The parts of him that were still connected to his central nervous system were as thoroughly conditioned as I was. But Benny had too many things going on in his head to sleep much; his mind prodded him out of bed early so that he could get busy in his on-site electronics shop.

Benny lived in what used to be a good-sized duplex at the edge of the sand in West Newport, the only sector of Newport Beach that tolerated much in the way of residential or human diversity. He started out using half the duplex as a workshop. Gradually his work invaded the living quarters to the point that it was hard to distinguish where the shop left off and everything else began. Even the bathroom cupboards had widgets stored along with the towels and toilet paper.

Newport was kind of a humorless place for a bearded New Zealander with a fully developed sense of the sardonic, but Benny liked the duplex because the sound of the waves soothed his restless mind. Soothing was also how he described surfing on a stubby little board that was about halfway between a belly board and a full-sized surf stick. The truncated board fit very nicely on the back of his wide-wheeled "beach chair," which Benny cranked through the sand with sweeps of his muscular arms. He could have cooked up a black box to power the chair at Mach 3, but he preferred the workout he got doing it by hand.

I parked in the driveway beside his van. When nobody answered my knock on the front door, I went around to the side. Sure enough, Benny's chair was standing sentinel just above the high-water mark. The waves were California symmetrical, about four feet high, with occasional bigger sets to make life interesting. There were about a dozen teenagers floating out there in wet suits, plus the muscular, bearded Ice Cream King of Saigon.

It had been a long time since Benny had been a quality-control man in an ice cream factory in Vietnam. *Nuc mahm* sherbet had been his specialty. When the sun went down, Benny had had a second job. I guess you could call him a quality-control expert in that one, too. When he found a bad lot, he took care of it. Unfortunately, the bullet that did for Benny's spinal cord came from the muzzle of an M-16 in the hands of a drunken American. Just an accident, mind you, since Benny was in the employ of one of the more esoteric units in what is now called the "U.S. intelligence community."

That term contains its own contradiction, since there's less communal spirit among U.S. spy agencies than there is between Ford and GM. But everybody involved in the Saigon mishap agreed that Benny had bought his U.S. permanent residency the hard way. The hirsute New Zealander had long since quit worrying about the fairness of life, death and paralysis. He had a genius for the blacker applications of high tech, and he consulted with all members of the intelligence community, even the agency whose drunken sentry had almost killed him.

Ever since the accident, Benny had made his way on wheels through a two-legged world, substituting upper-body strength for leg muscle. As a result, he could propel himself through choppy fifty-eight-degree water on a surfboard and leave a wake like an outboard motor. He gauged the approach of a building breaker, lunged forward on his short board and paddled like hell with his enormous arms and shoulders. He caught the wave at the perfect spot, read the break to the left, went with it and let the wave's power fling him headlong down the rolling incline, steering the board with his palms instead of his feet.

The curl of the wave built up over Benny in a churning question mark, but the wave's shape held. He rode into the roaring tunnel of froth. I lost sight of him for ten seconds before he came shooting out the other end of the tube, howling and grinning like a Viking. He must have seen me standing next to his chair, because instead of kicking out and heading back toward the applauding surfers, he kept his board pointed toward shore. A minute later the spent wave beached him gently.

I rolled the beach chair over to the tide line as Benny pulled himself across the wet sand like a muscular elephant seal, trailing his board on a leash behind him.

"G'day, mate," he said happily, still pumped up from the ride. "You want to use one of my boards? They're small, but they've got great shape."

I shook my head. I didn't have one bit of Benny's fondness for cold water.

Smiling, Benny hauled himself into the chair and toweled off with a heavy terry cloth robe while I stowed the board on the rack. He is as fierce about his independence as Fiora is, but once in a while he lets me give him a hand, particularly if his own are already busy.

"So you're not here to go surfing," he said. "Too cold and too bloody early in the morning for you to be doing anything legal, right?"

"You've seen that Nicholson movie, *Going South?*" I asked.

Benny ran the terry toweling through his water-tangled hair and beard, then looked at me with clear black eyes.

"I heard about Sharp on the eleven-o'clock follies," Benny said. He had a cool opinion about the educational value of news. "I figured you'd be wanting to do something. You need company?"

I shook my head. "I'm just going to make a courtesy call. Paying my respects to an old friend, that's all."

"Bullshit," Benny mumbled into the towel.

"Codswallop, actually."

Benny ducked out from behind the towel and gave me a look.

"Codswallop? Bloody hell, boyo, who have you been hanging out with?"

"Jane Austen. Look, if you happen to be out this evening, could you drop by and check on Fiora? She may stay in L.A., but if she comes home, I'd just as soon she wasn't alone."

Benny tried not to show his surprise. He needn't have bothered. I was a bit surprised at myself, too. Until the words had come out of my mouth, I had had no intention of dragging anyone else into this.

"I know you well enough to know you aren't inviting me to spend a night with your lady," Benny said, grinning wolfishly. "So what, exactly, is it that you want me to do?"

"Nothing. I'm not even awake. Forget it."

"Don't bullshit an old bullshitter," Benny interrupted, tossing his head to get the mane of wet black hair out of his eyes.

There was a brief struggle with my conscience. It lost. It wasn't nearly as well exercised as my body.

"Somebody was watching the house yesterday afternoon, shortly before I heard about Sharp," I said. "Last night I did a moonlight maneuver with a couple more clowns. They were either piss-poor shots or they lacked the emotional commitment to be hit men, but they sure didn't want me to find out who they were. They pinned me down and then got in the wind."

"You think it has to do with Sharp?"

"Could be, but that's hard to make fly. The guys were government issue, high-ticket items. But that doesn't figure, either. I haven't tangled with the FBI for six, seven months."

"You onto something you haven't told me about?"

"Not that I know of."

Benny's eyes narrowed suddenly. "Is Fiora dreaming?"

I winced. "Ask her tonight. We're barely speaking at the moment."

"Bloody wonderful. So what are you going to do?"

"Same thing you were doing out in the surf—going with the flow and seeing where it takes me."

"Lots of guys have been hammered headfirst into the sand that way."

"That's why I thought I'd see what you had in the way of crash helmets."

Benny closed his eyes for a moment, thinking. After a bit he opened them and absently scratched his bearded chin, where the ocean water had already started to dry, leaving a faint crust of salt behind. Then he nodded once. Muscles in his arms and shoulders bunched as he spun the wheels of the sand chair in opposite directions, smartly turning himself around. The chair hissed through the sand. I followed, stretching my legs to stay even. The door to Benny's workshop opened at an electronic signal from his chair. As soon as we were inside, the door closed, shutting out the sun.

Black magic doesn't do well with too much light.

By seven I was on the road again, carrying another suitcase full of odds and ends that Benny had been concocting and saving for just the right occasion. I never fail to be amazed by how subtle and devious he can be. It's a damn good thing he's on the side of keeping things together, because he'd be horrifyingly effective at pulling them apart.

Over the years he's given me more equipment than I've been able to use. I'm still carrying around one of his gifts, a handful of nine-millimeter cartridges loaded with chromium-plated ball shot. They're ultra-short-range loads, as they tend to take on unpredictable trajectories beyond three feet. But the steel balls are guaranteed to take no ballistics marks, which makes them ideal for one job—whacking somebody out and leaving no traceable evidence behind.

The implication of the steel balls wasn't comforting, but neither were some of the people I'd dealt with over the years. Somewhere along the way from Puerto Peñasco I had come to believe that there was a place for everything in the world, even for nine-millimeter cartridges that can't be held against you in a court of law. I'd never used one of those cartridges.

And I'd never thrown them away, either.

Back on Newport Boulevard I joined the early lemmings headed for the 405. I had to fight through a few clots of vehicles southbound on the San Diego Freeway past John Wayne Airport, but by the time I passed Jamboree, I could kick the TII up to the new unofficial interurban speed limit—sixty-five MPH. Once the powers-that-be had lifted the fifty-five-MPH limit out in the countryside, the city slickers caught on real quick.

Northern San Diego County has become too crowded for my taste. I thought about heading inland at Oceanside and crossing the Santa Rosas at Julian. The scenery would be a lot prettier, but the roads would be two-lane relics inhabited by farmers going ten miles per hour. If I stayed with the freeway, once I shook loose of the temporary impediments of the workaday lemmings, I would be able to make as much speed as I thought I could get away with. So I stayed with the freeway.

The Top Guns from Miramar were out, shooting landings and takeoffs and muddying up the clear morning air with their kerosene exhausts. I would have given a hundred bucks for fifteen minutes in one of their F-14s. That would have put me in El Centro, many miles and hours closer to whatever was waiting for me.

Two days didn't leave me much time.

As soon as I turned east on Interstate 8 past El Cajon, I cranked the TII up to ninety. After that there was nothing to do but watch for the CHP and admire the countryside as chaparral gave way to cold, sandy desert on the east side of the Tecate Divide. There were long, straight stretches of road between Coyote Wells and Seeley where nothing moved but the TII's flying shadow.

And then Mount Señalado, the signal mountain that sits on the west-side desert border, rose up sharp and clean, triggering memories.

Jake had used two landmarks when he was walking backpack loads of weed across the desert. One was the transmission tower of the little radio station in El Centro, the one that plays "Okie from Muskogee" three times a day, three hundred sixty-five days a year. The other landmark was Signal Mountain, which was almost always visible, even by starlight, on the desert floor.

As the brown-sugar pyramid of the mountain rose up from the desert, I felt a little bit like I was driving into yesterday.

7

Calexico was only three hours from the Gold Coast of California by freeway, but coming down the Ocotillo Grade was like sliding fifty years into the past. The Imperial Valley desert barely had a fingerhold on the modern high-tech world. Except for the television antennae and the K Mart, life hadn't changed much since the Depression.

The February temperature was balmy. The July temperature would be brutal. For nine months of the year, the sun relentlessly hammered down on the buildings. The local architecture had made some allowances for that. Almost everything was one story and flat-roofed. Adobe was still the building material of choice, because it moderated temperature very well, and did it much more cheaply than air conditioners or even desert coolers. In the commercial district, Calexico's sidewalks were overhung with verandas, because shade was at a premium no matter what the time of year. As with most hot country small towns, the streets were nearly deserted. People around here didn't make any unnecessary moves, even in the winter.

The Customs Investigative Service office was purposely hard to find. It used to be in the port of entry building, until one night when an irate smuggler stuck an altered M-1 carbine through a hole in the chain link border fence and held the trigger down until he ran out of ammo, blowing out the building's front windows in retaliation for something Sharp had done.

Afterward Sharp had moved his whole contingent north a few blocks, out of easy gunshot range. The new Customs Investigations office was now camouflaged in a run-down commercial building that had an outdated, sun-faded McMahan's Furniture sign on it. I pulled into one of the diagonal parking spots out in front of the building. There was no shade. The dumpling of a Latina who had answered the phone yesterday was still talking today. She lowered the receiver an inch and looked at me inquiringly.

"Dana around?" I asked.

She must have been used to strangers in blue jeans asking for Lighter, because she waved her hand toward a big room behind an opaque glass divider and picked up her conversation.

Lighter was sitting in a straight-backed chair, his Tony Lama lizard-skin boots propped on a cluttered desktop next to a clean white straw Stetson. He was hard asleep, his head thrown back and his mouth wide open like a hungry baby bird.

For a moment I almost didn't recognize the sun- and wind-burned border cop. His face was gray with exhaustion. He looked as though this was the first sleep he had gotten since his partner had been killed. I was going to withdraw and let him rest when the back door of the office clattered open and two men entered. They weren't making any effort to be quiet.

One of the men had an angular face, dark brown hair and eyes, and was somewhere in his middle twenties. He wore a white straw Stetson like Lighter's and a Levi riding jacket and jeans. The heels of his black boots rang on the uncarpeted floor of the office. I guessed that his name would be Suarez. The other guy wore a dark blue business suit and a cool, quietly disdainful air that suggested he was a city cop in a backcountry world. The suit could have been from anywhere, but the attitude was pure FBI.

Lighter's head snapped upright at the sound of the screen door slamming. His eyes flicked open, focused somewhere on the wall for a moment, then shifted toward me. He knew he had seen me somewhere, but he wasn't sure where and he wasn't sure whether I was friend or foe.

"Hi, Dana," I said. "Fiddler. Sharp introduced us down south one night. I think it was in a bar called Montezuma's Revenge."

Lighter's face relaxed. "Oh, uh, yeah," he said, swinging his feet off the desk and straightening up. "I guess you heard, then."

I nodded. "It's hard to believe."

His face became grim. "You seen his brains splattered all over the rocks like I did and you'd have no trouble believing." He stared at the toes of his boots for a moment, then shook his head as though he was trying to banish the memory. He was a cop. He'd seen his share of dead bodies and then some, maybe even had a hand in producing a few.

But he would never see another one without thinking of Sharp. Your first dead friend is like that. For an instant, every corpse I see is Jake.

"You get some sleep, Dana?" asked the Latino.

"Some," replied Lighter. He sounded as though he wished he hadn't. He glanced sourly at the city man in the blue suit. "Your lab people come up with anything yet?"

The man glanced at me as though he was expecting an introduction. None was offered. Finally he shook his head. "We aren't going to be able to work that crime scene, Lighter. I think you know why."

Lighter stood up slowly, uncoiling to his full six feet four. "That's fine with me," he said with disgust. "We can take care of our own messes down here without any help from the likes of you."

The man in the suit glanced at me again. He still couldn't tell whether I was a cop, a snitch or a civilian, and he didn't want to say anything until he knew.

Lighter let the FBI agent squirm for a while, then shook his head in angry disbelief.

"Don't worry about him," Lighter snarled. "Worry about doing your job or getting the hell out of my way while I do it!"

I had remembered Lighter as a mild, laconic type of country cop, a perfect foil for Sharp's sardonic, aggressive tactics. But now the lanky cop was playing a different role. For an eerie instant, it was like Sharp's ghost was in the room.

"Headquarters says we aren't going to work that crime scene without full cooperation from the Mexican authorities," the FBI agent said calmly.

"Screw the federales," Lighter said loudly. "It was an American cop who got his head blown off. That might not mean too much back in Washington, but down here we take such matters seriously. We have to. If one of those bastards out there gets away with murder, we'll be in a shooting war every night of the week. You hear what I'm saying, or are you one of those Fan-Belt Inspectors who never worked the street?"

The agent's face flushed with anger.

"Look, Lighter," he said, clipping each word. "You want to stumble around beating on your chest and creating international incidents, go right ahead. But if you decide you'd rather find out who killed your partner, let us know."

"That'll be the day," Lighter said, his eyes narrowed. "That'll be the goddam *day*."

The agent glared back for a moment, then spun around and stalked off, slamming the back door behind him, leaving two Customs cops and me in the middle of the room.

"Tight-assed prick," Lighter grumbled at the closed back door. "We can do better without their help, can't we, Matt?" Lighter looked at me again, trying to remember where I fit in the picture. His eyes were rimmed and bloodshot, but his color was better now than when he'd been asleep.

"I'd like to hear how it happened," I said to Lighter.

He studied me silently for another minute.

"I still know some people on the other side of the line," I said. "It might help." I could see that Lighter didn't buy it entirely, but the full story would have taken an hour to tell, so I took a shortcut. "Sharp saved my life."

That explanation seemed to satisfy Lighter.

"Matt Suarez, this is Fiddler," he said to the young cop. "Sharp thought he was all right, even if some of his people were smugglers."

I nodded at Suarez. "Only one was a smuggler, and he's dead." I looked back at Lighter. "You had breakfast?"

He shook his head, grabbed his hat off the desk, clapped the white

Stetson onto his head and clumped across the room with the gait of a very tired man. Then he turned around and went back to the desk. He yanked open the belly drawer, pulled out a flat, well-worn .45 automatic and shoved it in his belt, handle pointing forward. The gun fit inside the waistband of his jeans as though there were a holster. Lighter didn't bother to hide the weapon beneath his shirt.

"Let's go south," he said. "Food's cheaper there."

A dusty Ford Ranchero was parked under a pepper tree out back. Lighter drove. Suarez, the smallest of us, sat in the middle. Nobody said much while we went the few blocks to the Mexican port of entry. The aduanal at the border recognized Lighter's car and raised the crossing gate before we got there. We sailed into the Third World without a pause and picked our way two more blocks through snarling bobtail diesels and beaten-up refugees from American junkyards. Lighter found a potholed spot in front of a place called the Café Norteño and parked.

The Norteño was smudged and unprepossessing on the outside, but the inside was clean, cool tile and elegant rattan. Lighter and Suarez must have been regulars, because the slender Mexicana at the reception desk gave them both a dimpled smile and ushered us to a table. She also gave Suarez a sideways look when he wasn't watching.

Thirty seconds after we had been seated, a waitress appeared with three cups of good black coffee norteamericano, three cold Bohemias and tortillas. All three of us drank—first beer, then coffee. The dark Bohemia was as rich as cream, and the coffee was triple-roasted. I buttered a tortilla. It tasted like corn. The feeling of having slipped into yesterday increased, and with it came a light-headed adrenaline rush. Part of me was a lot like Jake, fascinated by every border.

Lighter was more relaxed now. "Best food in Mexicali," he said. "Best spot for a restaurant, too. Farm workers headed north may sneak through the fence, but when they go home to Mexico, they make a big deal out of walking right down the main street of Los Estados Unidos and through the front door into Mexico. And the first thing they want is a real home-cooked meal, huevos and chorizo and tortillas." He picked up a warm tortilla, rolled it up, and bit off a third of it. "You ever notice how a good tortilla tastes pretty much like hominy? That's what Aaron used to say, anyway. His people came from Oklahoma, you know."

"Is that where the body is going?" I asked.

Lighter shook his head. "No way. The Sharps have been in this valley since 1913, even if they still did eat hominy. He'll get buried over to Holtville, on Saturday. That's where his people are."

"Was he ever married?"

Lighter and Suarez traded sideways looks. "He had a pretty blond wife a long time ago, but she got sick of waiting for him to come home from Mexico," Lighter said finally. "I think whatever home life he had was south of the line."

"Family?"

The shrug Lighter gave showed how long he had lived in a Latin culture. The gesture looked eloquent but said nothing.

Suarez grimaced a bit, studying me as though he was still trying to figure me out. I wondered if he had recognized my voice yet from our telephone conversation yesterday.

"Sounds like Sharp lived the same place he died—south of the line," I said quietly.

Lighter looked at me through narrowed eyes. The wrinkles around his eyes became more pronounced. The lines were the legacy of a life squinting into the desert sun. Sharp's eyes had been like that. Jake's would have been, but he had died too young.

"Who gave you the idea that Aaron Sharp died south of the line?"

"The FBI agent who didn't want the dust of Mexico on his shiny shoes," I said.

Lighter took a pull on his Bohemia and squinted at me some more. When he put the beer bottle down and gave me a tired flicker of a grin, I knew that I had guessed right.

Sharp hadn't died in America.

"The FBI detailed twenty-five agents down here to help us find Sharp's killer," Lighter explained. "But a fat lot of good all that high-priced manpower is going to do us. You see, the wing-tip brigade thinks that ratty little fence back there is the Berlin Wall."

Suarez was still young enough to be nervous about plain cop talk in front of civilians. "I don't know if you understand, but the line's not always marked," he said quietly to me. "Anyone, even someone as expert as Aaron, could easily cross the line at night and never know it."

I nodded neutrally and kept on watching Lighter. He picked a shred of tortilla from beneath a molar with his tongue, chewed on the morsel, and washed it down with a sip of coffee. Then he smiled at Suarez.

"Relax, Matt. This guy's uncle was the only smuggler who ever took a right hand from Aaron and didn't whimper. Fiddler doesn't need a map to know what it's like down here." Then Lighter turned to me. "You know the tunnel east of Campo on the Arizona Eastern railroad?"

I couldn't help but smile slightly. The Arizona Eastern Railway was a now abandoned railroad line that ran along the international border from San Diego through the Imperial Valley. The railroad had been built before the turn of the century, back in the days before the actual boundary between the countries was even surveyed. Since the location of the border in any given place was unclear, but the demands of a railroad grade were both clear and inexorable, some of the right-of-way ended up inside Mexico.

The Campo tunnel started in Mexico and ended up in the United States. It was one of the best smuggler's crossings on that harsh, dry stretch of border. Men and mules could walk the carefully graded railroad right-of-way instead of having to scramble up and down brushy rises and steep-sided dry washes. You could also strap on a kidney belt, put a pickup truck on the rails and go like a bat out of hell.

"Yeah, I know the tunnel," I said. "Jake always claimed he invented that smuggling route."

"Invented it?" scoffed Lighter. "Hell, man, Mexicans were whipping mule trains of hooch through the tunnel in the twenties, and Chinese opium merchants used it long before that. But if you know the tunnel, you also know which country the west end of that tunnel is in."

"Mexico."

"That's where Aaron bought it," Lighter said, rubbing his face tiredly. "The official version says the group was coming out the tunnel on the U.S. side, but they were actually still inside Mexico."

"How did you know about the group? Or were you waiting for something else and just happened to find the weed?"

"No. We had a snitch," Lighter said, sighing a cloud of smoke across the table. "Little Mexican punk who picks up a hundred a month telling us lies. Aaron ran into him at a place called Camacho's Store—a little restaurant and beer bar west of town—about nine o'clock. The snitch's name is José Sánchez-Huerta. He had a hot tip about a load of weed moving through the tunnel. So Aaron called me at home and we took a little ride out there just before midnight and laid in at the south end of the tunnel." Lighter drank again, frowned at his memories, and then shrugged them off. "You probably know the rest. The newspapers got that part mostly right."

"Who is this Sánchez?"

"Just a snitch," Lighter said, sighing. "He hangs out in the *coyote* bars and bus stations, picking up cigarette butts and information. We got him a permiso, a crossing card, so he trots north when he hears something good and peddles it to us or to the Border Patrol, depending on whether it's dope or mojados."

Lighter's use of the Mexican slang for "wetbacks" brought a grimace from Suarez, but the young Customs investigator said nothing.

"You talk to Sánchez since then?" I asked.

"I've spent the last thirty-six hours looking for that little shit, but he's really in the wind," Lighter said. "I can't find anyone who'll admit knowing him, much less having seen him recently."

Lighter rubbed his face again with a blunt, gritty hand. He looked old, as though just talking about the last day and a half had worn him out.

A smiling waitress with an indio face and thick black pigtails brought three big clay platters covered with fried eggs floating on ranchero sauce, great reddish chunks of chorizo sausage, beans, rice and nopales, which was pickled cactus chopped like piccalilli. The clay platters were oven-hot. We had to work carefully, scooping up runny golden egg yolks, bright red salsa and tan frijoles with pieces of tortilla. The plate took on the look of a Jackson Pollock canvas, but I ate as though I hadn't seen food since last year.

Lighter lost his appetite after a few bites. He smeared the eggs and beans around with a tortilla but ate little. A few minutes later the waitress brought him another beer and took our plates away. Suarez leaned back and fished a cigarette from his shirt pocket. I caught a glimpse of what looked like the butt of a Walther .380 stuffed into a hideout holster inside his jeans. He set fire to the cigarette. When he blew smoke across the table, I caught a whiff of the past.

I'm not sure what Mexican tobacco companies do to their cigarettes, but nothing in the world smells like a Delicado. They were the Mexican incarnation of Camels, a macho smoke for the workingman, cheap Turkish tobacco powerful enough to take off the top of your head. The sweet odor of their smoke is distinctive, almost overwhelming. If American cigarettes smelled like that, they would have been outlawed in public a long time ago.

I associated the smell of Delicados with Jake, who had smoked them in Mexico. I was surprised that Suarez smoked them. He looked a bit too much like a gringo for such a pronounced Mexicano taste. But I've never been one to question another man's choice in cigarettes, politics or sex.

Suarez finished his smoke, Lighter his beer, and we stood up to leave. Not surprisingly, a check had never arrived. In Mexico, cops pay for nothing. It isn't corruption in the classic sense of the word. It's just the way things are. When I peeled off a few bucks as a tip, Suarez gave me a shake of his head.

"No es necesario. It's not necessary here."

"That's why I'm doing it."

He shrugged, not as gracefully as Lighter had, but with more vigor, the way an American would.

When we got to the Ranchero, Lighter climbed in over the side like a tired hunting dog and stretched out full length in the bed of the pickup.

"Give me an hour," Lighter said to Suarez. "Then I want to take a run out to Niland. Seems to me Sánchez-Huerta used to spend time with a woman who lives in a little ranchería next to a date grove there." Lighter glanced at me. "See you around, Fiddler."

With that Lighter curled up, using his arm as a pillow. He must have finally drunk enough beer to wash away the bad taste of death, because he was asleep before Suarez drove through the port of entry two blocks away. Suarez had about as much to say to me as an adobe brick would. Back at the office, he positioned the truck carefully beneath the shade of the pepper tree. When we got out he closed the car door very quietly. He led me off ten or fifteen yards before he turned on me.

"You get answers to all your questions this time?" Suarez said.

The cold tone of his voice told me that he had remembered the telephone call yesterday. I looked down at the toe of my boot. Already the leather had taken on a desert patina, dust and heat and dryness sucking out the shine. I looked back at Suarez. I didn't know where he fit in with Sharp. I did know grief and anger when I saw it. Suarez wanted to kill something. I could have told him that revenge wouldn't make him feel better, but it was too dry and windy for me to stand around telling lies.

"This may be hard for you to believe, Suarez, but I've got more questions now than when I talked to you yesterday."

He gave me a slow look that reminded me oddly of Sharp. Then he shrugged abruptly and looked away. "Don't know why he put up with you, Fiddler. No accounting for tastes, I guess."

The wind picked up suddenly. The sun was past its zenith, heading for the long slide into night. In the shade of the building, the air had already caught the coolness rising out of the winter desert's rocky ground. Suarez pulled his hat into place with a hard jerk, then turned and disappeared into the office. A minute later he came back carrying a folded wool army blanket. He shook it out and threw it over Lighter.

When Suarez turned back toward me, I caught a glimpse of something in his features, a hard-edged echo of Sharp or Jake or even myself long ago. There was something about spending a few years with the border and the desert that made men move and talk and look alike. It came from watching over your shoulder and squinting into shadows, and whispering at midnight because sound carries forever in those deserted ravines.

"You need anything else, gringo?" Suarez asked coldly.

The choirboy Spanish softness of his voice was suffused with a familiar hardness. Sharp all over again, Sharp and the border and death.

"Not right now. I'll be back again, though. Count on it."

I walked away before Suarez started making threats he couldn't keep.

8

La frontera is where cultures collide. On the flat desert floor I had a choice of three kinds of radio music for company: shit-kicking country-western, rancheras, which are the Mexican version of shit-kicking country-western, and something called XTRA.

XTRA used to be one of those fifty-thousand-watt south-of-the-border Bible stations that blared sermons and ads for plastic dashboard Jesus statues across the western states. On a good winter night, you could pick up the signal all the way to Saskatchewan. The Jesus merchants have gone on to the greener pastures of satellite television, forcing the border radio dinosaurs to look elsewhere for ad revenue and listeners. XTRA, with studios in San Diego and a renegade transmitter in Tijuana the size of Radio Free Europe's, tried an elevator music format for a time. Everybody tuned out. No surprise, really. If they had an off button in elevators, the canned-music folks would be reduced to wiring stairwells for sound.

XTRA had been saved by a new format, a blast from the past, a.k.a. golden oldies. The songs were for baby boomers and their children who waxed nostalgic about a decade when daisies grew out of ROTC rifle barrels and sex came with a money-back guarantee plus the assurance that anything you caught could be cured by penicillin.

Yeah, I suppose we believed in the Tooth Fairy, too. Why not? The believing, like the love, was free. Or seemed to be. It took us too long to figure out what our parents had already learned: there ain't no such thing as a free lunch, baby.

Somehow XTRA's nostalgia rock format seemed right for poking around the time warp known as the Imperial Valley. Jake and the Jefferson Airplane were still completely at home here. I couldn't say the same for me. I would have been, once upon a time, but that time was no more.

Yesterday.

I turned down the radio. Paul McCartney's melancholy paean to twenty-twenty hindsight wasn't telling me anything I didn't already know. I pointed the TII west again, heading for the other side of the line. International incidents didn't appall me as much as they did the FBI. But then, I didn't have to fill out forms in quintuplicate detailing who had done what and with which weapon and to whom . . . and, most important, *where.*

Daylight was thickening into dusk by the time I came up over the top of the Mountain Springs Grade. I turned off the interstate to gas in Jacumba, a tiny city that sits a few thousand feet up off the desert floor. The wind had forty-five-degree teeth in it, and nothing to break its sweeping attack but a lunar landscape of boulders and parched ground.

Apparently the old Anglo with bad teeth hadn't gotten the word about self-serve stations. He was determined to pump the gas, so I stretched my legs and admired the cold blue sky over Jácame, Jacumba's sister village across the border. Yesterday ran very close to the surface here, like an underground river forced upward by substrata of unyielding rock. It was only about a decade ago that Mexico finally got around to running power lines over to Jácame's three hundred residents. The good folks of Jácame weren't overjoyed by the government electricity. Most of them made their living smuggling something. Anything. Illegal aliens and dope north or consumer goods and appliances south. Either direction, there was a profit to be made. Lights cut into that profit.

The cold wind swirled around me, tightening my neck and shoulders. Stretching didn't help. Neither did the taste of dust on the wind. Finally I dug a down vest out of the trunk. A few minutes later I was warmer but just as edgy.

I climbed back into the car and headed west on the chipped, cracked two-lane concrete road that used to be called the Friendship Highway. The road runs within a pistol shot of the border for twenty miles, finishing the climb up the dry side of the Laguna Mountains and leveling out into high chaparral and scrub oaks around Campo. Springtime can be pretty here, but that was a month or two off. Winter was cold and barren as a stone. Summer's fire was a memory. Finally I turned on the heater to keep my feet warm. There was still a trace of daylight lingering around the high places. I kept the accelerator down and the engine at high revs, asking myself too many questions about yesterdays that never seem to stay decently buried in the past.

My memory is all too good. I found the old turnoff as though it had been a day rather than a lifetime since I'd last driven that lonely dirt road. There were a few leftover puddles in the low spots, dregs of a recent winter storm. Tire tracks were thickly layered, indecipherable. I knew without getting out to look that one set of tracks belonged to the hearse that had carried Aaron Sharp away.

The road ran beside the abandoned San Diego and Arizona Eastern Railway tracks. Fifty yards short of the entrance to the tunnel, the road simply vanished into the monochrome landscape. I pulled the TII over to the side of the track and sat for a moment, listening to the little engine turning over slow and smooth. There were 165,234 miles on the motor, but somebody standing ten yards away would have had to strain to hear it idling.

From the looks of the place, there wasn't anyone within a dozen miles, much less yards, to hear or see me, but I knew just how deceptive that appearance of emptiness could be. The desert around here was so rugged you could hide a regiment with ease.

Was that what had happened to Sharp? Had someone hidden a regiment and then opened fire? If so, there would be signs—spent shell casings, cigarette butts, splatter spots where a man had taken a piss in a drift of loose sand. Only ghosts and memories could move without leaving a trace, but ghosts and memories don't carry nine-millimeter pistols.

I turned off the engine and stepped out. The wind had died in the shelter of the rocky hills between me and Mexico, but the air was chill and crisp. A pair of ravens flew by slowly, their wings whispering a warning of just how silent something must be to remain hidden. Off in the distance a scrub jay jeered the fading light. There was no other sound.

The TII's trunk opened with a muted squeak of metal hinges. I took Jake's .45 out of the case and shoved a loaded magazine into the butt. The gun was clean and oiled, but it hadn't been fired in years. Right now, miles from the nearest human being, seemed like a good time to find out whether the .45 still threw a foot to the right at fifty yards. Darkness wasn't far away, so I also grabbed the thin Maglite out of the tool kit and stuck the flashlight into my hip pocket.

The single-track tunnel was a hundred years old. Now that it was no longer maintained, the rock interior had begun to deteriorate, sloughing head-sized boulders down onto the roadbed at the entrance. A chilly wind from Mexico blew through the rounded, glowing arch of the opposite end of the tunnel as the last of the sunlight disappeared south of the line. I shoved the .45 into my waistband and started walking.

The midpoint of the tunnel was like a meat locker, cold and dead. I walked along as silently as I could, trying to imagine what I might find that the dozen or two investigators who had already been here could have missed. It was a fool's errand in many ways, but I was just the fool to run it. I didn't want one more dead man asking questions in my dreams. I had left Jake's corpse wrapped in unanswered questions, the most urgent being who had killed him, and why. Jake had deserved better. So did Sharp. Jake's answers were beyond my reach. Sharp's weren't. I know a lot more about finding answers now than I had known when Jake died.

At the far end of the tunnel, the level of illumination improved. There was a perfectly framed vista out across the Baja del Norte desert, a landscape washed by cool, fading light. I was still in the dark, thirty yards from the tunnel mouth, when I caught a whiff of Jake . . . like a memory and a ghostly presence all at once. I froze in my tracks, unable to shake the feeling that Jake was behind me and I was a very young man again.

Slowly I took another breath. Along with the oxygen came the realization that it wasn't Jake or the past I was smelling. It was fresh smoke from a cigarette. Not too far away, somebody had just lit up a Delicado. Somebody who hadn't left a car in sight at either end of the tunnel. Somebody who was careless enough not to have noticed my arrival, or lazy enough not to care. Perhaps the Mexicans had posted a bored federal at their end to preserve the evidence.

And perhaps pigs flew.

I moved to the wall of the tunnel and stood silently for a moment, listening. I heard nothing, not even the distant cry of scrub jays. But I caught another faint, unmistakable whiff of sweet tobacco smoke on the breeze that was funneling in from the rocks beyond the entrance. Another smoker would have missed the smell, which is one of the reasons I quit smoking long ago.

Staying close to the wall, I crept another ten yards toward Mexico. Even though I was still hidden in darkness, I had a fair view of the natural rock amphitheater beyond the mouth of the tunnel. I stood motionless for another five minutes, examining the rocks for ambush sites.

There were several places out there where a man could watch the tunnel exit from good cover. Nothing suggested that any of the spots was occupied. But someone was smoking Delicados. Whoever was up there had been on station long enough to get very restless or simply careless enough to risk a smoke. That was understandable; he was probably packing it in for the day. Ambush or legitimate surveillance, his light was fading fast.

As darkness suffused the sky, I edged closer to the end of the tunnel. At one point I glanced down and saw a discarded beer bottle just before I would have kicked it. The label said Bohemia. I wondered if Sharp and Lighter had brought a six-pack along to kill time on their own ambush, or if the folks who used the tunnel regularly brought beer with them to wash the dust of Mexico from their mouths.

Venus shone clear and steady, a knife-point of silver twenty degrees above the western horizon. Stars began condensing from the hushed darkness. There was still some twilight indigo in the sky, just enough to backlight the man when he finally stood up and stretched slowly. He had been crouching below the lip of the bowl; from that position he would have had a clean view of the tunnel mouth and not a hell of a lot else.

A sniper scope was clearly silhouetted on the receiver when the man slung the rifle over his shoulder and began to pick his way down the hillside, moving with the awkward motions of someone who has been cramped in a small place too long in a cold wind. A few seconds later he disappeared behind a steep rock hogback. He was probably making his way down the hill toward the railroad right-of-way. From there, I guessed he would turn and go south, toward Mexico's Highway 2, the little gravel road that parallels the border between Mexicali and Tijuana. Unless he intended to hitchhike into town with a sniper's rifle on his shoulder, he had a car stashed somewhere close to that road.

The railway roadbed had begun to fill in with the coarse sand that was constantly sloughed off by the decomposing granite boulders. The drift muffled the sound of my boots as I jogged the two hundred yards to the point where I judged the man would reappear. He must have loosened up quickly; I barely had time to hide behind a rock the size of a Cadillac before he arrived.

Even stiff from a day in a blind, the man moved quietly. I heard only one little stone come dribbling down the hillside during his descent. But he had to jump off a three-foot ledge onto the roadbed at the end. The small, flat *whump* of his landing came clearly in the silence. He stopped to light another Delicado. I couldn't see him, but I was close enough to hear the scratch of the match and the soft scrabble of his boots as he turned and headed away from me down the tracks.

I stepped out of concealment and moved forward a few feet. There was enough light to let me see his back clearly. For an instant my attention was caught by the odd configuration of the sniper weapon slung on his shoulder. Its stock had been cut away and reworked into a wooden skeleton, like the stock of a bench-rest rifle. The scope was matte black, uncluttered and businesslike. Everything from the man's dusty, stone-colored clothing to his gliding walk suggested that he was equally uncluttered and businesslike.

It was the only warning I would get, and probably more than Sharp had gotten.

I picked up a palm-sized rock and lobbed it off to the man's right. While the rock was finishing its trajectory, I covered some ground myself. When the stone came down and clattered around, the man froze for an instant before spinning to face the noise, reaching around to pull the rifle off his shoulder and bring it to bear as he moved. His hand was still on the sling of the long gun when I racked the slide on the .45. It was an unmistakable announcement that he was in deadly danger.

"¡Párese!" I called.

To make sure there was no language barrier, I started to repeat the command in English, but was too late. He had already made his decision. It was a tactical error, because his half-unslung rifle got in the way of his quick drop and roll to the left. He made most of the turn, but the long rifle barrel caught in the sand and stalled him for a quarter second.

Crouching, I followed his roll with the .45, expecting him to quit when he saw the dark eye of my pistol muzzle staring at him. He saw, but he didn't even hesitate. He completed the roll, pivoted around his right hand and was coming away from his waistband with a pistol when I fired the first time.

Jake's .45 hadn't changed. The first shot was wide to the right. The sniper didn't flinch. His pistol was coming to bear on me when I fired again. My second shot caught him flush in the chest, all but lifting him out of his boots as he went over backward. His only shot passed over my head and into the blue-black sky. The reports were still echoing around the rock amphitheater when I straightened and moved forward.

The sniper lay on his back, his arms flung over his head in a parody of surrender, his unfocused eyes staring toward the few stars that had poked through the twilight. I kicked the pistol away from his right hand and frisked him. Then I knelt beside him and put the flashlight to work. I wasn't looking for ways and means of applying emergency first aid; a .45 slug in the chest at close range doesn't leave enough for even a hot dog paramedic team to fix, much less a citizen like me.

The man was about thirty, with dark, fine hair and pale skin, slender yet muscular, rather like a snake. A long, deeply indented scar puckered his cheek. No indio heritage showed in his build or in the bone structure of his face. His blood was the way fresh blood always is—shiny and much too red.

"You don't warn worth a damn," I said.

His eyes slowly focused. He looked at me without comprehension for an instant.

I tried Spanish. *"Lo siento, hombre."*

His eyes cleared, then widened as though he recognized me as his killer. *"Chinga tu ma . . ."*

He died before he finished, but the sneer remained on his face, livid as a fresh wound.

"Fuck your mother, too, pal," I said softly.

Then I sat back on my heels in the sand, swallowed hard and waited for my heart rate to slow to double time. At that moment I felt almost nothing. I could still look at the sneer on the man's face and write him off as a poor loser. Later, after the adrenaline wore off, it would be different.

When I could hear the sound of the wind over the roaring of blood in my ears, I stood up and looked around at the empty land. The bleak chill of night welled up behind the rock rim where a man had lain in ambush. The sky paled in front of the rising moon. I couldn't see the horizon, but I could sense it in all directions, a hundred miles away and receding fast, leaving only me and a corpse and questions.

Again.

"Why did you have to kill yourself like that? I had you cold. You saw that. Why didn't you throw it in? You're no cherry. You didn't think you were bulletproof. Why did you do it? *Why!"*

More unanswered questions asked of a dead man. My list was growing. Maybe the sniper had thought he was quicker than my trigger finger. Maybe he had decided that death was better than being captured. Maybe he hadn't thought at all. Maybe the killer reflex simply had overwhelmed the survival reflex.

The body was losing heat to the cold ground. I checked the sniper's front pockets before rolling him over and checking the back of his pants. Except for the half-smoked pack of Delicados in his shirt pocket and a book of matches from a Tijuana bar, he couldn't have been cleaner if he had been vacuumed. The clothing itself could have been worn by any Mexican. *Hecho en Méjico,* cheap and polyester. He must have been one cold son of a bitch, sitting up there in the rocks with nothing to cut the wind but a thin synthetic cloth. He was getting a lot colder now.

The only thing about the sniper that wasn't cheap was the rifle he carried. Both the steel and the wood were European-made and carefully maintained. The receiver was as blocky as an AK-47's. The ejector lever and safety were conventionally placed, but the rifle itself bore neither manufacturer's mark nor serial number. The glass in the scope was as clear as springwater. Even in the pale moonlight, the scope brought the timber framework around the end of the tunnel into fine-grained clarity.

The pistol the man had carried in his waistband was less exotic, a nine-millimeter Llama automatic. Nothing fancy, but serviceable and well oiled. I shoved it behind the waistband of my pants.

"Wish to hell you'd lived, pal. I'd sure like to know why you were camped out here with a rifle, a sniper scope, a nine-millimeter pistol and a great deal of eagerness to use them."

I slung the rifle over my shoulder and walked away from the dead man. There was nothing more for either of us to say. He could have been a lookout for cocaine or heroin smugglers. He could have been part of one of the dozen red brigades that operate out of sympathetic, corrupt Mexico. He even could have been hired by a border bandit with a grudge against American cops in general or one Aaron Sharp in particular.

Except that none of those descriptions would explain why he was still hanging around, thirty-six hours after the fact.

The only place I might find any answers was the dead man's ambush site. It was probably vacuumed as clean as his pockets, but a long shot was better than no shot at all. I took to the rocks, scrambling up the little bank by the roadbed and picking up the tracks of his shoes in the coarse granite sand. The trail up the hogback was easy to follow. Five minutes later I found the spot near the rim of the amphitheater where his tracks disappeared up a rock face. I kept going without a pause. It's easier to track a man across decomposed granite at night than it is in the daytime. A flashlight makes the fresh scratches stand out like diamonds in a goat's ass, as an old border tracker once put it.

At the end of the scratch marks was the coziest little sniper's den I've even seen—out of sight, out of the wind, surrounded on all sides by boulders. The spot was roofed over with big rocks, almost a natural cave. Between two of the rocks there was a narrow gap, a natural gun port, which looked out on the amphitheater and the tunnel mouth. It would have been a 250-yard shot to the tunnel entrance. I knew without looking that the scope on the sniper's rifle had been calibrated for 250 yards.

The place showed signs of having been occupied for some time. The ground was thoroughly scuffed and tracked. There was a small tin can full of Delicados butts and paper matches, a half-full canteen of coffee and a makeshift honey bucket that hadn't been emptied today. There was also a heavy jacket, a sleeping bag and a small knapsack that had once contained food but now was empty except for one can of pineapple bits in heavy syrup.

There was an eerie feeling about the place, as though an animal had gone feral and holed up here. The empty knapsack did tell me one thing. The shooter had misjudged the length of his wait. He had been forced to break cover because he was running out of food. Probably he had intended to return with fresh supplies. He had been a pro; if he had been leaving for good, he would have removed all traces of his former presence. Even with those traces intact, the den was devoid of personal touches. The sniper remained as anonymous as a coffin nail.

As the small cone of light slid around the cave once more, I caught a flash of white at the corner of my eye. I played the flashlight over the area again and saw that something had slipped into a crevice in the rocks beside the gun port. A moment later I realized that the papers hadn't been misplaced. They were photographs that had been put within easy reach for a sniper crouched over a scope at the gun port.

The first three photographs were of Sharp. Though dark and unfocused, as surveillance photos often were, they gave a very good idea of what Sharp had looked like from his right side, his left side, and head-on as he leaned his elbows against a little bar in Mexico and surveyed the room. I recognized the bar. I had been there with Sharp not a month ago. We had drunk the moon under the horizon while we sat and watched assorted border bandits come and go from the room.

I wondered which photo had triggered the sniper's recognition pattern. Had Sharp been shot from the left, the right, or the front? Not that it mattered. Dead was dead, no matter what the angle of entry.

Shuffling quickly through the photos, I wondered what other unlucky Customs agent was on the sniper's hit list. The fourth photo was so blurred that it was almost useless. If it hadn't been for the unmistakable lines of a Shelby Cobra in the background, I wouldn't have guessed the identity of the man leaning on the fender. The fifth and sixth photos took all the guesswork out of the game. I tried to remember where I had been when the pictures were taken. I couldn't. Sharp and I had been to more than one Mexican bar. Even if memory hadn't told me that the pictures had been taken under cover, the expression on my face would have. I wasn't aware of the camera.

Right side. Left side. Center.

I switched off the flashlight and stood there in the dark for a long time, wondering why Sharp and I had been paired for an executioner.

9

I kept the rifle for the same reason that I had hung on to Benny's spherical chrome-plated slugs. I kept the photos as a reminder of how unpredictable life can be, and death. I had other plans for the pistol.

By the time I got back to the corpse, the moon was shedding so much light that the two expended shell casings from Jake's old .45 gleamed back at me like fallen stars. I picked up the casings and the Delicados pack with its matchbook shoved among the cigarettes.

I left the body where it lay. The coyotes weren't going to drag it very far in the next few hours.

When I was four miles down the Friendship Highway, I turned on the headlights. Back on the interstate, going against the evening commuters, I made good time to El Cajon. There was a Denny's just off the freeway at Wintergardens Boulevard. The coffee shop was crowded, but the phone booth beside the john was empty. I punched in the Customs office number in Calexico. Suarez answered. He sounded more tired than he had that morning.

"Nine-millimeter? Luger cartridge, like maybe a Llama?" I asked without preamble. Sometimes official phone calls are recorded. I didn't want my name attached to this one.

Suarez remembered my voice very quickly this time. "Yeah, why?"

"In about fifteen minutes, call the El Cajon cops and have somebody check the trash bin in the men's room at Denny's on Wintergardens. Tell them not to worry about smudging the prints on the piece because there won't be any."

The second pause was longer.

"Hey, Ace. You going to tell me what the hell is going on?" Suarez asked finally, not bothering to mute the anger in his voice.

"If it's the gun that killed Sharp, you can find the man who carried it lying on the San Diego and Arizona Eastern tracks about a quarter mile from the Mexican end of the tunnel."

"And if it isn't the gun?"

"The guy will still be there, but you can let the coyotes and the Mexicans worry about him. In the meantime, see if you can find anything in your intelligence files on a place called the Blue Parrot in Tijuana."

"Hold it, Ace. I'm not your gofer. This is a federal murder investigation, not some—"

"This anonymous recorded message will self-destruct in three seconds," I said, cutting him off and hanging up.

The john was empty. I stepped into a stall long enough to wipe down the Llama thoroughly with toilet paper. Carrying it by the checkering on the handle to avoid leaving usable fingerprints, I dropped the gun into the trash receptacle beneath the sink. A few minutes later I was back on the interstate.

I checked into a Best Western motel in San Ysidro, the last gringo town before the border. I wasn't going to sleep on the south side of the line if I could help it. Especially not this particular stretch of the line. Sharp had told me it was the most active piece of the two-thousand-mile U.S.-Mexican border.

The motel was only half a mile away from the line. As I carried my bags to the room, a Border Patrol helicopter circled over Spring Canyon just east of Interstate 5, trying to turn back the nightly flood of illegal Mexican immigrants. As Benny would say, "S.S.D.D." Same Shit, Different Day.

Once inside the room, I called home and got nothing but my own voice on the answering machine. Fiora's answering service had no idea where she was. Benny wasn't home, either. I was uneasy as hell, but I'd made my choice when I headed for the border.

Finally I called Suarez again.

"It's El Papagayo Azul, Ace," he said. "Not the Blue Parrot. Smugglers up the ass."

"Tell me something I don't know."

"That shouldn't be hard. They aren't smuggling dope. The place is kind of a staging area for los mojados—wetbacks, as you gringos call them."

I grunted.

"Customs files had nothing on the place," Suarez continued in a clipped voice, "but Bill Glenn, who's with Immigration Service intelligence in El Centro, got a whole bunch of hits on the place in his data base."

"I'm listening."

"Good for you, Ace. El Papagayo Azul is in the Zona Norte, just back from the River in T.J. It's owned by a guy named Rickie Hernández. He's a pocho from East L.A., but he went south for good several years ago, after he was indicted here for alien smuggling. He hasn't been seen north of the line since. Glenn says Rickie is big time. In the past few years, he's gone international. Seems like about half the OTMs in Baja come through Rickie's bar."

"OTM? What's that?"

"That's Immigration Service talk," he said. "It means Other Than Mexicans. Could be anything from Guatemalan to Ghanian or Guamanian."

"I thought Mexicans had the franchise on fence jumping."

"Haven't you heard, Ace? The rest of the world finally discovered that you don't have to wait in line to get into the U.S. You just go to Tijuana, pony up the smuggler's fee, and wake up on streets paved with gold. There's big money smuggling Chinese bankers from Hong Kong and Sikh separatists from the Punjab."

"Bigger money that smuggling Mexicans?"

His laugh was derisive. "Hey, Ace, Mexicans are a volume business, didn't you know? Three hundred bucks a head, max. A Hong Kong banker will pay twenty grand to get himself and his wife smuggled to L.A., and ten grand apiece for the kids. Besides, smart Mexicans don't need smugglers anymore. You ever see Spring Canyon at twilight? The Mexicans have all made the trip so often, the paths across are worn a foot deep. I suppose an ace like you would call them cattle trails."

"Only if cattle made them. I don't know about you, *Ace*, but the last time I counted, a cow had four legs. Now, if you're through being a prick, you can give me the rest of what you know about the Blue Parrot."

Suarez was silent for a long five-count.

"El Papagayo Azul has a very tight dress code," Suarez said. "Glenn said he has a friend who got his skull caved in last month for wearing a snitch jacket into the place. You might want somebody to ride shotgun for you."

"You're a federal officer. You can't go to Mexico on a criminal investigation without an invitation. That would be a violation of international neutrality or something, wouldn't it?"

"The percentages aren't with neutrality," Suarez said in a bleak voice. "I just talked to the criminalists. They've been going crazy trying to figure out what make of gun killed Aaron. Llama's kind of an esoteric weapon, but it leaves the right number of lands and grooves to fill the bill. They want to do a test-firing as soon as somebody can get the gun back from El Cajon, but I'm betting that's the piece."

"Well, if you're getting itchy sitting around the office, I'm sure the Baja judiciales wouldn't mind if you went out and shifted some carrion north about three quarters of a mile."

There was absolute silence, then a low laugh.

"Hell of an idea, amigo. Then I'll know where the carrion is buried. I can piss on its grave every Sunday."

Suarez might have been young, but he had a healthy streak of mean in him. He must have known Sharp better than I'd thought.

"With any luck, I'll give you the bastard who killed Sharp," I said.

"What do you mean?" Suarez demanded. "The one near the tunnel —isn't he the man who killed Aaron?"

"He was the weapon somebody bought. The weapon is out of

commission. Now I want the buyer. If I don't call by morning, check El Papagayo Azul."

I hung up and tried the cottage again but got no answer. Then I tried the Beverly Glen Hotel. Fiora was registered for the night, but she wasn't in her room. I was glad as hell she wasn't hanging around the cottage all by herself.

Benny was home. I told him about the Llama, the sniper's roost and the photos.

Benny laughed.

"I didn't find it all that funny," I said.

"You always sound so amazed to discover that you've acquired enemies." He chuckled some more, but I could hear the wheels turning, too. "Sharp and you . . . There's only one link that I can think of."

"Volker," I said flatly. "But it doesn't wash. No motive."

"Ever heard of revenge?"

I made a disgusted sound. "C'mon, Benny. Volker was—is—a professional. Win some, lose some, some never had a chance. Revenge is no part of that equation. Oh, I'm not saying that Volker wouldn't dump me if he happened to walk by me and had a loaded gun and a dead-bang escape at hand. But waste a lot of money and brain time on killing me? No way. I don't mean that much to him."

"What about you? Would you take a crack at him if you had the chance?"

I hesitated. Part of me would have leaped at the chance to kill Volker. And part of me knew that kind of exorcism doesn't work in the long run. Killing Volker wouldn't erase the fact that in many acutely uncomfortable ways, Volker and I were as close as brothers, perhaps twins.

He had been Fiora's lover when I first met him. I had been prepared to hate him for that. He had been prepared to return the favor. We both had been astonished to discover that in many ways we were mirror images. In retrospect, it shouldn't have surprised us. Fiora had chosen us both. Volker was blond and I was dark, he had intense blue eyes and mine were pale gray, he was under six feet and I was over; but those were only superficial differences.

Volker moved like a hunting cat and smiled like a fallen angel. He had been a world-class gymnast and had become a world-class intelligence operative. Fiora hadn't known about the latter until too late. She had sensed that something was wrong beneath Volker's incredible flexible voice, and she had come to me because she didn't trust her own judgment where Volker was concerned.

Lucifer, Lord of Light. The most charming man I've ever known. And the coldest.

Yet Volker had loved Fiora as much as he could love anything. He had calmly asked me to take her and to disappear for a few weeks, and when the weeks had passed, Fiora could choose between us. It was the most deftly presented bribe I'd ever been offered . . . and one that I have often regretted not taking.

But I did refuse it, which was how I had learned the true difference between Volker and myself. He would have accepted either outcome. More important, he would have killed Fiora in order to get his job done. I couldn't imagine deliberately killing any innocent person, much less the woman I loved.

The ability to kill exists in nearly everyone. Some just come to it more quickly than others, and suffer fewer aftershocks. Volker could kill and never suffer a qualm. I couldn't. There have been times when I wished I could, but only a few, and the desire never lingered for long.

"Fiddler, you still there?" Benny sounded suddenly lonely.

"I'm still here," I said.

"Well?"

"I spent the first year after Danny's death hunting Volker. If I'd found him, I'd have dumped him."

"And now?"

"I'd think twice."

"That's a better break than he'd give you."

"He doesn't have to live with my conscience."

"Too bloody right. So what makes you think Volker wouldn't go out of his way to bugger you?"

"It's been years, Benny. I live in the same place, do the same kinds of things, love the same woman. If Volker had wanted me, I'd have been easy to find. He'd have come after me a long time ago."

Benny grunted, telling me that he had thought of that little kicker, too. Volker had been hard to find. I hadn't.

"Well, mate, you might be right," he said, "but Volker's my candidate unless you and Sharp both pissed somebody off the last time you went slumming south of the border."

"Not that I remember," I said. "Oh, there was the normal amount of shouldering, but nothing to make a vendetta out of."

Benny muttered something unflattering about men who drank so much they couldn't find their own cocks. I ignored it.

"The Blue Parrot is the only lead I've got," I said. "I don't know what that string is tied to, but I'm going to keep pulling on it. Sooner or later, something will unravel."

"I can be there in an hour, maybe less at this time of night," Benny said.

"I've had more offers of help tonight than anytime in the past six months. I didn't know T.J. had become such a popular destination."

"Just make sure your shots are up-to-date, mate."

"Penicillin or hollow-point?"

"Both."

Benny's warning was running around the back of my mind as I drove back down Interstate 5 toward Tijuana. If the desert border is an exercise in cat-and-mouse skirmishes, the urban border is full-scale guerrilla warfare. The Border Patrol's Hughes 500C was hovering about fifty feet above the levee on the south side of the Tijuana River. The chopper's million-candlepower searchlight picked out small groups of men and women wading through the foot-deep pools in the river channel.

The chopper was new, a replacement. A few years ago the old one had hovered a little too low over a group of Mexican kids on the south levee. One of them pegged a rock through the whirling rotor, knocking a chip out of the blade. The bird settled rather unceremoniously into the river bottom—on the U.S. side—and the gang of kids proceeded to storm across the line and rout the chopper's crew with a hail of rocks and bottles. The chopper remained behind. The kids swarmed over it and reduced it to high-tech trash in a good deal less than ten minutes.

So much for hands across the border. Down here it's more like fists.

The stretch of border between Imperial Beach and Otay Mesa is about seven miles long, but it generates more than half the illegal crossings recorded each year along the entire two thousand miles of U.S.-Mexico frontage. On an average night, between fifteen hundred and two thousand people are arrested trying to crash that seven-mile line. Some Mexicans commute regularly, if illegally, from homes in Tijuana to jobs in San Diego. The ground is literally beaten flat in places by the constant traffic.

The green-shirted Border Patrol agents are shoveling sand against the tide, and they know it.

It's easy to make the no-man's-land of Spring Canyon into a setting for modern melodrama—ask any media type, Chicano politician or Immigration bureaucrat bucking for a bigger bite of the national budget. The word "invasion" is usually mentioned. If los nortenōs, as the illegals call themselves, constitute an invasion, it's a relatively friendly one. Although some ugly specimens of humanity are on the loose in Spring Canyon at night, they aren't the immigrants themselves. Border bandits—many of them Mexican cops—rob and rape at will and slip back across the line Pancho Villa–style when the American authorities intervene.

Some people see the immigrants as utterly benign folks who had been victimized by man and circumstance: the poor and huddled masses yearning to breathe free. Others regard immigrants as utterly malignant: alien hordes, Vandals and Visigoths storming the walls of the New World's Rome and bringing with them the germs that will destroy civilization as we know it.

There's a touch of truth in both views, I suppose, but not enough to write law over. The illegal immigrants I've known are pretty much like the legal variety, no more or less human for their lack of documents. Los nortenōs are neither the poorest nor the least educated of Mexicans. The poorest are frozen in place by their poverty, unable to raise even the price of a bus ticket north, much less the three hundred collars a *coyote* would charge to move a man across the border; and the uneducated have no notion at all of the larger world. Los nortenōs, like all immigrants everywhere, are the ones with imagination, hope, guts, and enough aggression to go for the brass ring no matter how rough the ride.

The alien smugglers, however, are a different lot. In Mexican slang, the customers waiting to be smuggled across are called pollos, chickens, and the smugglers are called polleros, chicken hawks, or *coyotes.* Pollero or *coyote*, the relationship to their clients is the same: predator to prey.

I parked the TII in a lot close to the San Ysidro port of entry and walked over to the gate carrying the briefcase I had carefully packed in my room. Mexico frowns on gringos carrying guns, and while I probably could have taken the Detonics south in my boot, there was no need to risk a smuggling charge so early in the game. Besides, customs cops aren't the only ones who frown on guns. Crooks do, too—at least if you're the one who's armed. That was why the briefcase contained some of the gear Benny had loaned me, including a hand-sized plastic package call the Nova XR5000. It looks a bit like a Sony travel radio, an appearance I'd underlined by wrapping a pair of stereo earphones around the shell.

The Mexican aduanal was having a hard time staying warm in the wind. He gave me and my briefcase a thorough, skeptical look, which was unusual. Most aduanales weren't excited about anything you carried into Mexico.

"Good evening, sir," he said in lightly accented English. "Will you be long in Mexico?"

"I just thought I'd go down and see the sights."

I lifted the briefcase onto the long table. Mexican Customs officers don't usually hassle the tourists, but this one was either bored or looking for a little extra money.

"What are you carrying of value?"

He looked at my face, not my briefcase. Nervous smugglers don't like to make eye contact with the Customs guard.

"Nothing much," I said, looking him in the eye.

He wasn't buying it. So I volunteered a red herring.

"Just some cash I'm taking down to a bank in Tijuana."

That piqued his interest. Many dope dealers maintain Tijuana bank accounts in order to avoid reporting currency transactions to the U.S.

government. The guard was probably getting a little bounty from American Customs for any currency smugglers he caught. Or he could be collecting a little of the southbound greenery for his own personal garden.

"How much money are you carrying?" he asked blandly.

"About five grand."

At the motel I had withdrawn five bills from the stash in my money belt and placed them in an envelope. The envelope also contained a single fifty. I hadn't figured to need it so soon, but it looked as though the guard had nominated me to pay a onetime user's fee for entrance into Mexico.

"That is five thousand dollars?" he asked carefully.

"Yes."

"May I see it?"

I opened the briefcase, pulled out the envelope and handed it to him.

"You know that you are allowed to bring only five thousand dollars in cash into Mexico at one time, do you not?" he asked when he saw the bills.

"Yes," I said. "I would have had to file a U.S. export declaration if I had more."

"Then what is this?" he said, showing me the corner of the fifty.

I did a double take. "Damn. I must have miscounted."

"You know the penalty for failing to report excess currency, do you not?"

"Confiscation?" I offered, watching his eyes.

"*Sí, señor. Exactamente.*"

He palmed the fifty and handed me back the envelope. Then he glanced with an utter lack of interest at the rest of the contents of the briefcase and nodded, indicating that he was satisfied. As I moved to shut the briefcase, he pointed at the Nova.

"What is that?"

"A communications device."

He looked puzzled, as though defeated by the fancy English. "A radio?"

"Close enough," I agreed. "Fifty thousand volts of easy listening."

The idiom confused him even more. He shrugged and waved me through. *"Pásele."*

I closed up the case and walked into Mexico. The aduanal was already looking north again, straightening his khaki uniform, waiting for another customer.

La mordida. The bite. Every official is a tax collector of sorts. There are times when I prefer la mordida to the IRS.

This was one of them.

10

"Hey, man, what you after tonight? You look like a gringo who wants a little panoche, huh?"

The kid wore a black and green flannel shirt and black Levi's. He was maybe twelve and his English was utterly without accent, as though he'd learned it from "Sesame Street." Television signals being what they are, he probably had.

"Candy rots your teeth, kid," I said, shaking my head.

"Not that kind of brown sugar, man, the other kind."

For a kid so young, he had a pretty good leer.

"I thought kids couldn't pimp anymore in Tijuana," I said, digging in my pocket for a buck to get rid of him.

"I'm not a pimp," he said, rejecting the dollar, "and I'm not a beggar. I'm a businessman. Now, what's your pleasure? You need a guide or a ride, a blow job or a burrito? You name it and I'll tell you where to get it."

"You know a place called El Papagayo Azul?"

The kid blinked and then gave me a second once-over. "There's lots of Blue Parrots. Which one do you have in mind?"

"The one where *los pollos exóticos* hang out."

"You into smuggling foreigners? You don't look like the type."

"Why?"

"They're weird," he said flatly. "I mean, real foreigners—Japanese and Koreans and black Africans. What are you?"

"Me? I'm a real foreigner, too. I'm from the United States."

He gave me a grin and looked me over again. "Sure you don't want a little panoche?"

"Just a parrot. A blue one."

The kid shrugged. "You want to go there, that's fine with me. But it's a hard place to find. I can show you how to get there."

This time he took the buck when I offered it.

"I'm Jaime, *a sus órdenes.*"

The kid's Spanish was as quick and unaccented as his English. Brown, tough, wiry, bright, child of two cultures and master of both. Today he was hustling me. Tomorrow, the world.

Jaime led me past the thin, tubercular men selling plaster bulls and the heavy indio women who stood expressionlessly peddling paintings of saints on black velvet. A six-year-old dusty-faced child with a runny nose tried to dart in and sell me a pack of Chiclets from her nearly empty tray. Jaime offered her the back of his hand. I stopped him, dug out another buck and gave it to her.

Suddenly another pair of waifs appeared from nowhere and zeroed in on me.

"Now see what you've done," Jaime said, disgusted. "Keep that shit up and we'll never get out of here."

He dispersed the children with shrill Spanish epithets and led me toward the foot of the Tijuana River bridge, where a line of taxis waited.

"Competition looks pretty tough, Jaime."

"Brutal, man," he said, shaking his head. "Some of those kids would slit your throat for a U.S. dollar. Ever since the exchange rate went over twelve hundred pesos, the competition's been unreal."

"What's the secret of your success?"

He grinned, suddenly a kid again. "I'm a USC," he said, "a United States Citizen. My mama sneaked across the border when she felt the first pains. I was born in a Border Patrol holding cell in Chula Vista."

He motioned back toward the Customs shed, which stood precisely on the border. "That means I've got a right to stand right there, right on the line. I get the first shot at customers like you."

"You ever think of moving north yourself?"

"Mama got tired of the hassle. I could stay, but not her. Besides, things are cheaper in T.J., and I don't have to go to school anymore."

"If you ever change your mind, you might think about Wharton, or maybe a Harvard M.B.A. You'd knock 'em dead on Wall Street."

Jaime's smile flashed, but he shook his head. The only street he wanted right now was the one we were on. He led the way to a rank of taxis, all of them at least two decades old and looking like their last paint job had been done with a wire brush. The cab at the head of the line was a 1963 Plymouth that had once been white and green. The driver, a big-bellied Mexican whose face was shaped like Jaime's, held the back door open for me.

"You meet my boy already," he said. "My name is Héctor. Where you want to go?"

"This is a very sophisticated gringo," Jaime said. "He wants to go to the Blue Parrot."

The boy slid into the front seat. The back seat was rump-sprung, but the cab itself was clean and didn't smell of raw gas, so I relaxed. Héctor swung out of line and headed across the bridge into town.

"You come here much?" Héctor asked.

I shrugged "Not lately."

"You meeting a friend?"

"Never can tell. It's a small world."

Héctor gave up on me and drove. I looked out the window at the seething streets.

If you ask people to name the biggest cities on the West Coast, you get names like L.A., San Francisco, Portland, Seattle, and if the person is vaguely sophisticated, Vancouver and possibly even Anchorage. No one mentions Tijuana, but it's bigger than every city on the West Coast except Los Angeles.

Even on a cold night like tonight, about half of T.J.'s million residents were on the streets, walking purposefully or wandering or merely huddled around flickering fires built in fifty-five-gallon steel barrels. There has been a relentless housing shortage in the city ever since it became the staging area for the vast illegal migration north. People rent rooms in shifts and then stand in the streets waiting for their twelve hours out of the wind to begin.

It was the same in the Zona Norte—a sprawling collection of cantinas, flophouses and tortillarías. Groups of young men from the interior of Mexico thronged the streets. The men were going north, headed toward the river levees, where they would cross the border in a darkness shattered by searchlights. To cut the raw wind, a few of the men wore makeshift ponchos created from trash can liners. Most simply hunched their shoulders and endured.

"You want some mariscos?" Jaime asked.

I shook my head.

"I can get you tacos that won't make you sick."

"Yeah? What's the trick?"

"If the meat has claws in it, you don't eat it."

From the corner of my eye I saw two Chinese slip in and out of the dim light thrown by a streetlamp. Dark on dark, other figures hurried by just beyond the cone of illumination. No one else on the street gave the Chinese a second look. That alone told me how routine their presence had become. I remembered what Sharp had told me about the Chinese having a regular pipeline laid out. They flew in through Mexico City with the other tourists from Hong Kong, then hopped on Aeroméxico and flew straight to Tijuana.

Once here, the Chinese were met and taken to houses near the Blue Parrot, or some similar smugglers' hangout. When a vanload had been collected, the pollero would load 'em up and head 'em out like so many cattle. If they were going on the cheap, the Chinese might be mixed in with a group of Mexicans and walked north. Three hours later a car would pick them up near National City, north of the border. Bang, the pollos are on the freeway, and three hours after that, they're in Los Angeles International Airport, waiting for a plane to take them to San Francisco, Chicago or New York.

Sharp had watched them all, the frightened, the diffident, the Chinese, the Koreans, the Pacific Islanders, the Turks and Germans, the chestnut-haired Argentinians and discreet Iranians, the pale Scandinavians who had tired of lists seven years long. They all passed through Tijuana on their way to the Promised Land . . . and most of them were guided by kids not much older than Jaime.

"You know the guy who runs the Blue Parrot?" I asked. "Name of Rickie?"

"*Sí,* Rickie Hernández is a heavy dude, El Mero Gallo," Jaime said.

"What's his reputation like? Do his customers get what they pay for?"

Héctor gave me a long look in the rearview mirror. Jaime wasn't that subtle. He simply stared over his shoulder at me.

"You got a special reason for asking, or are you just curious?" Jaime asked.

"That's right," I said.

Jaime was quick. It took him only two seconds to figure out that I'd answered both his questions—and neither of them.

"Señor Rickie is the best," Jaime said simply. "He pays the local federales and judiciales more than the government does. A thousand dollars a week, U.S." He shrugged. "At least, that's what I hear on the streets. He only hires family."

There was both bitterness and resignation in Jaime's voice. In Mexico, family connections were everything.

"I'd like to meet him. Does he hang out at the club?" I asked.

"Sometimes, but you won't be able to see him, señor. He was many bodyguards, and he never drinks with the customers." Jaime smiled meanly. "I've heard that la Migra has offered a thousand dollars and a case of pistol ammunition to any Tijuana policeman who delivers Señor Rickie north of the border."

"Any takers?"

"*¿Quién sabe?*" Jaime said. "There are more rumors in the streets than cockroaches. People, even policemen, are always for sale, but they do not always stay bought. El Mero Gallo is still here. The money and ammunition are still north of the border."

We had passed through the roughest part of the Zona Norte and were on the fringe of downtown Tijuana. Héctor pulled off the potholed street half a block short of a whitewashed facade that was the backdrop for a blue neon Art Deco creature roughly resembling a parrot.

"There it is, señor." Jaime waved toward the sign. "We're not afraid, you understand, but Papa doesn't want to deliver you to the front door. He does not wish to be seen in the company of a gringo asking questions about Rickie Hernández."

I understood. In some ways Mexico was more like a collection of feudal states than a modern country; law was dictated by whoever got there first with the most firepower, which meant that Mexico was riddled with fiefdoms. That was one of the reasons Sharp—and Jake—had liked the place. The rules were both very clear and geographically limited. South of the border, a man could be as good or as bad as he dared. The idea has a certain appeal. . . .

Jaime reached for the five I offered. When he tried to take it, I held on.

"I'd hate to be stranded without a ride if things don't go well here. If you wait two hours for me, it would be worth a hundred U.S., fifty now and fifty when I get back."

I let go of the five. Father and son discussed my proposition in pragmatic, very rapid Spanish. There were risks, but at the current exchange rates, I was offering them a month's salary.

Finally, Héctor pointed up a side street. "We will park there and sleep."

"But first the fifty," Jaime said, holding out his hand.

I gave him two twenties and a ten from my wallet, got out and quietly closed the Plymouth's door behind me. As I waited in the shadows, Héctor pulled away from the curb, drove past the front door of the Blue Parrot and turned up the little side street. I strolled down the cracked and buckled sidewalk into the flickering pool of blue light thrown by the buzzing neon parrot. It was just after ten o'clock.

The Blue Parrot was cleaner and better-lighted than most Tijuana dives. The big room was a cabaret, complete with a parquet dance floor and fifteen or twenty tables. A little combo—a black man on an electric keyboard and a Latino on electric guitar—played something relatively innocuous but loud. A bar stretched along the entire length of the back wall, where potted palms and overhead fans lent a Mediterranean flavor. Business was good. Maybe fifty people, men and women, were strung out along the bar or seated at small tables.

I stood for a moment, letting my eyes adjust to the smoky light.

Rickie Hernández went to great lengths to maintain an orderly café. A pair of watchdogs in polyester leisure suits and open-collared shirts were studying me from either end of the bar. They must not have liked what they saw. One of them dropped off his stool and headed up a flight of stairs to a suite of offices. The other one, a beefy guy with a head the size of a large pumpkin, put down his Dos Equis and studied me coolly. He was clean-shaven, except for a dark swatch of beard that covered the point of his chin. He scratched the beard thoughtfully while he studied me, assigning me a weight class and trying to see whether I would lead with my left or my right. I pretended he wasn't there.

"Good evening, señor; would you care for a table?" A waiter slid out of the shadows, looking patient and incurious. He spoke with a thick accent that was Latino but not Mexican. He had the look of a Colombian in his dark suit and rose-colored shirt.

"I thought I'd try the bar," I said.

"Then perhaps I could take that for you," he said, reaching for the briefcase.

"I don't mind carrying it."

His look told me that he could have taken it away from me, but it wasn't his job.

"As you wish," he said.

Now that I could hear it more clearly, his accent sounded Cuban: muted sighs and blurred consonants and swallowed syllables. Somehow it reminded me of the hit man's dying curse. I pulled a twenty out of my wallet, folded the bill and palmed it, leaving only an edge showing. That was more than enough to attract the waiter's trained eye.

"I'm supposed to meet a man here," I said. "Maybe you can help me, because I think he's one of your countrymen. Six feet tall, thin, muscular. Like a snake. He has a long scar down his face. A knife scar."

The Cuban gave me a skeptical look. "This man you describe sounds *muy malo.*"

"Oh, I don't think so, at least not anymore," I said. "He been in here lately?"

"No, I'm sorry," the maître d' said promptly.

"Too bad."

He was very cool. His eyelids didn't even flicker when I pocketed my twenty and walked past him toward the bar.

There were three empty stools at one end. I sat on the middle one and wedged the briefcase against the bar with my foot. After my beer came, I watched the room in the mirror that ran the full length of the bar. The music was salsa, and the crowd sounded like Saturday night in mid-Wilshire, L.A., an undifferentiated mob of nationalities and ethnic groups on the prowl. There were a dozen distinct clusters of people, all of whom bore the unmistakable tentative look of strangers in a strange land. Subtle differences among nationalities—haircuts, clothing styles, even physical mannerisms—showed up very clearly in such a setting.

While there was a Latino bias to the crowd, it was not Mexican. There were Guatemalans wearing black felt fedoras, Argentines looking and sounding more like Italians despite the fact they were speaking Spanish, and a knot of black men—probably Dominicans—gathered around a table cluttered with empty Corona bottles. The men spoke Spanish and had a subdued, wary look about them. Next to them, a turbaned Sikh sat drinking an orange soda. He was the only man in the crowd who seemed not to be nervous.

In one corner, almost hidden in the shadows, sat a well-dressed Chinese couple. They looked like tourists out on the town for the night, but they weren't having much fun. They stared numbly at the untouched drinks before them on the table.

A Mexican with a limp came down the stairs from the office suite and walked straight across the room to the Chinese. He spoke quietly. Instantly the couple stood up and followed him out the front door. They walked quickly, jerkily, in the manner of obedient but unwilling schoolchildren. Their expressions were a mixture of fear and eagerness.

I wondered if the couple would wake up tomorrow in Los Angeles or in the Baja desert without their wallets. They were probably wondering the same thing.

The bar's polyglot crowd of expectant immigrants was oddly energizing. Wherever these people were coming from, the United States looked to them like heaven just over the hill, just beyond the ragged chain link fence on the north bank of the Tijuana River. Rickie's Blue Parrot bar was a film noir advertisement for America with a salsa score.

An Anglo came from somewhere down the bar and slid onto the stool beside me.

"Hey, mate, you're a Yank, right?" The accent was somewhere between Liverpool and King's English. The face was pale, sweaty, and unevenly covered with sandy beard stubble. He looked like he was behind on his rent and smelled like he'd been eating the wrong kind of tacos.

"I'm American, yeah," I said, turning back to my drink.

"Just the bloke to appreciate a bargain," he said enthusiastically, making eye contact in the mirror. He held up his hand like a traffic cop as he accurately read my expression. "I know what you're thinking, but this isn't a hustle. I'm just a wee bit down on my luck, but my bad luck is your good fortune, mate. See?"

He pulled a Rolex Oyster out of the pocket of his jacket. The watch was used, which was probably a sign of its authenticity. If it had been brand-new, there would have been a 98 percent probability that it was a Japanese knockoff. He offered me the watch. I didn't take it. He laid it on the bar, propping it so that the crystal face caught colored reflections from the lights overhead.

"That's a two-thousand-dollar watch where you come from, mate, but I've worn it for a few months, so I can afford to sacrifice it to a bloke like you with taste and five hundred dollars cash in his pocket."

"I don't wear watches."

"Three hundred," he said quickly. "How about three, mate? That's a bloody good bargain. You look like a man of the world, so I can tell you that I only paid five hundred bucks for it myself. Bought it from a longshoreman in Marseilles. He and some of his mates had lifted a container full of the bastards."

"Then you'd probably settle for fifty, wouldn't you?" I asked in a bored voice.

He looked away, considering the offer. His hands were shaking. There was the faintly acrid smell of desperation beneath the odor of unwashed Englishman.

"Look, mate, I can't afford to haggle, but I can't take less than three hundred, either."

"Trying to get north?"

He looked shocked. "You're not some kind of cop, are you?"

I shook my head. "Three hundred's a popular number, particularly in a place like this. But I thought Rickie charged more than three hundred for pollos with white skin."

"I'll have to walk with the Mexican field-workers," the Brit said sourly, "but it was the best deal I could make. I jumped ship off a freighter that made a call in La Paz. I was going to go north and cross the border in style, under a load of bananas, like some of these blokes here." He sighed. "But a tart rolled me last night in a hotel over by the jai alai stadium, whatever it's called . . ."

"Fronton."

"Yes, well, anyway, she pinched my pecker and then my wallet, and this watch is the only thing left. Three hundred is really a bloody good . . ."

His voice died as he looked over my shoulder. He glanced away and tried to slide his hand down the bar to collect the watch. A brown hand reached over his shoulder and stopped him.

"Señor Hardy, this is a place of business. Our business. This is not a —¿cómo se dice?—a garage meet, no?"

"Swap meet," I said, taking another swallow of beer.

"Sí. Swap meet. Gracias, señor."

The hand and the insincere thanks belonged to the bouncer with the billy goat beard. He was very compact, very quiet, like a python. He had Hardy's pinky finger and was coolly bending it backward with enough force to bring a stifled little yelp from the sailor.

"I will break this finger if you disturb our customers again. ¿Me entiende?"

Hardy's face was beaded with sweat. He nodded because he hurt too much to speak.

The bouncer released his grip. "We still have our agreement, Señor Hardy," he said softly. "But you must raise your payment in the street. ¡Vaya!"

Hardy almost fell off the stool in his hurry. The bouncer turned to me, making sure I had been watching. I got the impression the performance had been as much for my benefit as it had been for poor Hardy's.

"Sorry, señor, for the rudeness of our customer," the bouncer said.

His smile was as empty as his apology. The only thing sincere about the man was the butt of the blue steel Colt that made his coat tent across his chest as he reached in and leaned toward me.

"And now, señor, what is in that leather case?"

The bouncer did a lot of frijoles and tortillas. His belly had begun to pull at the buttons of his black and white polka-dot shirt, and a jowl was threatening to swallow the gold chain around his neck. But he was big and he must have done some iron along with the beans; he had a neck and a pair of shoulders that seemed to invite a matador's estoque. I could have stood and put us on the same level, but that would have meant letting go of the briefcase. Instead I reached for the beer on the bar, took a sip and held the bottle carelessly by the neck.

Without moving his head, the bouncer measured the distance from the beer bottle to the side of his face. Then he straightened and smiled, showing me the caps on his incisors. They were made of a reddish gold, as though the native metal had a lot of copper in it. They matched the color of the fifty-peso gold piece on the chain around his neck and the five-peso gold piece in the ring on his pinky.

"Rickie around?" I asked, smiling, giving the bouncer a chance to see that I had teeth too.

His expression didn't change, but his mouth got thinner. "You want Señor Rickie? Why?"

"The usual reason."

"Business?"

"I doubt that it's going to be a pleasure."

"What kind is your business?" he demanded.

I took another sip of the beer, wrapped my fingers around the barrel of the bottle and looked at the bouncer. He was *muy macho*. That was his job. My job was to convince him that leaning on me was more trouble than it was worth.

"Hey, pal," I said, hefting the bottle. "Fight, fuck or hit the wall."

The bouncer might not have done enough jail time to understand my exact meaning, but he got the drift. He drew a sharp breath through his nostrils.

I waited.

He pawed the ground for a moment or two, swinging his scrotum as though he thought it was too big to fit between his legs. When his bearded chin dropped for the charge, I swiveled on the stool to face him, flipped the bottle six inches in the air and caught it neck-down. The last of the beer drained impolitely onto the floor between us.

"Which ear are you willing to lose, toro?"

He snorted a warning. "Pendejo. Do not start trouble you no can finish."

"Good advice. Try taking it."

I rotated the bottle idly, making light run like white water over the curved glass. The bouncer watched and moved no closer. I nodded.

"I came in here to do business with your boss, and you're acting like I'm a drunk selling bad watches. I don't know what your problem is, and I don't care. We're wasting time. Either get out of my face or lose yours."

That idiom, too, was unfamiliar but self-explanatory. The bouncer thought it over. Mexicans understand insults better than anybody except, perhaps, the French. He had been the one looking for trouble, not me, and he knew it as well as I did. But he had been looking for only a *little* trouble, the kind that could be taken care of with a bit of pinky twisting. I was offering him the kind of trouble that would clear the bar and bring in the cops. He wasn't about to accept my offer without a better reason than he'd had up to now.

The bouncer straightened and dropped his hands below belt level.

"My name is César," he said. "I work for Señor Rickie. I do not start fights. I keep order."

I shrugged and lowered the beer bottle to match César's peace offering. "I, too, am an employee. I represent a group of wealthy but disconsolate Americans. Their families are separated by politics, clerical errors and the Pacific Ocean. A friend of mine in Monterey Park tells me that Rickie is a humanitarian who makes it his business to reunite such families."

César blinked and relaxed another notch. Even if he had only understood half my speech, I had said the magic words: Monterey Park. That city had become a modern shibboleth to Chinese immigrants, legal and otherwise. It was the new Chinatown of Los Angeles, the destination of choice for half the Pacific Rim's immigrants.

"And how is Señor Rickie to help los pobres?" César asked, spreading his hands in a gesture that could mean empathy or disbelief.

"Who said these families were poor? God helps the poor. The rich have to find their own way. With money, usually. Lots of it."

The corners of César's mustache twitched. "Señor Rickie is a man of much family. He understand. Perhaps he help you. Come, we drink *más* beer."

He signaled for two beers from the bartender. I traded in the empty bottle for a full one. Briefcase in one hand and beer in the other, I followed César to a small table close to the combo, whose salsa was loud enough to prevent casual eavesdropping.

"Speak now, señor," César said expansively.

I gave him a cool look. "Thanks, but I'd rather explain it to your boss. Nothing formal, mind you. Maybe over a drink."

"You must speak first to me. Señor Rickie, he never drink with customer."

Win some, lose some. The first round had been mine. The second would be the bouncer's.

"Okay, but take notes or something so I don't have to repeat everything twice."

He gave me a cold flash of teeth again. "Where you hear the name of Rickie Hernández?"

I shook my head. "No names. All I can tell you is that my source is a very substantial member of a Los Angeles area bank. Until two years ago, he was the sole owner of a bank in Hong Kong, but with the impending change in government there, he decided to emigrate. He has no desire to practice capitalism under the Communist regime of the People's Republic."

César nodded. "Much chinos come to Tijuana."

"And those Chinese have paid Rickie very well to smuggle them into the United States," I added blandly, just so there was no mistake about where the conversation was going.

The bouncer neither agreed nor disagreed.

I shrugged. My movements were too Anglo to give the gesture its full Mexican grace, but César got the point—I cared enough to come to Tijuana and the Blue Parrot, but my life wouldn't be significantly blighted if I couldn't do business with Rickie Hernández.

"I don't object to the profit motive, even in humanitarian endeavors," I said. "After all, I'm an attorney."

Attorney was the second shibboleth. César was very accustomed to American lawyers purchasing illegal acts. With one swallow César finished half his beer. He set the bottle on the table with a decisive rap.

"How many?" he asked.

"Fifty."

His eyelids flickered. "Fifty peoples? That is very much."

"Fifty *families*. We're talking nearly three hundred relatives. What kind of money does Rickie get per head?"

César's eyebrows bobbed as he drank more beer. He was doing the mathematics on three hundred times Rickie's going price. When César put the bottle down, a little beer trickled from the side of his mouth. He wiped it with the back of his hand.

"Five thousand dollar," he said.

"Jesus Christ. These people are economic refugees, even if they are bankers. They're fleeing Communist repression in their native lands or something. Where's your sense of decency? Have you no—"

"Is bargain," he said, cutting me off. "We do everything. We buy ticket from Hong Kong. We give entrance visa for Mexico City. We have bus to go from there to the frontera. Our system is good, señor, very good. We promise you get north or we do it second time for nothing. It is a mero—¿cómo se dice?—a bag tour?"

"Package tour."

"*¡Sí! Exactamente.* A package tour, everything in neat little box."

"Visas included?" I asked mildly.

"*Sí,*" he nodded, smiling to himself. "The Hernández family, she is very big in Mexico City. The pasaportes look real. *¿Cómo no?* They are real. But they are very, very precious. Money, *me entiende?*"

I understood. "Welcome to Mexico, the best government money can buy," I said, watching bubbles rise in the beer. I swallowed some of the brew and thought it over, as César would expect me to do. "It might be worth five grand to these people, with Rickie's guarantee that, if they're caught, you bring them through again for free," I said finally. "Hell, I might be able to boost these bankers up to six grand, if you make it worth my while."

César's smile flashed in shades of gold.

"Of course, I'd have to make that kind of arrangement with Rickie himself," I added blandly. "I'm not about to drop nearly two million American dollars into the hands of anyone but el jefe himself. Personally."

César's smile vanished. "No is possible. Señor Rickie, he no do business himself," the bouncer said, shaking his head sadly.

"Too bad. I've got five grand in earnest money in my briefcase, but it goes only to the boss." I swallowed some beer, set the bottle down and picked up the briefcase. "Thanks for the drink."

For an instant César was too startled to stand up. He hadn't expected the negotiations to end so soon.

"Maybe you can tell me which is closer to the Blue Parrot—Paco's Café Norteño, or Chico's Salsa Verde?" I asked.

The names of Rickie's two closest competitors for the OTM trade focused César even more quickly than the mention of five thousand dollars had.

"Earnest money?" César asked. "What is this?"

"Five grand up front just to prove I'm serious. But I deliver the money to Rickie, and only to Rickie."

César chewed on the inside of his cheek for a moment, then stood up on feet that were as small for his size as his hands were.

"Stay here, señor. I will speak to Señor Rickie."

"I'll make a phone call while I wait."

You can direct-dial Los Angeles from Mexico. I got a sleepy hotel operator in Brentwood, but Fiora nailed the receiver halfway through the first ring. Her voice was wide awake.

"Fiddler," she said.

Not a question. She knew. That should have made me feel good, but it didn't. She had been thinking or dreaming the wrong things; neither activity was good news for our chances of living together.

"Hope I'm not interrupting anything," I said.

"I don't think that's terribly funny, particularly since Richard Toye is here in bed with me."

"In that case I know I'm not interrupting anything."

She made a sound that could have been strangled laughter or a teary sigh. I could see her in my mind's eye, stretched out on top of the covers, staring at the blank ceiling of the hotel room, thinking about things that separated her from sleep and from me.

"Having trouble getting to sleep?" I asked.

"No. Just staying asleep."

"Street noise?"

"No," she said with finality. "Just a dream."

A dream. Just a dream.

A dead man counting stars while coyotes circled.

"Want to talk about it?" I asked, hoping that she didn't. I didn't want to lie to Fiora. Nor did I want to tell her the truth over the phone.

"I'd rather talk about Dickie-bird," Fiora said, her voice tight, almost brittle. "He's beginning to make me angry. He spent half the afternoon with some foreign bankers, rounding up enough capital to buy back my stock or make a run at Mia Portman's, or both."

"You sure?"

"Positive. His secretary and I shared the powder room. She hates her boss more than I do."

"You must have him panicked. What kind of foreign bankers?"

"His secretary guessed Europeans, maybe Swiss, maybe Italian. But it doesn't make sense. Why are Europeans trying to get into the Pacific Basin Fund?"

"Maybe they've seen the end of the European era as surely as Teddy Portman did. Maybe you should just take your profit and get out."

"But that's just it," she said. "There won't be any profit. With the right kind of support from the board, Toye could force me out at about eighty cents on the dollar. I'd have no recourse except maybe to go to court. That would take months or years and cost thousands, and by the time anything was settled, he would have cemented himself into position so deeply at PBF that I could never get rid of him."

"So what are your options?"

"Now, of course, you're asking me what my options are. . . ."

It was an old gag between us, stolen from some English comedian and used like code between us. But suddenly Fiora was out of humor.

"Dammit, Fiddler. Why aren't you here? I have enough to worry about without knowing that someone is chasing you all over hell and maybe—" Her voice broke. She took a careful breath. "Are you still in Calexico?"

"I came back over through San Diego, trying to get a line on something."

"Something." Her voice was flat. "What caliber?"

"Not to worry. Everything's fine. I had a little trouble with a guy earlier, but things are so cool right now that I'm not even carrying a gun."

"You're a shitty liar, Fiddler."

"I'm telling the truth. The Detonics is in the car."

"Then that's where you should be. In the car. Heading home."

The salsa combo had come back from a break. The guitarist began running arpeggios up and down the fingerboard of his Fender.

"That doesn't sound like San Diego," Fiora said. "It sounds like a cheap T.J. bar. Why do you always end up in places like that? On second thought, forget I asked. I don't want to hear any more cool half-truths or salsa lies right now."

I saw César working his way toward me through the high-strung crowd.

"I've got to go," I said quickly to Fiora.

"Fiddler—call me?"

"Tonight?"

"Yes. No. Whenever you can." She drew a broken breath. *"Be careful."*

She hung up before I could answer. When I turned around, César was there.

"You are ver' lucky, señor. Rickie say to tell you he has a free minute."

"No shit," I said, unimpressed. "I'd have a free minute, too, if somebody was going to give me five grand."

César led me across the big room, up the stairs and down a short hallway. He knocked on a door before he pushed it open and went in with me behind him.

The second bouncer was behind the door when it closed. Suddenly I found myself kissing the cold, hard tile wall, but it wasn't nearly as cold and hard as the pistol muzzle tucked up against the base of my skull.

"*Perdóneme*, señor, but is necessary to look for weapons," César said calmly.

You bet. That's why the Detonics was in the car.

The other bouncer, the one with the fat mustache, was thorough and deft. He patted me down politely but didn't miss a trick. The Detonics in the boot wouldn't have passed muster. Neither would the hideout knife in the belt buckle. He even examined my knuckles and the edges of my palms for calluses like the ones that karate practitioners build.

Satisfied, the bouncer stepped back and held out his hand for the briefcase. I handed it over without objection, letting him discover for himself that it was locked.

"*La llave, por favor*," he said with faint impatience.

I gave him the key.

The room looked like a receptionist's office with nobody home. The briefcase hit the desk with a soft thud. A few moments later the locks were open. Through it all, César stood between me and what I took to be the doorway to Rickie's office.

"Your boss is a little paranoid," I observed.

Nobody answered. César didn't even look over at me. Now that he was certain I wasn't armed, and that whatever the briefcase might hold was under the control of his partner, César was quite relaxed.

"*¡Hijo de la chingada!*" the Mustache said in a startled voice.

Five one-thousand-dollar bills computes to millions of pesos. A lot of millions. Either one of these guys probably would have killed me for a good deal less than that. As a matter of fact, I think the idea occurred to Mustache. He looked at the contents of the unsealed envelope, then at me, then at the money again.

"Naughty, naughty," I said, shaking my finger at him.

He spoke little or no English, but he got my meaning. He grinned sheepishly. Then he fanned the five bills and showed them to César.

"Hijo de la chingada," he repeated.

César had more class. He walked over, snatched the money from his partner's hand and shoved it back into the envelope. He showed me that he was putting the envelope back in the case. Then he picked up the plastic box wrapped in the earphone cords.

"What is this?" he asked skeptically, telling me that he had at least heard about room bugs even if he had no idea what they looked like.

I gave him my best city-boy smile. "Haven't these made it to T.J. yet? It's the latest radio from Sony."

I took the thing from César and unwrapped the earphones, working quickly without seeming to, and talking the same way.

"It's called a Crawlman, a kissing cousin of the Walkman," I said. "You can listen to it with headphones, just like a regular radio. Or you can carry it in your pocket and listen without earphones. It transmits right through your body. Wildest sensation since your last blow job. I'll show you."

César was a bit uncertain, but before he could object, I pressed the electrodes on the bottom of the box right against his chest and punched the button. He caught the fifty thousand volts flush on the sternum. His whole body stiffened like somebody had rammed a yard of steel rebar up his ass. Before he could even groan, I zapped him again and simultaneously reached for the pistol in his shoulder holster with my free hand.

César was already headed for the floor, so I let his momentum pull the gun from the holster. He turned out to be a very traditional Mexican; the gun was a .45. I stepped back, pointed the muzzle at the other bouncer and thumbed the hammer back. I was gambling that César was macho enough to carry a round in the chamber.

Either I was right or Mustache was less of a gambler than I was. His eyes got real big and his hands went up like they were on rubber bands. I kept the gun trained on him while I checked César, who was groaning weakly on the floor. He was pale, but he was breathing steady. That was one tough man. I straightened up, picked up the stun gun and dropped it in my jacket pocket, then retrieved Mustache's .38 from the desk, where he had laid it. That, plus the envelope full of money, and I was ready for my job interview.

"*Vámonos*, Mustache," I said, pointing toward the door. "*Ahora, ya.*" He obeyed and moved to the door.

"*Manos abajos,*" I warned softly.

Mustache understood border Spanglish. He lowered his hands. I screwed the muzzle into the back of his neck, reached over his shoulder and knocked on the door to Rickie's office. Someone answered from inside.

"*Pásele.*"

I opened the door and shoved the bouncer through in front of me. By the time Rickie Hernández looked up from the papers on his desk, I had a .45 pointed right at his clean-shaven face.

Rickie was a dark-skinned man with black hair and hooded black eyes. He was in his late thirties, wiry and dressed in a well-made white silk jacket, a white tie and a white cotton shirt. An unfiltered cigarette smoldered in the ashtray at his fingertips. I expected Delicados instead of the pack of Pall Malls at his elbow. He was trimming his nails with a small silver pocketknife.

Rickie might keep bodyguards, but he wasn't a coward. He watched me with unflinching black eyes.

"Keep your hands on the desk, Rickie."

I shoved the bouncer toward the floor. He got the idea and went facedown on the tile. I stepped out of his range.

"All I have is a few thousand pesos from the bar," Rickie said in a bored tone. "I'd pay you five times that to be my bodyguard, since you're obviously worth more than the ones I have."

I ignored Rickie and cataloged the room in a glance. Like most hunted men, Rickie had a bolt hole. Just beyond the office a back door opened onto a stairway.

"You don't want money and you don't want a job," Rickie said, reading my silence. "What do you want?"

"I want you to get up and cut the cords off those blinds," I said, nodding toward the windows.

Rickie moved slowly, keeping his hands in plain sight. The knife was

---

104

very sharp. It went through those tough braided cords in a single stroke.

"Drop the knife in the wastebasket, then tie up our friend with the mustache. Feet first. Then hands."

Rickie was cute, but he wasn't obvious. He did Mustache's feet real well, but a baby could have undone the granny knots on his hands. I made Rickie do the knots over again. I wasn't quite as fussy about the cord holding the gag in place. I wanted the bouncer quiet, not dead of suffocation.

"Looking good, Rickie," I said, testing the bouncer's bonds without looking away from his boss. "Now take off that fancy silk tie and wrap it around your eyes."

"I can face my executioner without a blindfold," Rickie said coolly.

"Good for you."

I put the barrel of the .45 on the ridge of bone between Rickie's eyes. He went absolutely still. His tie came off with a couple of quick pulls. I held it beneath his nose.

"Wear it or eat it."

12

Rickie didn't like either idea. He stared at me with those dark, hooded eyes, a man used to instilling frightened obedience with a glance. I stared back while I draped the tie over his shoulder and pulled the stun gun out of my pocket.

"The nice thing about electricity," I said conversationally, "is that it's quiet and it doesn't turn the target into wallpaper. Ask César. Of course, I'm told it's rather painful when applied to certain parts of the male anatomy, but you can't have everything."

Without a word Rickie picked up the tie and blindfolded himself. Maybe he had had some experience with cattle prods and testicles, a favorite interrogation technique the world over. The instant that the blindfold was in place, Rickie changed. He seemed to shrink inward. Being blind does that to people who aren't used to it.

I pulled off his belt, strapped his wrists behind his back and half dragged, half carried him down the stairs to the alley below. He moved tentatively, reminding me of the Oriental couple as they had followed their guide out the door of the Blue Parrot.

"Look, man," Rickie said softly, "la Migra is only offering, what, a thousand bucks U.S.? That's nothing. I can raise ten grand in ten minutes. Just give me the chance."

I had wondered when Rickie would decide that I was an unruly emissary of the U.S. Immigration and Naturalization Service, a.k.a. la Migra south of the border. Rickie was getting worried now, starting to break a sweat. I wanted him more than worried. I needed outright terror to loosen his tongue.

"Rickie, Rickie, Rickie," I said soothingly, massaging the tense muscles beneath his shirt collar with the hand I was using to control him. "You keep misjudging me. I don't want your money."

"Then what do you want? Who the hell are you?"

The words were half demand, half cry of frustration and fear. Rickie tilted his head back, trying to see under the blindfold. I tapped the butt of the .45 against the base of his skull. He stumbled. I jerked him upright with one hand, letting him feel my strength, reminding him of exactly how helpless he was. Just short of the rumpled sidewalk I shoved him against a dark alley wall, told him not to move, and stepped out onto the sidewalk to check the street where Héctor was supposed to be waiting.

Héctor must have wanted the other fifty. The cab was right where it was supposed to be, parked in front of a little upholstery shop. I reached back into the alley's black mouth, grabbed Rickie and frog-marched him quickly to the cab.

Héctor was slumped behind the wheel, his chin on his chest. Jaime was in the front seat. His eyes widened when he saw the blindfolded Rickie and the metallic gleam of a gun in my hand. I put my finger to my lips to warn Jaime to be quiet. He nodded. I pulled open the back door and shoved Rickie forward until his shins collided with the rocker panel of the old Plymouth.

"On your knees."

Héctor woke up with a start. Instantly Jaime leaned over the put his hand across his father's mouth. Slowly Héctor turned toward the backseat, saw what was happening and sighed.

I pointed at the now prone Rickie and said to Jaime, "Watch him very closely. If he moves, blow his brains out."

Jaime nodded and perched on the front seat, where he could watch Rickie. The kid didn't have a gun, but he was more than smart enough to holler if Rickie moved. I signaled to Héctor. Together we got out of the car and walked about twenty feet away, where we could talk quietly without being overheard.

"*Hijo, señor,*" Héctor hissed. "Is that Señor Rickie?"

"*Sí,*" I said. "But don't worry. I'm the only one he's seen. As long as that blindfold stays put, you're all right. I need ten minutes in your cab. Here's the fare in advance."

I flicked a bill out of the envelope and handed it to Héctor. He moved a few feet so the streetlight could shine on the zeros behind the one. I could see his lips move as he counted, one, two, three. He swallowed hard and counted again, and then a third time.

"*Madre de Dios,* is it real?" he asked, looking up at me.

"Yes."

"I am not a bandido," Héctor said doubtfully. "What must I do?"

"Just show me where the Border Patrol concentrates its men at this time of night."

There was a long four-count. Suddenly Héctor's face lit up like a shooter's moon. He had figured out what I wanted to do.

"I know just the place, señor," he said, laughing softly, "and do not worry about Jaime and me. It will be good for my clever son to see that even a rich cabrón like Rickie pays for what he does."

When we got back to the cab, Rickie hadn't moved. I slid into the backseat and pulled the door of the cab shut. When Rickie raised his head a few inches to find out what was happening, I tapped his skull with the barrel of the .45, then rested the weight of the gun on the muzzle pressed against the base of his head.

"You better pray we don't hit any potholes on the way to the border," I said.

Rickie tried to shrink away from the muzzle. He couldn't.

Traffic thinned out as we passed through the Zona Norte. After a few minutes we left the commercial district and turned into a neighborhood of increasingly dilapidated houses and, finally, shacks.

"Colonia Independencia," I said, recognizing the area. "Your kind of place, Rickie. This is where the *coyotes* round up their pollos for the run across Spring Canyon. Bet la Migra is all over the border here like green on a frog."

Rickie muttered something.

"Louder," I said, tapping him lightly on the back of the head with the gun.

He raised his head a few inches. "I said somebody's going to pay for this, pendejo."

"The trip's free, baby," I said, punctuating my words with the pistol barrel. "And it's a one-way ticket unless you get real smart, real fast." I rapped him again with the gun. "You say something?"

"Nothing," he said carefully. "I didn't say a thing."

"You're learning."

I rapped him again, just hard enough to get the job done. The Ice Cream King had taught me this variation on the game of one-upsmanship. He had learned it in Vietnam, but I was never sure from which side, ours or theirs. The whole process was like Chinese water torture, only more so. Just keep chipping away at the prisoner's confidence with the barrel of the gun, reminding him every few seconds that the next tap might be a bullet.

It isn't a nice game, but then, I never play it with nice people.

Colonia Independencia's jumble of cardboard shanties and adobe hovels ran right up to the border fence and then stopped. The fence was ten-foot chain link that hung slackly from its steel posts to discourage climbing. It hadn't worked. Smugglers had simply cut holes in the fence big enough to drive cars through. It took less time to cut fence than to string it up, so there was never a lack of holes. Just beyond the fence was Spring Canyon, a network of chaparral and cactus-choked finger canyons that was decorated by a madman's scrimshaw of footpaths.

Technically, everything north of the fence was the good old U.S. of A. In reality, the first mile north of the line had become a kind of no-man's-land that belonged to whoever had the balls to occupy it.

By day, Spring Canyon was largely deserted. By night, the illegals ebbed and flowed through the canyon in a living tide. Years ago the Border Patrol gave up all pretense of being able to stem the flow. Patrolmen were too few and the illegals were too many, so the Border Patrol simply erected temporary dams to channel and contain the flood, skimming off a percentage of the human flow, processing it, then funneling it back south of the border to try again another time.

At night, Spring Canyon is as grim as Hogarth. White searchlights and the headlights on Border Patrol vehicles sweep across the barren landscapes, seeking the furtive, fleeing groups headed north. Everything is black and white, and the night itself seethes with life hiding just beyond the reach of light.

Héctor drove silently, pretending this was just one more cab fare. He pulled up at the stub end of a street that looked out onto Spring Canyon. Jaime gestured. I leaned close so that he could whisper in my ear.

"Out there is the Soccer Field," Jaime said. "It's a bad place, *muy malo*. Pollos, *coyotes*, and border bandits all mixed together. The American patrols are heaviest here."

"How about Mexican cops? The word about Rickie being taken is probably out on the street already. The cops might want to rescue their little meal ticket," I said, tapping Rickie on the skull with the pistol muzzle.

"The policía only come here to shake down the wetbacks," Jaime whispered.

"Figures," I grunted. I opened the car door and heaved Rickie out onto the dirt. "Come on, pal. Let's make like international tourists."

The ocean was only a few miles to the west, which meant that the wind was cold and damp. I yanked Rickie to his feet. He moved slowly, stiffly, but he said nothing. At least he wasn't a whiner. As a reward, I eased up on the pistol muzzle in his neck.

The narrow little street was lumpy with discarded cans and rocks. The hovels on either side were dark. I pushed Rickie ahead of me and watched the shadows in case some brave soul decided to start asking questions. When we left the street and scrambled up a low bank, I caught a flicker of movement at the corner of my eye—a feral dog or a true coyote dashing off into the night. There was a raw stink in the air, like a skunk had cut loose somewhere upwind.

The moon was past its zenith. The few high clouds let through enough light to see the border clearly. In several places all that remained of the fence was a few shreds of twisted chain link hanging from support posts that had been bent and nearly flattened. It had been a long time since the fence had been patched or replaced. I steered Rickie through a large gap and pulled him to a halt about ten feet inside the United States.

"Welcome home, Rickie," I said, yanking off his blindfold. "We've all missed you, boy."

He blinked rapidly, letting his eyes adjust to the moonlight after a time of total darkness. Suddenly he saw the ratty fence between himself and Mexico. He went very pale beneath his dark skin. Up until that instant he had still believed that this was all an elaborate shakedown. Sweat gleamed clearly on his forehead and cheeks.

I backed up into Mexico.

"A border is a funny thing," I said as I pulled Mustache's .38 from my belt. Moonlight gleamed off the whites of Rickie's eyes. "I could drop you in your shoes right now and get away with it. Mexico won't prosecute me for firing a pistol, and the United States can't cross the line to grab me. But you already know that, don't you? You've been playing the touch-me-not border game for a long time."

"What do you want, man?" Rickie asked. "Just tell me what you want!"

There was an edge of panic in his voice. Just what I had been waiting to hear. I lifted the pistol shoulder-high and pointed it at him.

"We'll start with the easy questions. And Rickie . . ."

"¿Sí?"

"Don't lie to me."

Moonlight ran over the barrel of the gun that was pointing at Rickie. He nodded jerkily.

"What do they want you for in the United States?" I asked.

"Smuggling," he said quickly. "Federal grand jury indictment in Los Angeles. They caught a semi-truck of mine loaded with a hundred and forty-three Mexicans."

That wasn't good enough. The Border Patrol doesn't offer to make an unofficial swap of money and ammunition for a generic alien smuggler.

"What else?"

"That's all, man. I swear on my—"

I cut off the lies by lifting the muzzle of the revolver to the sky and firing three evenly spaced rounds. Rickie flinched with each shot as though the bullets were burning into him.

"Don't, man! You'll bring every cop in five miles!" he said desperately.

I shrugged and leveled the pistol back at him.

"Some of my drivers have abandoned loads out in the desert," Rickie said hurriedly. "Sometimes people die. An accident, no more. It's very hot out there. Last summer four pollos died of the heat, and my lawyer thinks the Border Patrol is just waiting until they get me back across the line. Then they'll prosecute me for murder."

"You should have vetted your drivers more carefully."

"Shit, man, drivers come and go like clap, and pollos have been dying for years and nobody kicked. But I'm the biggest smuggler in Tijuana, so la Migra wants me. An example, you know?"

"Yeah."

Down in the canyon a pair of headlights suddenly appeared. The nearest public road was at least a mile away. The headlights could only belong to one of the Border Patrol's off-road vehicles, probably a hulking Dodge Ramcharger that had been lying in ambush at the bottom of one of the finger canyons. Slowly the headlights began to move as the patrol pushed tentatively into Spring Canyon's no-man's-land, investigating the gunfire.

"Looks like your ride is coming, Rickie."

He took a step back toward Mexico. I pointed the gun at the bridge of his nose. He stared down the bore but said nothing.

"What do you know about a Cuban with a scar on his face?" I asked, tracing the line of the scar on my own face with my finger.

For a moment Rickie forgot to breathe. "I've handled thousands of pollos. How am I supposed to know just one?"

I raised the gun in the air and fired three more rounds. Suddenly a spotlight on the vehicle's side snapped on. The beam lanced through two hundred yards of cold, damp air and caught Rickie in a narrow sword of light. He was trembling with cold or fear or both.

"This one wasn't a pollo looking for a good wage," I said. "He was a sniper, un asesino. Very professional. He smoked Delicados and lit them with matches from the Blue Parrot."

The big Dodge engine growled through the night, louder every second as the Ramcharger climbed up out of the canyon in low range, sending pebbles and small rocks flying.

"Come on, man, come on," Rickie said urgently. "I'll give you twenty thousand. Just let me back over there!"

I dropped the empty .38 onto the gravel and went back to the .45. I cocked the hammer and waited.

The beam of the searchlight was jerking unpredictably as the vehicle hit rocks and ruts. More sounds came, the gabble of a police radio on an outside speaker and the grinding crunch of gravel beneath huge all-terrain tires. The vehicle approached slowly, as though the Border Patrol suspected a feint or a smuggler's diversion or even an ambush. From another angle came the headlights of a backup vehicle deploying a quarter mile away. Gunshots were heard often enough on the border, but they were never taken for granted.

"Man, give me a break!" Rickie wailed.

"The Cuban," I said flatly.

Rickie lasted another thirty seconds. By then, the Ramcharger was barely a hundred yards away.

"¡Manos arriba!"

The border Spanish sounded tinny and very threatening over the outside speaker, but there was no way Rickie could comply with the order, because his hands were belted behind his back.

"Put up your hands and walk toward the vehicle!"

The English sounded just as tinny and was just as impossible for Rickie to obey.

"Mother of God," he said, measuring the shrinking distance between himself and the vehicle. He turned back to me. "All right, man, all right! I'll give you the Cuban, but first you have to let me through the fence!"

"Just to the line."

Rickie stumbled twice getting back to the fence post that marked the border.

The patrol wagon didn't move. The driver was playing it by the book, waiting for his backup before he approached the fence.

"What did you do for the Cuban?" I asked.

"Just a tour of the border, man, that's all. I didn't even move him north."

"Why did he come to you?"

"I've moved Cuban pollos before. They know me."

Rickie looked more unhappy than gratified by his fame. If all the Cuban pollos he had moved had been of the same stripe as the one I'd killed, I could understand why. I doubted that Rickie had been passing boat people up the line. True refugees didn't have the money to pay Rickie's freight charges. But not all Cubans were poor and desperate political refugees.

"Were they Fidelistas?" I asked.

Before Rickie could answer, the patrol wagon began to move forward, gravel crunching and popping under its tires.

"Stand where you are!" an American voice ordered. *"¡Párense, pendejos!"*

"Well?" I asked.

Rickie slumped in defeat and started to turn away from me. I grabbed his shirtfront and shook him hard.

"¡Dígame!" I said.

"If I tell you, the Cuban will kill me," Rickie said simply.

"Wrong. I killed him about sundown."

"You killed him?"

"Yes."

For the first time I saw real fear on Rickie's face. He started to back away, as though a U.S. murder charge looked better to him than any more of my company. I yanked him back into Mexico, dragged him into a slit between two hovels and slammed him up against a wall.

"Maybe you'll like me better once you get to know me," I said.

13

The winning of hearts and minds is a haphazard process, so I wrapped the silk tie around Rickie's eyes for the ride back to the Zona Norte. It didn't matter how much he had seen of me, but Héctor and Jaime had to go on living in Tijuana. Rickie wouldn't have thought twice about killing both of them if he knew who they were.

Héctor pulled into a dark alley behind a cabaret whose walls vibrated with norteño music. I dragged Rickie out of the backseat. Jaime leaned out the front window and handed me a smudged business card with his father's name and phone number on it.

"Anytime you need wheels, man," Jaime whispered.

Before he had finished, the Plymouth lurched off down the potholed alley. A few seconds later the cab turned onto the next street and disappeared. I removed the belt and silk tie from Rickie.

"Tell me more about the Cuban with the scar," I said.

Rickie was less frightened now. His eyes glittered with anger and calculation.

"I told you. This bunch of radicals—"

"What bunch?" I said, interrupting him. "Do they have a name or are you just passing the buck?"

"They call themselves the Che Guevara Battalion of the Aztlán Liberation Front."

I couldn't help it. I laughed. The name must have sounded a hell of a lot more impressive in Spanish than it did in English.

"It's true!" Rickie said.

"Oh, I believe you," I said. "You couldn't make up a name like that on your own."

He shrugged. "Politics aren't my thing, man. I just move people. Once in a while the Battalion wants to move somebody important. Like everybody else in T.J., they come to me because I'm the best."

"Who have you moved?"

"We don't ask for passports, chico."

I moved fast. Rickie thumped up against the wall, hard.

"How'd you like a fifty-thousand-volt honk, chico?" I asked, reaching into my pocket.

The old Fiddler charm still worked. Rickie went from cocky to cooperative before he could lick his lips.

"I don't know who I've moved because I don't care," Rickie said quickly. "They're mostly Mexicans, probably political fugitives from down south. The hills in Oaxaca and Chiapas are full of guerrillas. When things get too hot down there, they head north and hide out in the peach orchards around Fresno."

"What about the non-Mexicans you've moved?"

"Well, maybe once in a while a Central American comes through—a Nicaraguan or a Salvadoreño. Probably guerrillas who got tired of fighting."

"Or whacked-out terrorists?" I suggested softly.

His eyelids flickered, answering the question for me.

"Maybe some of them were freedom fighters," he conceded grudgingly, "but they sure as hell weren't carrying any bombs when I moved them. I got at least that much patriotism."

As my mother would have said, we should thank the Lord for small favors. "What kind of arrangements do you have with the Che Guevara Battalion?"

"Same as everybody else—cash on the bar. We give them a volume discount because they send us a lot of business. Right now they're only paying twenty-five hundred a head. Half when they walk in the door and the rest before we turn them loose at the other end."

"Where's the other end?"

"We've got drop houses all over, but usually either Santa Ana or East L.A., anywhere north of the Border Patrol checkpoint at San Clemente."

"What about the Cuban?"

"I just saw him once, the night he came in with this chick from the main Aztlán group," he said. "She counted out four grand on my desk and said we had to cooperate with the Cuban if we wanted to do more business with her organization."

"So you took him, no questions asked."

"What's to ask? The money was real."

"What happened after the Cuban arrived?"

"César spent a week with the dude, showed him every bit of border between here and the Arizona line." Rickie paused, started to speak, then shrugged. "Don't know how to describe it, but the Cuban was a real bad-ass. Never raised his voice. Never leaned on anyone, but . . ." Rickie shrugged again. "He even had César making the cross on himself. They spent another week over in Mexicali."

"Doing what?"

Rickie thought about making a smart remark, then dropped it as a bad idea.

"Hanging around bars, man," he said. "Drinking and talking and spreading money around. César said the Cuban kept doing dumb things, like talking to pendejos who were known to be snitches. After a week César and the Cuban came back over here. The Cuban bought a knapsack full of supplies, like he was going camping, and disappeared."

Silently I wondered if one of those snitches happened to be named Sánchez-Huerta.

"Where did the Cuban go?" I asked.

"¿Quién sabe? We were happy to see him leave."

"Did he mention why he was here or what he was going to do after he left?"

"That one? No way, man. He never said nothing he didn't have to. Like a snake without rattles. I never did figure out what he was doing."

"You hear about the American Customs cop who got killed day before yesterday?"

Rickie narrowed his eyes. He looked at me for a long moment, then glanced away and muttered a complicated Mexican oath under his breath. He reached toward his shirt pocket with the automatic gesture of a man hooked on nicotine. Then he remembered. He looked quickly at me. I nodded. He dug out a pack of American Pall Malls, shook one out and lit it with a Bic. He took down a half inch of tobacco in one long hit, swallowed smoke and breathed out. Very little smoke escaped. He took another drag, swallowed again, and sighed.

"You gotta believe me, man. I didn't know the Cuban was going to hit an American cop or I'd never have helped him. If the judiciales thought that my organization was involved with killing a gringo cop, my ass wouldn't be worth a peso."

Rickie might have been lying, but I doubted it. He was sucking on that cigarette like a man with a lot on his mind, and none of it comforting.

"What do you know about this Aztlán group?"

"They're into automatic weapons and taking off banks," Rickie said. He hit the cigarette hard again. "You know what Aztlán is?"

"Isn't that where the Seven Cities of Gold were supposed to be?"

Rickie nodded and finally blew out smoke, making a rippling gray streamer in the alley's dim light.

"Aztlán was supposed to be in the land the gringos stole from Mexico with the Treaty of Guadalupe Hidalgo. The Aztlán Liberation Front wants to take back that land. They've got a storefront out toward the colegio, and they're always agitating, picketing the American Border Patrol or demanding the return of the Southwest to Mexico, that sort of thing."

There was a cross between amusement and scorn in Rickie's voice.

"You don't like that idea?" I asked.

He dragged on the Pall Mall again. His black eyes reflected the glow as twin points of burning orange. "Like I said, man, politics ain't my thing. Besides, if the crazy dudes at Aztlán got their way, there wouldn't be a border and I'd be out of business."

"You could always start smuggling Americans from Nebraska back into the Sunbelt."

Rickie smiled sardonically but said nothing.

"You mentioned some girl. . . ." I said.

His smile shifted into a masculine leer. "Small bones, big tits and a mouth wide enough for any man. Mercedes."

"Does she run this Che Guevara Battalion?"

"César said there was another man, a cripple. But mean, you know? Everyone kissed his ring. César said Mercedes was real quiet around him, and that's not like her. She likes to give orders."

I stood in the cold alley and listened for a while longer. Rickie gave me an address and description of the Aztlán storefront, but he was beginning to run out of anything I was interested in hearing. It was getting too cold to stand around with a little black shock box in my hand. I stowed the Nova away, did the same for César's gun and turned to leave.

"Hey, man," Rickie said softly, "you weren't really going to kick me back across the border, were you?"

There was enough ambivalence in his voice to leave a distinct impression that he might have liked an excuse to go home. Looking at Tijuana, I could understand.

"See you around," I said.

"It better not be around Tijuana. If I see you, you're dead meat."

"Don't bet anything important on it. Like your life."

I left Rickie in the alley, smoking the last hot inch of his cigarette.

It was ten minutes before I could find a cab stand in Zona Norte's disheveled sprawl. The cab stand was in front of the open-air carnival known as the downtown bus station. It was at the edge of the Zona. Because Mexico tolerates, perhaps even encourages, the migration of its own jobless citizens from the interior to la frontera, at midnight the transit station was alive with immigrants, smugglers and the human parasites who attach themselves to any sublegal activity.

As I waited for a cab, a recruiter greeted a dusty bus that had just arrived from Zacatecas, Culiacán and points in between. The recruiter had a carnival barker's brass voice and a spiel that went from colloquial Spanish to English-flavored idioms to pure Spanglish. Border argot, as distinctive as a homeboy tattoo.

"Hey there, boys and girls, welcome to the Last Frontier. Time to join your brothers and cousins in Los Estados Unidos, get rich and come back a norteño, *muy importante*. But first you have to cross. I'm the dude to help you. I know all the best routes, all the easy ways to gringo money. I know when la Migra sleeps and when they are awake, and for two hundred dollars, just two hundred American dollars, I'll make sure you get to L.A. by noon tomorrow.

"Not only that, amigos, but if you don't have two hundred dollars, I can arrange a little loan for you. Follow me, amigos, I'll get you a job at the other end and take our fee out of your wages. There's a small service charge, of course, but what's *un poco dinero* when you'll be rich? There's plenty for everybody in the north."

The come-on sounded like an invitation to indentured servitude to me, but I guess I was jaundiced. There was no lack of business for the recruiter. People stumbled off the bus into the bright lights and honky-tonk atmosphere, blinking like sleepy children. Fully half of them lined up behind the man with the brass voice and dreams to match. There was no fuss, no real hesitation. For all the emotion the future immigrants showed, they might be doing nothing more than transferring from one bus to another.

The other half of the passengers were already spoken for. Many of the smuggling rings recruited their customers in the interior, offering a package trip from the town square in San Luis Potosí to a ramshackle bunkhouse in a peach orchard north of Fresno. You could pick out the little groups of country cousins in cheap polyester clothes and soup-bowl haircuts, all trooping obediently along behind a guide who was recognizable by his Tijuana-cowboy pegged pants and punker hair-cut. The guides had to keep close tabs on their clients. The bus station was an open-air smugglers' market. Competition was intense and cutthroat. Between the eager immigrants and the hucksters selling streets of gold, there was a seamy, untrammeled energy to the place. The air crackled with fear and greed, adventure and hope.

By the time I found a cab, the empty bus had been replaced by a full one and the recruiters were spinning shrill dreams into the night once more. I opened the back door of the cab and came face-to-face with two blond-wigged prostitutes who were trying to hustle a pair of norteños in the opposite door of the cab. The two women stood there giving me hell in machine-gun gutter Spanish while their two customers watched, nervous grins on their sunbaked faces. Finally I shrugged and surrendered the cab. All I had waiting for me was a cold bed in San Ysidro. These pollos were going to get laid one last time before embarking on a six-month voyage with their live-in girlfriend, Manuela.

When the next cab came, I invested ten bucks in reconnaissance. The Che Guevara Battalion of the Aztlán Liberation Front turned out to be a small building in a commercial district toward the south edge of the city. A flag hung limply in the damp night air out front, adorned by a single yellow star on a red field. A stylized portrait of Che sneered down at the passing bourgeoisie. The streets were almost deserted, but the cantina next door was doing a healthy business. The neighborhood felt more like Mexico City than the frenetic frontera.

For an extra five bucks, the cabbie made two complete circuits of the place and then drove slowly down the alley behind the storefront. I caught the brassy glint of a surprisingly efficient-looking dead bolt in the back door. Apparently this was another group of revolutionaries that believed in private property—as long as it was theirs.

Big fat dead bolts are more of a challenge than a wave-off, but the cantina looked like it was going to be open for a while. From the smell of the place, more than one drunk came out in the alley to piss. Getting the kind of privacy I needed for a run at that dead bolt wasn't likely. Besides, I needed more equipment than I had with me.

When I got out of the cab at the border, a sleepy-looking U.S. Customs inspector waved me back into the United States without a second glance. I didn't even remember until I got to the car that I still had César's pistol shoved into my belt under my jacket. The smuggler with a clear conscience is unstoppable. I snapped the shells out of the gun's magazine, wiped down the metal and dropped the piece in a trash barrel in the parking lot. One at a time I flicked the shells out the window as I drove slowly back to the motel.

The problem with a motel room less than two hours from home is that you keep remembering how good your own bed feels. I took one look at the pronounced dip in the middle of the motel's queen-sized mattress and decided to hell with it. I threw my gear back in the car and was ready to leave when I thought of Fiora. The whole thing with

Rickie had taken just over an hour. She was probably still lying in the hotel bed, staring at the ceiling, waiting for me to call. I went back into the room, dialed the Beverly Glen and asked for Fiora's room.

"Ms. Flynn checked out," the operator said after a moment.

"When?"

"Perhaps thirty minutes ago, sir."

"Did she leave a message for Fiddler?"

"One moment, please,"

I heard papers being rearranged, and then the clerk picked up the phone again.

"Ms. Flynn said she would see you back at the cottage."

I spent the entire drive trying to figure out how Fiora had known that I'd taken care of business fast enough to make the drive home look good. There was no logical explanation, of course. The woman is a Scots witch.

But I got even with her. I didn't turn on the heater the entire trip. By the time I hit Crystal Cove, my feet were as cold as the sea. Fiora was already asleep under the down comforter. Her feet were warm.

After a while, so were mine.

14

The instant I awakened the next morning, I knew that the strain had gotten to Fiora. It was two minutes before nine and she was still lying in my arms, her eyes tightly closed against the light that was seeping in through a parted drape. The day that woman misses her five-o'clock wake-up is the day she is very, very tired.

I lay there listening to her even breathing, enjoying the warmth of tangled arms and legs beneath the comforter. I could feel my own pulse, slow and deep and steady, and at the same time her heart beating beneath her soft breast. I remembered the chill of the desert, the pictures of me, and the dead Cuban with his long rifle and short pistol.

No guarantees.

Fiora stirred softly, arching against my fingers and murmuring something.

"Hmmm?" I asked.

"You sound like a big, contented cat. You don't feel like one, though."

My breath caught as her hand slid down my body. "No fur?" I offered.

"Oh, there's plenty of fur," she said, tugging lightly to prove her point. "It's the contentment that's lacking."

There was something I wanted to say, but all I could think of was how good her hand felt. And she was right. Contented didn't exactly describe my condition.

She laughed softly.

Lazy mornings are a luxury with Fiora. Usually, by the time I roll out of bed, she's fully dressed and as tightly wound as a human dynamo. But this morning I was up and she was unwound, languid, steamy, trying to sink as deeply into me as I was into her. She remained in the same mood even after we lay flushed and satisfied in one another's arms.

"Please stay just a little while," Fiora whispered, pressing herself against me in a caress that was both a plea and a bribe. "You were so cold last night. . . . Don't go yet, love. Not yet."

It was not a request I could turn down. We lay for several minutes, listening to each slowly breaking wave against the bluff in front of the cottage.

"Sorry about the cold feet last night," I finally said.

Fiora's smile was small and had a marked inclination to turn upside down. "I wasn't talking about your body." She looked at me with eyes that were dark. "You want to tell me about Mexico?"

I tucked her face against my neck, knowing that it would be easier to talk about Mexico if she wasn't watching me with those uncanny green eyes. As long as I didn't have to see her concern and her empathy, I could be fairly dispassionate and even a little wry, particularly when I got to the Cuban's dying words.

Fiora simply held on to me and began stroking my chest as though she could somehow smooth away all the violence and cold.

When I got to the head game I'd used to get Rickie Hernández to talk, her whole body stiffened. With a minimum of fuss I described what I had done to enlist his cooperation. I didn't bother to point out that Rickie hadn't exactly been a candidate for sainthood in the first place. She knew it as well as I did. Just as she knew that violence was like cocaine—the more you used it, the less it affected you.

Fiora was right, of course. More than my body had been cold last night. When it came to getting certain jobs done, warmth was a handicap.

Her long, ragged sigh warmed my chest. "Did you find out why Sharp died?"

"No."

"Do you have any ideas?"

"None that make sense. How about you?" I asked bluntly.

"What do you mean?"

"Do you still feel like I'm in danger?"

"Yes."

Fiora's voice was like her body, suddenly tight. Sometimes I think she's even less comfortable with her fey Scots mind than I am. Even tangled by a night of sleep and a morning of love, her hair was still soft as I stroked it. I kissed her forehead very gently, waiting. I would bring the name up if I had to, but I'd rather that she did.

"Volker," she said finally, the word both a sigh and a curse. "Is that what you're waiting to hear?"

"Is he keeping you awake nights?"

"I never . . . my dreams . . ." Fiora took a deep breath and tried again. "No names or dates or faces or places. Just . . . someone wants you dead, Fiddler. Someone wants it very badly."

"And you think it's Volker."

She moved slightly, restlessly, like a wary animal being driven into a tight place. "Who else is connected to you through Sharp?"

I shook my head. "Benny tried that on me last night."

"It didn't work?"

"If I were certain Volker was behind Sharp's killing, I wouldn't be lying here."

"Where would you be?" Fiora reached over and touched the white scars on the back of my left hand. "What would you be doing?"

"You don't want to know."

Fiora was urgent, tight, humming like a violin string. "Can't you let it go? Bury the dead and get on with life. Life, Fiddler, not more death."

It was the cutting edge of an old argument, but still so sharp and fresh that we both bled every time it touched us.

"Whoever hired the Cuban to murder Sharp knew me well enough to know that I'd investigate Sharp's death. So he hired an assassin to sit up in the rocks and stare at snapshots and wait for me to turn up in the cross hairs. But I had to make nice at a charity soiree that night, so I was late for my appointment in Samara and the assassin got impatient and lit a cigarette and died."

Fiora flinched, but never looked away. "I don't think Volker knows you that well."

"He knows *himself* that well. Neither one of us likes it, but Volker and I are too much alike in too many ways. And even if I'd been inclined to just bury the dead and walk away, he left me a message on the machine that I couldn't overlook and still face myself in the shaving mirror."

"Pride," she said harshly, wrenching away from me. "Is that what this is all about? You're risking your neck for some warped masculine notion of pride?"

"Call it self-respect if it makes you feel better, and if I didn't have it, you wouldn't be in my bed, and you damn well know it."

Can't live with it. Can't live without it.

Neither of us said anything. We didn't have to. The knowledge vibrated between us in the silence.

Suddenly Fiora made a small sound deep in her throat, anger and despair and fear. Fear most of all. She didn't bother concealing it now. She just looked at me like a woman saying good-bye.

And then she looked away.

I put my fingers under Fiora's chin and forced her to look at me again.

"When an assassin is trying to kill you, guessing who paid him isn't good enough," I said flatly. "Sometimes the obvious answer isn't the right one. Volker has no more reason to kill me now than he had at any time in the past. I've never tried to hide. If he wanted me, I was always here. And never, not once, did he take the bait."

Fiora shivered despite the warmth of the comforter and my body, but she didn't disagree. "I know."

"If Volker is after me now, he's got more than revenge on his mind. Vengeance isn't in his repertoire. That would require the ability to feel. His emotions don't run that deep."

Her smile was sad. "I know that, too. But you have emotions, Fiddler. Volker doesn't have that problem. He can kill or betray and leave without a backward look. You can't. You pay. You get . . . cold."

"Look," I said impatiently, cutting across her words. "Even if I had Volker in the cross hairs right now, I'd be a fool to pull the trigger. I have to know why he—"

"That's just it," Fiora said, talking over me, talking fast, words spilling out before I could stop them. "You would hesitate before you killed him, but he wouldn't hesitate one bit. He's utterly ruthless. You aren't. Not like he is, all the way to the core. That's a terrible edge to give him. Don't you realize that, Fiddler? You'll give Volker an even break and he'll kill you and walk away just like he killed—" Her voice broke.

Danny.

Neither one of us said the name, but it was there between us. Fiora's twin brother had been a hell of a lot less lethal and more charming than I'd ever be, but Volker had snuffed him anyway; and Volker had done it knowing how much it would hurt Fiora, the woman he had loved as much as he could ever love anything.

"If Volker is suddenly after me, I have to know why," I said patiently. "Just killing him isn't good enough. If it isn't Volker trying to kill me, I have to find out who it is. Then I'll probably know why. That's the only way to be sure assassins won't keep turning up until I get careless or run out of luck. Like Sharp."

"The FBI—"

"Wouldn't break a sweat if I got dumped, and you know it," I interrupted. "Hell, they'll probably give the hit man a merit badge for marksmanship."

Fiora looked away, hiding her eyes. When she looked back, sad and bleak and angry, I wished that she hadn't.

"You do believe, really *believe*, that Volker won't give you an even break, don't you?" she asked softly.

"Yes."

"Yet you'll—"

"Yes," I said, interrupting again.

Fiora was silent for a moment. Then she reached up and smoothed her fingertips over my mustache in an old, familiar caress.

"No matter what happens," she whispered, "I love you. Remember that, Fiddler. I will always love you."

I moved my head slowly. Fiora's fingertips were cool against my lips, but when I took her hand to warm it between mine, she slipped out of bed.

"I have a meeting at ten, one of those private back-channel affairs with some people on the Pacific Basin Fund board. It would be stupid to be late."

When she came out of the bathroom, I lay in bed and watched her pull on her business persona along with her Alcott and Andrews suit. I waited for her to ask me where I was going and what I was doing and when I would be back. She didn't ask, so I filled her in.

"I'm going to Tijuana to see what I can find out about the Che Guevara Battalion. Benny is coming along. We probably won't be back tonight."

Fiora nodded as though I'd said that Benny and I were going surf-fishing next to the Newport pier. With graceful, efficient motions she gathered up papers and her leather briefcase. When she came over to get her watch off the nightstand, I snapped an arm around her waist. She was wearing lavender and an unsteady smile. Her neck was warm and smooth. She hadn't put any lipstick on yet. She knows I hate the taste of the stuff.

"Does that mean you'll let me kiss you?" I asked, running my fingertip over her naked lips.

Whatever she said was lost in the kiss.

When the door shut behind her, I dressed and walked down to use the pay phone beside Coast Highway. I was becoming as paranoid as Rickie.

Benny answered on the third ring.

"You interested in a little black-bag work?" I asked.

"I'm getting picky in my old age, mate. Who's the target?"

"Does the name Che Guevara strike a familiar note?"

He laughed with a wicked kind of pleasure. "Sold, boyo. I haven't done a number on a revolutionary cell in years."

I described the layout. The fact that the office we were going to black-bag was in Mexico didn't reduce Benny's enthusiasm one bit.

"I suppose you're going to want room coverage as well as a tap on the phone," he said cheerfully.

"Can you manage both?"

"Permanent installation or temporary?"

"I'm not a government agency with a task force and a year to burn. This is strictly rip and run, but it would be nice to have something that would work for a few days before it craps out."

Benny grunted.

An odd sibilant sound came through the receiver—tires hissing over smooth cement. Benny uses a cordless remote phone in his workshop. That way he can prowl without pulling wires out of the wall.

"Bloody hell," he mumbled. "That's not going to work."

"What isn't?"

"A sweet little line-powered unit I happen to have."

"Sounds good to me."

"It wouldn't to them. It draws too much juice. The Mexican phone system operates on about as much voltage as your average flashlight. Slap this little puppy on the line and you'll get a noticeable drop in sound quality. They'd have to be deaf as well as stupid to miss it."

There was more hissing of tires over concrete, punctuated by odd sounds as Benny rummaged in bins and muttered curses when he didn't find anything to meet his precise specifications. The vulgarities were entertaining; since he had gone back recently to New Zealand and Australia for a "consultation," Benny had reverted to native slang.

"I'm going to have to call some blokes and see about battery-powered third-wire possibilities. I'll get back to you."

"Call me at home. And Benny . . ."

He made an absent-minded noise.

"Until you sweep my home phone, assume that it's bugged."

He hung up without answering.

By the time I got home, the phone was ringing. I cut off the Ansafone and picked up the receiver.

"Got us covered, mate," Benny said. "It's a very simple unit. Even a maladroit like you should be able to install it. Need anything else?"

"You still have friends from the old school?"

"Fewer every year."

"You remember the gentleman we talked about last night?"

Benny grunted an affirmative.

"Would any of your old school friends still have his address?"

"Not a recent one. His own school kept him on the roster after you met him, but no one saw him. He was taken off the list after six months. Supposedly he went back home, but no one has seen him since."

"Did anybody see him outside of his home grounds?"

"No."

"You got all this in a single call? I'm impressed."

"No, you're just dense. I kept tabs on that little piece of sunshine long after you lost interest. Had him in mind as a birthday present."

"No thanks."

"For Fiora, mate, not you."

Benny hung up, leaving me staring at the phone.

15

It was evening when Benny's van reached the border. The vehicle was loaded with six hundred pounds of the sneakiest gear in the world, but when the Mexican Customs inspector stared in questioningly, Benny shrugged, pointed at the fishing poles on top of the pile and made motions like he was casting and reeling in a fish. The inspector was used to dealing with rich gringos headed for the world-class trophy fish around Cabo San Lucas. He smiled and nodded his head.

"Depth-founder," he said knowingly, waving us past.

"Right you are," Benny said, giving him a thumbs-up signal, which is the Down Under equivalent of "Up yours, mate."

As Benny picked his way through the Zona traffic, I sat cross-legged in the back of the van, studying the wiring diagrams of a dozen types of telephones and brushing up on my technique with wire strippers.

"The blokes at Pacific Bell said most of Baja runs on salvaged American equipment, so pay special attention to the Western Electric instruments before, say, 1960," Benny said, glancing in the rearview mirror and both side mirrors. "That's Stone Age stuff. It ought to be a piece of cake."

I took a page from Benny's repertoire of small talk and just grunted.

"How security-conscious are these dreary young blurters of yours?" Benny asked.

"Overhead light and a dead bolt at the back door. I've cracked a lot tougher nuts."

"Spoken like a baby squirrel," Benny retorted. "Sounds like they're typical Red leftists. Long on head trips and short on hardware. Black terrorists, the fascists, are just the opposite. They're simpleminded sods, but Lord God, they love their hardware."

There was more traffic around the storefront than there had been the previous night. Even worse, the lights were still on inside the building. Benny found a spot on a dark side street that gave us a good angle on the front door. After we parked, he levered himself out of the front seat and into the darkness at the back of the van. Anyone looking in wouldn't be able to see us.

After a few moments I heard him rustling around in one of the tool bins. Shortly afterward, a pair of oversize binoculars landed in my lap. I lifted them to my eyes and was almost blinded by the greenish wash of a powerful light amplifier. He laughed at my reaction.

"Starlight glasses," he said softly. "Old enough to vote and never been used, with USN stamped right in the crosspiece. The Navy designation got me to thinking, so I called the manufacturer and did a history one day, just for the practice."

"Don't tell me," I said. "General Westmoreland carried them during the Tet Offensive."

"Not bloody likely. The Navy ordered five thousand pairs in 1971, twenty-five hundred bucks a pair. These were shipped in 1973, and as near as anybody could figure, they were abandoned on the Saigon docks when we pulled the plug.

"From there it's guesswork, but it seems the new rulers of the People's Republic of South Vietnam snapped them up, then turned around and sold them to a Brazilian military surplus outfit. A decade later they surfaced in some junk store in Bellflower. I paid a hundred and a half for them, and no one had even opened their carrying case."

While he was talking, I had put down the glasses and dug the Detonics out of the hidey-hole where weapons had been stashed for the border crossing. The first four rounds in the clip were the ball-shot slugs Benny had given me a day or two before I met Volker for the first time. I peeled a bullet out and flipped it to Benny.

"Speaking of war surplus," I said, "are these still good?"

He held the cartridge up and looked at it. In the faint light from the main street, his mouth became a cold ivory grin.

"They're good for as long as you keep them dry. The Frog machinist who made them was a real artist. A round like this should stand up to at least a decade of careful storage."

"It's been two decades already, Benny."

He thought about it, then shook his head. "Lord God, how the time flies when you're having fun." He held the cartridge to his ear and shook it gently. "Sounds like it should be fine." He handed it back. "But I wouldn't keep it around too much longer. It's not a vintage wine, boyo. That bullet was intended to leave the world a better place than you found it."

In the faint light Benny's eyes were like his smile, cold and gleaming. He saw my glance and nodded.

"That's right," he said in a low voice. "I enjoyed my work. Revolutionaries give me a pain in the arse. May their enemies multiply."

"This isn't political. It's between Volker and me—assuming that it's Volker who paid the assassin."

Benny shrugged. "It's all political, boyo. Haven't you discovered that yet?"

I let it drop. Despite his occasional digressions, Benny isn't really a political animal. He's just a piss-poor loser. He has worn out a dozen T-shirts with the emblem, "Southeast Asia War Games, 1965–1975— Second Place." The logo is his way of reminding people how the last big war in the world turned out. And why.

Neither of us spoke for a long time, but we didn't mind the lack of conversation. We sat in the dark, drinking coffee from a Thermos and listening to the sounds coming from the neighborhood around us. There was some kind of meeting going on in the Battalion storefront. With the window rolled partway down, we could hear occasional phrases of revolutionary rhetoric on the evening air.

". . . the miserable gringos will capitulate to the people. The races of Aztlán will be restored to the territory that is rightfully theirs."

The voice sounded like it had been run through a Border Patrol megaphone, tinny, overamplified, unconvincing. Or maybe it was just the words that were unreal. The Spanish was baroque, all but incomprehensible.

The front door of the adjacent cantina popped open, emitting a few drunks and a blast of Bruce Springsteen, a workingman's lament with the kind of beat that could drive pilings into solid rock. The door slammed shut, cutting off all but a fading wail.

Thirty minutes passed and the cantina door slammed open again. This time it was Tina Turner asking what love had to do with anything. Three men staggered out. One of them pissed a couple of cervezas into the gutter. The door slammed shut.

Benny yawned widely enough to break his jaw.

". . . imperialist gringo dogs will take their feet from the bleeding necks of the workingman . . ." someone announced angrily from the meeting hall.

"Polly want a cracker?" muttered Benny.

"What's a little plagiarism among friends?" I whispered. "Besides, if Mexican radicals didn't have Uncle Sam, they would have had to invent him. The Great Devil Theory sells as well in Baja as it does in Bahrain. Maybe better."

"S.S.D.D."

We settled in and tried not to fall asleep. The meeting broke up about ten-thirty. The very small audience filed out of the storefront and into the night. With the starlight glasses, I could see the handful of people clearly—a collection of college students and proletarians, hardly the sort to need the services of an expensive alien smuggler like Rickie Hernández.

"Where'd you put the leash?" I asked.

Benny dug around in a gym bag and tossed me a three-foot leather leash with an empty chain collar on the end of it. I eased out of the van and strolled down the side street. At the corner across from the Battalion storefront, I paused and searched the street in both directions, holding the leash loosely in front of me. I peered up and down the street again, a vaguely helpless Anglo in blue jeans and a wool shirt looking for a lost pooch. When nothing came to my call, I crossed the street. In my most colloquial Spanish I asked one of the men who had just emerged from the meeting if he had seen a black dog around. He shook his head and kept walking, taking no more notice of me than he did of anyone else.

I stopped beneath the limp red-star flag to look up and down the street again. A woman wrapped in a wash-worn dress and a black cloth coat came out of the storefront. She had the face of a peasant, broad, stolid and quiet. She brushed past me and hurried away. I wondered what solace she found in the speech to keep her up past ten o'clock.

The dirt-streaked windows of the Che Guevara Battalion of the Aztlán Liberation Front were partly papered over with broadsides and handbills advertising everything from an upcoming rally in solidarity with the guerrillas of El Salvador to a flashy motorcycle that some well-off college rebel was trying to sell. There were messages imploring support for Nicaragua, Cuba, Angola and the Eritrean rebels.

The handbills were the kind you'd see on any moderate-sized college campus in the United States. But there was a hard edge to the messages that probably would have seemed overly serious north of the border. The people down here were orthodox leftists; Mexican radicals didn't seem to dilute their politics with Greenpeace, Love Animals Don't Eat Them, or the Lesbian Poetry League.

The podium was still occupied by a thin kid in a black beret and an olive-drab field jacket that looked grungy enough to have been liberated from some Camp Pendleton gyrene. The kid was painfully thin and his face was covered by a mangy attempt at a beard, but his eyes burned with the clarity of a true believer. He was lecturing some hapless member of the audience who must have asked him the wrong question.

The broadsides shielded me while I inspected the interior of the building. In the main room, two dozen chairs were arranged in free-form rows before a podium. The furniture was postmodern thrift shop, mismatched, and the walls were shedding streamers of paint. Behind a partition at the rear were several offices and perhaps a storeroom.

Like Benny said, a piece of cake . . . if everybody would just go home.

I walked down the street past the front door of the cantina. Someone had propped it open. Clouds of stale kitchen smells and cigarette smoke poured out along with some baile band whanging away on a hot version of an old Mexican standard called "La Bamba." The place looked like the taco meat had once had claws. The patrons weren't much better.

Still trailing the leash as cover, I turned the corner and walked down a side street. When I got to the midblock alley, I turned down it, whistling from time to time, still a man looking for a dog. The secret to surveillance is simple, Sharp used to say: *If you don't hide, nobody's going to find you.*

The alley was dark from one end of the block to the other, except for the illumination that was cast by one unshielded light bulb hanging above the back door of the Battalion's storefront. As I approached the pool of light, I slowed a little, inspecting the back of the building. There were no signs of an alarm box, no lead wires on the door casing. But the dead bolt was new enough to gleam. One look told me that someone had recently installed the back light as well.

A small thing, really, but troubling. This outfit looked like it would steal electricity to avoid the bourgeois constraints of a power bill, but somebody had made sure there was good light in the one spot that would repel prowlers, the back door. Then a new dead bolt had been added that would take a minimum of ten minutes to defeat, and that was ten minutes in the bright illumination of a two-hundred-watt light, also recently added.

Somebody seemed intent on turning a simple little black-bag job into a major undertaking. In Mañanaland, such attention to detail was uncharacteristic and, frankly, irritating. I studied the new fixture for a minute, then pulled a pair of dainty wire cutters from my hip pocket. The wires parted easily, ending the connection through the back wall into the building's circuitry. The light went out. I pushed the cut ends back against the wall before I strolled on down the alley. Tonight or perhaps tomorrow night, somebody would realize that the light was out. Probably it would take two or three days for them to figure out that it wasn't something as simple as a burned-out bulb. By the time they found the snipped wires, I intended to be in some other country.

I circled an extra block before returning to the van. Away from the main street the neighborhood was filled with small, well-kept houses with inner courtyards and head-high brick or wrought-iron fences along the street. Mexicans tend to be very private people. They orient themselves and their homes inward. That was a bonus. Benny and I could park on the street as anonymously as if we were in downtown L.A., where the windows face out but nobody gives a damn.

I tapped on the side door of the van gently, slid it open and climbed in. Benny was propped up against the bulkhead, watching the street door of the Battalion's storefront. A pistol gleamed dully as he lowered it.

"Expecting company?" I asked as I slid the door shut quietly behind me.

"Old habit," he said absently, not taking his attention from the storefront. "It comes from too many years in the war zone. In Saigon I used to sit on a Browning Hi-Power when I drove anywhere. Hard on the bum, but you always know where the gun is."

We sat in the darkness for another half hour, watching the last of the revolutionaries spill out into the night. The lights inside finally snapped off. The tall, thin kid in the field jacket came out with a girl. From Rickie's description, I decided that she must be the famed Mercedes, she of the big mouth and other local attractions.

The young orator locked the door behind Mercedes. They walked off down the street together, talking earnestly. The effect would have been more intellectual if he could have kept his eyes above her neck.

"He didn't set any front-door alarm," Benny said. "Going in that way might be simpler than diddling the dead bolt in back."

"The cantina next door stays open until two."

"Maybe there isn't much traffic."

Thirty minutes later we had watched seventeen people enter or leave the cantina. At no time had the street been deserted. It was the back alley and dead bolt for me; if we were parked on the street after the cantina closed, someone was sure to notice.

Benny handed me the tool kit and said, deadpan, "If you or any member of your team is discovered, the President will disclaim any knowledge of your activities. Have a nice day." Suddenly Benny's grin faded. "Sometime I'll tell you about the wanker who said that to me—and meant it."

The dead bolt wasn't as tough as it looked, mainly because the intense young man in the field jacket had forgotten to use it. Big tits can be a real distraction for young revolutionaries. I picked the door-knob lock in two minutes flat and was inside.

Through the wall I could hear the norteño music from the jukebox in the cantina next door. The air in the storefront was still and stale. Letting out my breath and keeping it that way, I listened. All I could hear was the sound of my own blood rushing through me. Then I snapped on the night glasses. The light amplifier spooled up with a faint whistling squeal.

The glasses were useless for close work, but I didn't think anyone else was around. With the glasses I could orient myself easily and move freely without showing a light. I dimmed the brightness on the glasses to save the batteries before I walked down the hallway, drag-ging my black bag behind me with one hand and holding the glasses with the other.

The telephone terminal box was in plain sight on the back wall beside the storeroom door. I chanced a pinhole flashlight to inspect the box closely. It looked a hell of a lot older than I was. The cover popped off easily, revealing two pairs of wires and no place to hide a transmitter. I closed the box and moved on.

The storeroom itself was empty except for a few cartons of papers, some discarded furniture and a few shelves stacked with office sup-plies. I closed the door behind me and thumbed through the boxes of papers quickly, using the pencil light. The stuff was mostly back copies of a magazine called *Shining Path—Sendero Luminoso* in Spanish. It was classic Marxist-Leninist stuff, shopworn yet still serviceable, except that the Battalion could use a new editor. Even I could pick holes in the Spanish grammar.

Using the night glasses, I scanned the main room, where the meet-ing had been held. The place smelled of people and cigarettes. There were no secrets and no good places to hide a transmitter. That left the two offices.

The front office contained a conventional secretarial desk that was scattered with papers, and a standing three-drawer file cabinet that was locked. No telephone. I finally found the cord extending from a closed and locked desk drawer. I picked the lock on the belly drawer of the desk in thirty seconds, automatically releasing the locks on the side drawers.

The phone was right out of Benny's short course in Stone Age bugging—a Western Electric Model 500 with a dial. I clamped the pinhole Maglite between my teeth and went to work with a screwdriver. Two screws in the base plate, three more holding the dial in place, and watch the instrument come apart in your hands.

Telephones of any age are straightforward devices designed to be repaired by any warm body wearing a tool belt. Wires come in twos, and the pairs are color-coded. They connect the basic components— dial, transmitter, receiver, ringer—in a nice, simple, logical package that even a maladroit like myself can follow. But this phone had a new wrinkle. A tiny high-tech black plastic cube had been wired directly into the guts of the phone. The insert was compact, state-of-the-art, and damn near identical to the bug in my pocket.

I looked at the phone and wondered who had beaten me to the punch.

16

An electronic listening device is as anonymous as a turd. You never know who the hell left it. Obviously this was no amateur job; the wires were nicely stripped, and round-head connectors had been soldered into place very cleanly. Other than that, there was damn-all I could tell from looking at the bug.

I sat in the rump-sprung desk chair, the disassembled phone in my lap, and worried about the placement of the bug. An on-line transmitter is designed to monitor all conversations on a particular phone line, but this little beauty was wired right into the guts of the instrument itself. I traced the paired wires. One of them crossed the switch hook. That meant the unit transmitted phone calls to the eavesdroppers. But when the phone was not in use, it turned into a room bug, monitoring every conversation in the little office and probably half the activities in the entire Battalion headquarters as well. That was exactly what I wanted to do.

Small world, isn't it?

I thought it, but I didn't say the cliché aloud, not with somebody listening at the other end of the bug.

Amazing to think that retread Marxist rhetoric could draw one bug in today's world, much less two. Nor was the interest recent. There was dust on the bug's connectors. It had been in place for some time.

The phone in my lap rang.

Adrenaline may be my drug of choice, but the jolt I got was no treat. It was the kind you get when you screw up somehow and the pain is so bad you toss your cookies. My skin tingled, my head got light, my heart stuttered like an AK-47. But the adrenaline did what it was supposed to do. The world snapped into hard-edged, crystalline focus before the phone rang again.

Three possibilities: a wrong number; a call for the Che Guevara Battalion headquarters; or the clown with night duty at Wiretap Central was trying to figure out what or who was making that screwball noise he was picking up through his earphones.

The phone rang a second time.

I lifted the receiver, disengaged the switch hook and turned loose my most nasal Spanish.

"Bueno."

The Spanish that came back to me was hard and flat. Anglo Spanish. *"¿Quién habla?"*

Who's talking, my ass. There was nothing I wanted to say to Wiretap Central, so I grabbed the professional wiring of the telephone bug and jerked. The high-tech plastic cube came out with one pull.

The sudden surge of feedback when the bug yanked free must have been painful. I heard someone hiss, "Shit!" before I hung up. Definitely an Anglo.

The next ten minutes were spent cleaning up the fancy wiring job I'd just trashed and replacing the old, dead transmitter with the one Benny had built. I reassembled the phone, set it on the desk and whistled the first four bars of "The Star-Spangled Banner." Then I dug out the Handi-Talkie in the black bag.

"How do you read?" I said into the radio.

A quavering whistle came back through the Handi-Talkie. I didn't recognize the tune.

"Come back?" I said.

"New Zealand's anthem, you clod," Benny explained. "Any troubles?"

"They should have this place exterminated. I had to evict a previous tenant of long standing. Anything going on outside?"

"Negatory," Benny said. "I've got the scanner on what passes for the Tijuana police radio band, but I haven't heard a dispatch call in the last five minutes."

"Give me ten more."

I tossed the detached bug into my bag in the hope that Benny would be able to do some entomology on it, cleaned up the stray wires and put the phone back in the desk drawer where I had found it. Relocking the belly drawer took more time than unlocking it had, but I finally got it done. I took a last look around, ready to clear the place in a hurry.

Halfway to the back door I realized how close I had just come to being a complete fool. The junction box had two sets of wires, not one. That meant there was another phone line into the storefront.

But I'd seen only one phone.

A quick search of the baseboards in both offices turned up nothing. I called Benny back on the Handi-Talkie and told him I'd be delayed. Then I shut off the pinhole light and sat on the floor for a minute, thinking.

Darkness is useful. It helps you to see things more clearly. It took me two minutes to realize that I had very nicely walked into the middle of a sly kind of trap. The skin on the back of my neck tightened suddenly, futilely, underlining my new awareness.

The security on the storefront had been so half-assed—so very, very Mañanaland—that it had been almost a caricature. I would have been a hell of a lot more suspicious if there had been no security whatsoever, or if it had been tighter, more efficient. But the combination I'd found—good prowler light on the back stoop but disengaged dead bolt, telephone secured inside a desk as easy to pick as your nose—was so perfect that it really had to be planned.

The intelligence that had dreamed up that little ruse was the same intelligence that left the first telephone bug in place. Whoever had planted the bug I trashed—probably either FBI Counterintelligence or the Central Intelligence Agency—had been suckered into believing that they had their finger on the pulse of the Aztlán Battalion because they had a line tap in place. What they had was thousand of hours of office chitchat and bullshit revolutionary rhetoric. If the setup was half as clever as it appeared to be, the telephone bug wouldn't have recorded a single conversation of substance. Real business would be done on a second phone.

Move, countermove. It had a familiar feel to it. Too familiar. Like fencing with a ghost.

Once I realized there had to be a second phone, it wasn't difficult to find. The offices were laid out so that the storeroom was the only spot in the building that was out of range of the bugged phone.

The jack for the second phone was hidden behind a very neat little sliding panel in the dusty baseboard of the storeroom. The phone itself was a few feet away in a small compartment at the bottom of a carton of outdated Communist newspapers. After that, my luck ran out. Whoever was running the show here definitely did class work. He had glued the base of the telephone instrument and the case together. There was no way in hell to tamper with that phone without leaving tracks.

I put everything back the way I'd found it and went out the back way. Benny had the gun leveled at the van door again when I opened it. I tossed the black bag in, followed it, and quietly pulled the door closed behind me.

"Order, genus, family and species," I said, handing him the dismantled bug from the first telephone.

"Its order, family, genus and species," he said absently, holding the plastic cube in his hand. "Where did you find this bad boy?"

"Right where you told me to plant mine. Where's the coffee Thermos?"

"Under the seat."

While I poured coffee, Benny used the pencil light to examine the bug. He found a sealed seam and cracked it with a precise blow from the edge of his hand. The plastic case fell open, revealing a small circuit board festooned with capacitors and resistors and all kinds of exotic electronic life.

"Bloody beautiful," Benny said appreciatively. "Not a manufacturer's mark on one of them, either."

"East or West?"

"It looks West, but that could mean it was devised to look that way by somebody from the East, just to throw blokes like you and me off the trail. Or, of course, it could have been designed by someone from the West to look like it was designed by someone from the East trying to make it look like it was designed by someone from the West. Then again, it could have been de—"

"Benny?" I interrupted.

"What?"

"Shut up." I drank coffee, enjoying the silence. Then I sighed. "What do you use when you can't use a phone bug?"

"A snitch."

"He wouldn't fit in the cubbyhole."

I poured more coffee while I explained the setup I'd found. When I got to the cold phone, Benny cocked his head to one side. When I described the sealed phone unit, he went real quiet.

"That's classic E-Bloc tradecraft," he said finally, "but it isn't the sort of thing the Soviets will teach a Mexican kid attending Patrice Lumumba University in Moscow. The sealed telephone is postgraduate work." He took my coffee cup, drank, and sighed. "Leave it to you to go fishing for carp and end up with shark. Whoever is running this show isn't a young revolutionary with shit for brains. The whole thing stinks of a professional intelligence officer. And a bloody clever one, at that."

"Volker?" I asked, but there was little question in my mind.

"You know him better than I do."

Benny brushed the high-tech trash on his palm into a Baggie and began rummaging through small cubbyholes. After a few minutes he swore and rustled around in one of his toolboxes, then jerked open a satchel and groped through its contents. Finally he pulled out a handful of ballpoint pens.

"Knew I'd find a use for it someday," he said. "Strictly Stone Age, but sometimes rocks are the only thing that gets it done." He stowed all but one of the pens.

I took the one he offered and looked at it. It looked like a pen. I looked at Benny. "What am I supposed to do, write him a poison-pen letter?"

"Were there office supplies in the storeroom?"

"Yes."

"Do you think anybody would notice this?"

I shrugged. "What's to notice?"

Benny took the pen back, unscrewed the barrel and handed me a short metal capsule. "Condenser mike, three-transistor amp and short-range FM transmitter. All you have to do is turn it on and hide it in plain sight."

I put the pen back together and looked at it closely. "I'll be damned. It really works?"

"Of course it works. There's a problem, though. Did you see a commercial radio receiver in there?"

I thought for a moment, then shook my head. "Nope. They probably listen to the stuff coming through the wall from the cantina."

"Good, because whatever is picked up by the pen goes straight out on an FM band. What's the most powerful FM transmitter in town?"

Border Radio came to my mind. "Try eighty-nine point five," I said. "That's the FM side of a blast from the past."

Benny grinned at the irony and went to work on the device, resetting its transmitter to the desired FM band.

"What's the range?" I asked.

"A few blocks is all you can count on. But right now that's all we need." He handed me the pen again. "Tuned in, turned on and ready to be dropped off."

"Where in hell did you get a unit like this? It's so damned simple compared to most of your stuff."

For a moment Benny looked almost embarrassed. Then he grinned. "I got it through a little survivalist mail-order outfit down in Kentucky. Three hundred ninety-nine dollars, cash, check, MasterCard or gold bullion, depending on how much of a survivalist you are. These blokes even have a WATS line and an eight hundred number. If you're in a hurry, they can ship it UPS next-day air freight."

"Stand down, double-oh-seven," I muttered. "The new generation is here."

"You don't know the half of it. Give me a few hours and six hundred bucks and I could put that storefront under full video surveillance with an off-the-shelf system from my Kentucky friends. Peephole lenses, low-light camera, Watchman monitor, all Sony, all quality, and you could hide the entire unit in your bloody briefcase, if you carried one."

I turned the pen over and over in my palm. Reflected light flashed back at me from the shiny metal barrel. "Is this thing waterproof?"

"Bloody right it is. I keep telling you, they ship quality stuff. Why?"

Without answering, I opened the door of the van and dropped the pen into a muddy puddle. Then I scuffed its shiny barrel on a flat rock. None of the supplies in the storefront had been new or expensive. When I was finished, the pen would fit right in.

"Any special instructions for placing it?" I asked.

"There's only one that matters, boyo. Don't get caught."

17

Early the following morning, Benny and I were back on a Tijuana side street with the FM radio turned on, waiting for something to happen. We should have slept. We sat there for four hours listening to oldies but goodies that bled over onto the bug's frequency from XTRA.

When it came to working hours, the Che Guevara Battalion of the Aztlán Liberation Front had it all over any bank. It was eleven o'clock before a plain-faced Mexicana in black slacks and a San Diego State sweatshirt came strolling down the street, unlocked the storefront door and went inside. Lights snapped on in the back. The bug in the storeroom began to pick up muffled sounds of activity in the adjacent office.

"I sure hope she didn't bring a radio to work with her," Benny said. "The feedback would probably break her eardrums."

"XTRA is border radio," I said. "It's for gringos, not for politically hip Marxists. Quit worrying."

"If you're going to play this game at the major-league level, you can't ever quit worrying," Benny said flatly.

Our first bite came on the bug I'd wired into the desk phone. Even with an earplug screwed into place, the ringing sounded very soft. A faint voice came through the radio speaker from the storeroom bug as well. It wasn't clear enough to make out what the woman was saying.

"It's the secretary's phone," I said. "Turn up your third-wire receiver."

Benny grabbed the battery-powered unit and increased the volume in time for both of us to hear the secretary.

"He's not here at the moment. Is there a message?"

She spoke unaccented English, which surprised me, but not the man at the other end of the line.

"Have him call me."

The voice was a man speaking English. After that, any kind of identification would have been impossible. The voice was disconcerting: hollow, disembodied, almost spectral. After a few seconds I realized that the man was using a speaker phone. He sounded rushed, very impatient, but it could have been only the odd distortions of a speaker phone working in combination with the Mexican telephone system.

"The usual phone number?" the secretary asked.

There was a grunt that must have been affirmative at the other end of the line, followed by the noisy disconnect sound you get on speaker phones. Very efficient, very clipped, nothing for an eavesdropper to use.

On the phone bug, we heard the secretary slap the switch hook and then quickly dial a seven-digit number. It was picked up after the second ring but not answered.

"*El cojo,*" she said in guttural Spanish. Then she hung up.

"Good phone security," Benny observed. "A cutout and a blind phone drop. Dead ends all over the place. What's a cojo?"

"A cripple. From what Rickie said, El Cojo calls the shots around the storefront."

"Then he'll probably show up here to return the call. That cold phone is there because somebody important uses it."

"You want to find better cover?"

Benny shook his head. "The best time to steal elevators is at noon. Nobody expects a thief in full sunlight."

We crawled into the back of the van and drew the sleep curtains.

Benny wedged himself against the bulkhead and I sat on a camp stool. For the next ten minutes, we waited without saying a word. I spent most of that time trying to decipher the strange popping sounds that were being picked up by the telephone bug in the secretary's office. Benny was doing the same thing.

"Gum," he said finally. "The cow has a bloody great cud of chewing gum."

"Maybe she'll swallow it."

She didn't.

Nothing else useful happened, either. There's no magic to surveillance. All it takes is a good bladder and cast-iron butt. I went into a half trance of waiting and staring through a thin crack in the sleep curtains at the street traffic, watching the Battalion's front door as though it were the only thing of interest in the universe. The deliberate trance was so thorough that the movement in the driving mirror on Benny's door didn't catch my eye at first.

Then the movement came again, and with it the tightening of the skin on the back of my neck as the primitive part of my brain tried frantically to get a message through to the rest of me. I stared intently into the mirror, wondering what had triggered that elemental fight-or-flee rush of adrenaline.

The man who was approaching the storefront looked neither familiar nor dangerous. He was under six feet, modestly dressed, dark-haired, fair-skinned, and walked with a limping gait, as though one knee was stiff. For all his awkwardness, he covered the ground well enough. In fact, despite the odd, rolling walk, he had a physical assurance about him that was almost feline, as though he knew that whatever came next, he would manage to land on his feet.

Someone made a startled sound. I realized it had been me.

"Got something?" Benny asked softly.

"I don't believe it."

And I didn't. My rational mind was telling me that the reality out there just didn't match up with the image in my memory banks.

"What?"

"That's Volker," I said in a low voice.

"Bloody hell, mate. Who else did you expect—Sharp's ghost? Move over. I want to see this sodding paragon of male perfection who seduced Fiora and nearly killed you."

I moved. Benny looked. Then he turned and stared at me as though I was crazy. I didn't really notice. The Detonics slid easily into my hand from the leather holster in the small of my back. Automatically I thumbed off the safety and drew the slide back to make sure that one of the spherical nine-millimeter rounds was in the chamber. Then I sat on my heels and waited. Volker was two hundred feet away, much too far for the ammunition I was using.

"I thought you said you cut his arm," Benny muttered.

"Arm or chest just below his armpit. He was wearing Kevlar underwear."

"Wonder who gave him the limp?"

I shrugged.

Benny kept watching Volker, who came up the street like a wounded jaguar, all that sleek feline strength reduced to compensating for the physical perfection that was gone and would never come back again. The mental habits of an athletically gifted hunter were still there . . . but the body was not.

The awkwardness in Volker's gait came from his right side. His right arm was bent slightly at the elbow, and his hand was tucked into the pocket of his suit coat instead of swinging freely with his stride. My single thrust with the shark's-tooth hideout knife must have cut nerves and muscles all the way up into his armpit. No wonder Sharp had described Volker's trail as "bloody as a lung-shot buck."

My hands ached suddenly, reminding me of the instant when the packing crate lid had slammed down, driving bright steel nails through my flesh and bone. Did Volker remember that moment, too? Did he remember loving Fiora but not enough, loving her and condemning her to die of a shotgun blast to the base of her brain? Did he ever wake up suddenly in the small hours before dawn, sweating and sick with regret? Were we that much alike?

Volker approached the van with his head up, alert to the world around him. He was getting close enough to the van for me to see his goddam handsome features, a clean regularity and harmony in the shape of eyes and nose, mouth and chin. His skin was pale and cool in the morning sun. When light struck his eyes, they would be the uncanny blue of glacier ice. When he spoke, his voice would be that of a cello—supple and vibrating with resonances of emotions he could never truly feel. But he could *seem* to feel them. He could make himself a mirror in which you saw yourself endlessly, perfectly, reflected.

It was not a comforting reflection for me. There was too much about Volker that I really didn't want to acknowledge as part of myself. Ruthless, predatory. Cold.

Then I remembered what Fiora had said only yesterday.

But you have emotions, Fiddler. Volker doesn't have that problem. He can kill or betray and leave without a backward look. You can't. You pay. You get . . . cold.

I knew that killing Volker wouldn't exorcise his likeness within me, but I still toyed with the idea in my mind. It had enough appeal to make my palms sweat.

Volker turned his head from side to side as though sensing that I was watching him over the matte black barrel of a pistol. He was close now, close enough for me to see the darkness where blue eyes should have been. Contacts. Another veil over Lucifer's lethal radiance. Like the brown hair dye. Like the pain that had drawn his smiling mouth into a thin line as he limped forward.

An odd sense of shame twisted through me. When I had gone for Volker's throat years before, I had meant to kill, not maim. A simple, quick death. Not this wounded lingering, a dark shadow of former beauty.

No wonder he had sent an assassin after me.

That thought set up other resonances in my mind, uneasy echoes of my earlier argument with Fiora, with Benny, with myself.

Volker has no more reason to kill me now than he had at any time in the past. I've never tried to hide. If he wanted me, I was always here. And never, not once, did he take the bait.

So why had he finally decided to have me killed?

Volker was abreast of the van now. For an instant I thought of opening the door, grabbing him and wrenching the truth out of him. If it had been anyone else, I might have given it a try. But not Volker. Whatever else I was capable of, I knew that Volker's capacity to withstand pain was greater than my capacity to inflict it.

And at that moment, I knew I had to let him live at least long enough to find out what he was doing.

Benny had his Browning out and was braced in shooting position with his hand on the latch of the sliding door. I touched his elbow and shook my head. He looked at me like I had lost my mind. When I lowered my gun to underscore my decision, his eyes flashed with the dark suspicion that I had lost not my mind but my nerve.

We waited, utterly motionless, while Volker passed three feet from us on the other side of the van's metal skin. The uneven rhythm of his step on the moist gravel of the street came to us clearly. Benny's head swiveled until he could see Volker through the crack in the front curtains. He watched blackly while Volker limped down the street and out of range.

"Fiddler, you know three eighths of five eighths of sweet fuck-all about killing people," Benny snarled. "We could have made it across the border long before the local cops knew what happened."

I shook my head without taking my eyes off Volker's back. When the storefront door opened and then closed behind him, I turned to Benny.

"If you had been killed back in Saigon, would somebody have been sent in as a replacement?" I asked.

Benny glared at me without answering. He was loaded with adrenaline, trying to control it. Finally he closed his eyes, took a deep breath and opened his eyes again. Waiting.

"The night I knifed Volker, there were five people on that mountain in Santa Cruz," I said. "Two of them are dead—Korchnoi and now Sharp. That leaves Volker and me and who?"

"Fiora," Benny said harshly.

I nodded.

The quartz-crystal clock in the dashboard marked off ninety seconds. It was so quiet in the van that I counted each one of them. Then I uncocked the Detonics, snapped on the safety and shoved the gun into the holster at the small of my back.

"You'll never have a better chance," Benny said.

"Killing him right now won't end it," I said. "They'd just send somebody else. Volker doesn't take things personally, Benny. He's running an operation. He's always running an operation. We've got to let him run long enough to find out what the punch line is. If we don't, somebody could still get killed. I would take that chance if it was just me, but I won't take that kind of risk with Fiora's life."

Suddenly the storeroom bug transmitted the sound of a door opening and then closing. Soft, slightly arrhythmic sounds came as Volker limped about the small room. I reached through the sleep curtains and turned up the volume on the FM dashboard radio.

"Now we've got to pray he doesn't do a room sweep," Benny said under his breath. "Spooky blurter like him probably goes over the toilet with a field-strength meter before he takes a crap."

The ballpoint room bug was as good as Benny had said it would be. There were scrabbling sounds when Volker uncovered the telephone hidden in the box of old magazines. There was a vague click when he plugged the cord into the hidden wall jack. We would be able to hear only Volker's end of the conversation, but that was better than nothing.

There was a creak and then a sigh.

"He just sat down in one of the old office chairs in the storeroom," I said.

Benny held up his hand, silencing me. Only then did I realize that he was taping the feed from the radio. That way he could play back the tape until he deciphered the mechanical clicks of the dial, telling us what number had been called. We both listened intently while Volker dialed.

"Ten digits," Benny said when it was quiet. "The first three were long, short, medium, but after that I lost it."

"Seven, one, four?"

Benny spread his fingers and tipped his hand back and forth in a "maybe" sign.

I wondered if I was going to listen to my own voice on the Ansafone again, or if it would be Fiora instead. The thought of Volker confronting her once more made me wish suddenly that I'd killed him while I had the chance.

There was still time to change my mind. I could be through the back door of the Battalion headquarters in less than a minute without attracting attention. Five seconds to kick down the storeroom door, three seconds for two shots followed by one in the back of the head to be sure, and run to the van. It would be so easy.

And so stupid.

"You needed me?"

Volker's voice hadn't changed. Even over the small condenser microphone, the sound was calm and assured, with just the faintest touch of an accent that could have been German or Scandinavian as easily as Russian. The trace of phonetic difference worked beautifully with Volker's supple voice, hinting that each word held special meaning, special emotion. I would have sold my soul for a voice like that. He probably had.

There was a pause while Volker listened. The pause got longer. The chair creaked as though its occupant was uncomfortable. Or impatient.

"Calm yourself, my friend. We will think together about this for a moment."

Sympathy and steel. The gentle stroke, and the stiletto hinted at but withheld. Volker's voice resonant with all the emotions he didn't feel.

"I have as much at risk as you do," Volker murmured, his voice soothing and warning at once. "There is no reason for you to do that. Forcing the vote at this moment would just make everything more difficult. Be patient, my friend. Give our plan time to work."

Silence stretched. Benny motioned me closer, then spoke into my ear with a bare thread of sound.

"Sounds like he's got a jittery agent in place."

I nodded.

"Any guess as to who or where?"

Before I could respond, Volker spoke again. "What did the board say? Do you have a majority or can she still hobble us?"

Benny stared at me suddenly, telling me that I'd made some kind of sound. I probably had—the sound a man makes when he can finally see the gleam of the tripwire across the path in front of him.

18

Benny continued to stare at me. He could tell I had figured something out, but he didn't know what. I shook my head and held my hand up, wanting to hear more and hoping like hell I was wrong.

"Calm yourself," Volker said gently. "There is a small delay, perhaps, but no true difficulty. What do bankers understand better than anything else?" He laughed softly. "Very good, my friend. So we will just offer more money. It is so simple, yes?"

In my mind I could see Volker's special smile, the one which assured you that you were charming, handsome, wealthy and bulletproof. Personally, I would have settled for one out of four—as long as that one was bulletproof.

"What about the others? Are they . . ."

There was a pause, then Volker began again, his voice suddenly cold, barely patient.

"I am afraid that you do not fully understand the situation," Volker said. "There is no possibility of your withdrawing."

That brought a reaction on the other end loud enough to be transmitted by the pen bug. No words, no meaning, just a faint yammering of outrage or fear.

"That is enough." Volker hadn't raised his voice, but the sympathy was gone, leaving only naked, glittering steel. He waited, then said softly, "Listen to me, my foolish friend. Listen very well. I will say it only once. My principals have invested many millions of dollars in you. We will not lose that investment simply because you have discovered unexpected scruples to go with your cold feet."

"Volker's a rooting yuppie," whispered Benny. "Sounds like he's having lunch at the Tower Club with his whinging mates from the Yale Club."

"Or the Harvard M.B.A. program."

Benny gave me a questioning look, but I said nothing more.

"Yes, I agree that it presents a difficulty. It is not, however, insurmountable for a man of your talents. The widow trusts your judgment, does she not? Your new offer is a brilliant stroke. Twenty-five million is enough to assure her of a comfortable profit in her grief, but not enough to arouse her curiosity."

Warmth had returned to Volker's voice. He was a falconer alternately exciting and soothing his bird, but it sounded as though the bird in question wasn't entirely buying the balm.

"Oh, I believe you, my friend. I am very sure that your adversary will not be so easily misled. She is as intelligent as she is beautiful. However, I am certain that she will have a change of heart. If necessary, I will speak to her on that very subject. Personally."

Suddenly Benny had it all figured out, too. His hand snaked out and gripped the butt of the Browning Hi-Power that showed discreetly beneath the corner of a sleeping bag. I caught his wrist and shook my head.

"Absolutely," Volker said, his voice mellow and reassuring. "You may count on that. Do not be disturbed, my friend. Things will work out as we have planned."

Benny looked at me after Volker hung up. "Tell me I'm wrong."

"You could be, but I wouldn't bet my life on it—much less Fiora's."

"Shit!"

Benny rewound the tape, jammed in an earphone jack, and listened to the dialing sounds over and over. I didn't even bother to lean across his arm and look at the numbers he was writing down. I had a cold certainty that I already knew the number.

"714-555-6868," he said finally, not looking up.

"6768."

"Bloody, bloody hell! So you do know who's on the other end of that number."

"Pacific Basin Fund's very own Dickie-bird. Richard Toye, to you."

"Cut to the chase, boyo."

Benny was ready to kill. The Ice Cream King loves very few people in the world. My ex-wife is one of them.

"It's a high-risk, high-return, high-tech venture capital fund. At least it was until Teddy Portman died. Then Richard Toye started preaching the joys of low-risk, low-return government projects. Or codswallop, as Fiora calls it. Of course, someone from the fund would have to actually *see* the specs on these top-secret government projects before loaning an eager company money to bid on Star Wars or whatever. . . ."

"Lord God, but that's one clever agent we just let live."

"Don't remind me."

"Why? You already regretting your lost chance to save the free world?" He asked sarcastically.

"Bugger off, Kiwi."

"Don't feel too bad, Yank. All advantages in the international game are only temporary. What's done today is undone tomorrow, if not sooner."

"Not quite," I said softly. "Sharp won't ever wink at a shooter's moon again."

The smile vanished from Benny's face. "Do you think Fiora knows about Volker?"

"She knows that someone is trying to kill me. But I don't think she knows that the next one in line after me is her."

"Are you going to dump Volker when he comes out?"

"Unfortunately, no. Better the devil we have under surveillance than a new entry."

"Then we'd better be somewhere else. I'm not as fussy about how and when I take somebody out as you are." He pulled himself into the driver's seat and looked back at me. "Where to?"

"Home. I've got to put Fiora under lock and key."

It was well after noon by the time we found her. The ex officio meeting of Fiora's supporters on the Fund's board was just breaking up. The meeting room was in a quiet corner of Antonello's restaurant, the power lunch place of South Coast Plaza. I caught Fiora's eye, signaled for her to stay put and waited for the last board member to leave. The chair was still warm when I slid into it. Benny hadn't come inside with me. He hated it when Fiora and I argued—and this tête-à-tête had all the earmarks of becoming a real screamer.

"Toye has an offer pending for Mia Portman's stock," I said. "Twenty-five million. He's giving her one day to respond."

That was the easy part to say. I took a sip of Fiora's sauvignon blanc, watching her over the rim. She looked at me, then focused on a spot about four feet behind me while she thought about what I'd said. She didn't ask me where I had gotten my information. Nor did she question its truth.

"It doesn't surprise me," she said absently. She tapped a breadstick against her teeth for a moment, still thinking. "After all, it's the only thing he can do. But I thought I had all his sources of capital covered and blocked."

Fiora looked around Antonello's dining room as though trying to discover which of the men bent over plates of pasta had betrayed her. No one looked back at us. Antonello's was a bit stiff in the dress-code division for my tastes, but they had good food, good California wine, heavy silver on the tables and fresh flowers all over the place. No one would be so crass as to stare at another table of diners.

"Toye got his money by tapping into a pool of foreign capital," I said, using a clean fork to pick at the remains of Fiora's lunch. The veal tortellini was excellent. Hunger probably added at least one star to the rating. "A very large pool, as a matter of fact."

"Iranian?"

I looked up. "It's call the Soviet national budget."

Don't ever play poker with that woman. If she blinked, I didn't catch it. After a long three-count, she reached over and took the glass of wine from my hand. She sipped the pale, fragrant liquid and handed the glass back to me.

"Don't you love clichés?" she asked, letting her fingertips trail over my hand.

"Like?"

"Small world, isn't it? Or, what goes around comes around. Or bad pennies coming back or . . . yesterday always comes." She began rubbing invisible seams from the linen tablecloth. "God must have a sense of humor. Black."

I caught Fiora's restless fingers and waited.

"It's really funny," she said bleakly. "I'd forgotten, but I'm the one who introduced Volker to Pacific Basin Fund in the first place. I helped him and Danny negotiate a loan when they started up Omnitronix. They both had dinner with Teddy Portman several times. I'll bet Volker picked up on the Star Wars connection right off and has been looking for a way to exploit it ever since." She looked at me. "Funny, huh? So why aren't you laughing?"

"Fiora, don't blame yourself."

She made an abrupt motion, removing her hand and cutting off my words. She knew what I was going to say. She crossed her arms and rested her elbows on the heavy white linen cloth.

"Volker hasn't lost his predator's touch, has he?" she continued neutrally. "He spotted Richard as the weak one right away. I wonder what he used to cut the poor baby out of the herd." Her smile got darker. "He probably promised our young Cornellian a position as international financial commissar."

"Volker was very careful on the phone," I said. "I don't think Toye knows that he's a stalking horse for the KGB any more than Danny did. Dickie-bird doesn't have the testicular sufficiency to pull off that kind of balancing act. But so long as he figures it's only paper dollars he's playing with, he'll spill green blood all over the place and never think a thing about it."

"Was anything said about my sources of money?" Fiora asked.

"What?"

"If they don't dry up my money," she said patiently, "all I have to do is make a counteroffer."

"That won't be a problem."

"Really?" she asked. "Why?"

"Because as of this moment, you're out of the bidding."

"Bullshit."

"Whatever happened to codswallop?"

"Fiddler—"

"Look," I interrupted. "Your takeover's finished. Kaput. History. The Pacific Basin Fund wasn't worth Sharp's life, and it sure as hell isn't worth yours."

"Just like that?" Fiora snapped her fingers. "Daddy strides in and tells the little girl to pick up her marbles and go home?"

"Dammit, woman, when I need money-shuffling advice, I don't sit around and bitch at you for giving it to me. But this isn't a money game anymore. It's real and the blood is red, not green. Sharp is dead, Volker has made a try for me and you're next. Got that? You're next!"

"So you just hand the bank over to the KGB and run for cover, is that it? Some knight in shining armor you are!"

"Fiora—" I began, but she talked right over me.

"If you can't stop Volker, I will," Fiora said, her eyes as hard as the emeralds they sometimes resemble.

"Like hell you will." I leaned forward. "I don't give a rat's ass about what games the KGB plays. The U.S. government employs thousands of professional world savers for just these magic little moments. But not one of those government-issue saints will take a bullet for you, pretty lady. So you're going to drop out of sight for a few days. When you come back, you can pick up whatever pieces of the fund are left."

"And if I don't hide?"

"You aren't that stupid."

"Don't bet on it."

Suddenly a sheen of tears replaced anger in Fiora's eyes.

"He almost killed you once before," she said, her voice desperately calm. "My fault, Fiddler, not yours. I knew that something wasn't quite right about Volker, but I was crazy for him and I didn't want to know the truth."

She closed her eyes, but her voice went on. "The only problem was, I kept having bad dreams, death dreams. They scared me, scared me more than I had ever been scared in my life. So I asked you for help and you almost died and I found out I loved you all over again. If you had died, it would have been my fault. I dreamed of Volker, but I refused to believe my dreams. *Stupid.*"

I caught a strand of Fiora's hair and smoothed it between my fingers. "That was a long time ago, love."

Her eyes opened. They were as bleak as her voice had been. "Was it? Or was I seeing my future? Don't you see, Fiddler? If you get hurt again or if you die because of my stupidity . . ." She shook her head. "I can't risk that. I couldn't live with myself."

"I'm free, gringo and over twenty-one. Whatever happened then, whatever happens now, it's all my doing, not yours."

"You aren't listening, are you? *I'm in this too.*"

"Not any longer."

Fiora shook her head again. She glanced at her watch, ran her fingers through her hair in an angry, unhappy way and looked back at me.

"I'm late," she said.

"I'll come with you."

"Don't bother," she said curtly. "I'm going to rent a room at the Ritz and make calls. How long am I supposed to be out of commission?"

"A few days. Four, max. Call me tonight."

She stood up, gathered her briefcase and turned away without a word.

"Fiora, there's no other choice."

"Bull. Shit."

She turned away as though I didn't exist anymore. Within seconds she had walked out of sight. Not a word. Not a look. Not even a one-finger salute. The woman was well and truly pissed.

My face must have carried the whole story, because Benny didn't say anything when I climbed back into the van. We had already made our plans on the way up from the border. We ran all the necessary errands in silence. That was the same way we ate dinner at the cottage later that night. The only noise was the sound of knives against plates as we cut our steaks, and Kwame's big teeth crunching through the bones. Finally Benny kicked back, laced his fingers over his full belly and gave me a long look.

"This little stunt's going to cost a pot of hoot," he said. "Hernández is a leech. He's used to sucking people dry."

I shrugged. "What's the use of having money if you never get a chance to spend it? Hell, maybe I'll just offer him a ride north in my trunk. I got the impression he was homesick. Or just sick of Tijuana, period."

Benny started to say something, but the phone rang. I knew it was Fiora before I picked it up. At least, I hoped that it was Fiora.

"Fiddler?"

"Where are you?"

"Your least favorite place—my office in Century City."

"Are you all right?" I asked, because Fiora's voice sounded strange.

"Fine. Just fine."

She didn't sound fine. Her voice was flat, as though all emotion had been squeezed out of her.

"Fiora?"

"We have to talk. Can you come see me?"

"When?"

"Now."

"At the office?" I asked.

"Yes."

"Are you sure you're all right?"

"Nobody has a gun in my back, if that's what you mean."

"That's what I mean. I'll leave in ten minutes."

"Fiddler?"

"Yes?"

"You have to understand one thing. Volker has earned worse than a clean death and an unmarked grave."

She hung up without giving me a chance to say one word.

19

Somehow I wasn't surprised to see Jason at his station in the reception area outside Fiora's suite of offices. She expected her secretary to work the same hours she did, and she paid twice the going rate to ensure it. Jason was on the phone, so I waved and walked past, heading toward the impressive oak door that shielded Fiora's private office from the attentions of the uninitiated.

"Fiddler, wait!"

Jason's yelp was so unexpected that I stopped. He and I had reached a rapprochement years ago. He's as gay as a day in May, but he is not given to yelps. He's also as shrewd and efficient an assistant as God ever made. Jason and I had tangled at first, but things mellowed when we agreed on one thing: his job was to keep everyone but me out of Fiora's hair.

"You'd better let me announce you," Jason said hurriedly, picking up the intercom phone.

"Why?" I asked, opening Fiora's office door. "Has she taken a lover since she talked to me tonight?"

It might have been easier if a lover had been the only thing awaiting me.

The man in her office was a three-dimensional definition of medium: medium gray-brown hair, medium gray eyes, medium height, medium features. He wore a gray medium-weight wool suit with a vest and an understated chalk stripe. A durable black leather briefcase sat on the floor beside his chair. I knew without looking inside the briefcase that it contained a pistol, a tape recorder and a blank notebook.

The recorder and notebook were rarely used. With his mind, he didn't need them. But the four-inch .38-caliber pistol was another matter. Supervisory special agents have to go to the shooting range once a month, even in an up-scale cop shop like the Federal Bureau of Investigation.

"Hello, Innes," I said. "I thought you'd have grayed out into nothingness by now."

Michael Innes studied me with his neutral eyes. They were a grand inquisitor's eyes. They didn't smirk, they didn't judge, they just invited you to talk and talk and talk until you hung yourself with your own words.

I glanced at Fiora. She looked as drained as her voice had sounded. Her eyes were dark, no glints of gold, watchful. And she was watching me, not Innes.

"You are under no obligation to talk to this ghost," I pointed out. "As a matter of fact, you shouldn't talk to him without an attorney present. I'm sure as hell not going to."

"Mr. Innes is here at my request."

For a moment I couldn't believe it.

"It was the only way," Fiora said in her tired voice, watching me. And then I believed it.

"The only way to what? Make sure I spend some time in jail for violation of the Neutrality Act?"

"The only way to make sure no one gets hurt this time but Volker!" she said in a husky, strained voice.

"Thanks for the vote of confidence, Fiora. Thank you all to hell."

"Fiddler, please . . ." she said, holding out her hand to me.

I turned my back on her and stared at Innes. He stared back with something close to sympathy in his eyes. It was like throwing gasoline onto a fire.

"Am I free to go or are you going to whip out the handcuffs that are wearing a round pattern in the hip pocket of your Robert Hall suit?"

"Robert Hall went bankrupt years ago," he said mildly. "Besides, you haven't broken any laws. Yet. But you will sometime in the next few hours, judging from what Ms. Flynn tells me. I'd like to prevent that, if I can."

"Good luck."

My back was turned and my hand was on the doorknob when Innes spoke again.

"One more step and I'll put you under protective custody."

I stopped moving. Protective custody. That lovely official umbrella that stretches to cover all kinds of unlovely official acts.

"On what grounds?" I asked.

"Somebody already tried to kill you once," Innes said.

"I suppose she told you about the mole on my ass, too."

"Ms. Flynn did what she thought she had to do. Now it's up to you. You can help us catch Volker or you can spend the next two weeks picking your nose in a cheap motel and playing cards with a couple of U.S. marshals, compliments of Uncle Sugar."

I glared at the door, trying to control myself long enough to consider all the possibilities. Innes was no cherry. I'd met him a day or two before Korchnoi splattered Danny Flynn's brains all over the wallpaper of an apartment in Silicon Valley. Innes had been the FBI case agent on the Omnitronix spy scam. Sharp and I finally had to end-run Innes and an entire flying squad of FBI foreign counterintelligence agents in order to rescue Fiora from Volker.

At the time I felt like we had done the world—and even the FBI—a favor, but the FBI had felt differently. Not that I've ever expected the Bureau to see things my way. It's matter of priorities. The FBI is a brilliant organization, one of the best in the world, as cop organizations go. But it is an organization, a bureaucracy. Even though J. Edgar died more than a few years ago, the FBI is still run from the top down. That means FBI agents still have one way of doing things—the Bureau way.

That leaves very little room for the rest of the people in the world to do their own thing.

Slowly I turned around. Innes looked a little older than he had the first time I'd met him. Not that there was much chance he was wiser in any way I could use. He was just more firmly set in the Bureau's ways than he had been a few years ago.

I looked out the window because my mood was too uncertain for me to face either of the other people in the room. An unmistakable shape arrowed by the huge wall of glass opposite me, catching my eye. We were eighteen stories up, and the shadow was a female peregrine falcon that lived on top of the building. She was part of the relocation experiment being sponsored by the Friends of Urban Wildlife. Everybody thought the experiment was spiffy and environmentally uplifting, a heartwarming reminder of that wilderness called life.

I had a warm spot for that peregrine, too. She was a thunderbolt, a killer, hard-edged and razor-sharp. The extinction of that pragmatic, predatory flame would be a true loss.

But the pigeon doesn't regard the peregrine as such a bargain. What's more, if the urban wildlife lovers ever saw the falcon make a 180-MPH stoop and turn a big fat pigeon into a cloud of blood-spotted feathers, they'd probably agree that falcons should be outlawed, or at least captured, rehabilitated and turned into gentler, fruit-eating creatures.

But the birds know what people don't want to know. Natural laws can't be repealed or amended. Pigeons must eat and so must peregrines. Something always dies as a result.

The trick is not to let your emotions get the best of you. There are lots of pigeons in the world. More than enough.

I waited a few moments longer, testing my own control, and decided that I could handle Innes. "You want to read me the Litany of St. Miranda now, padre?"

"I haven't made up my mind yet," Innes said. "Why don't you tell me what your next move is and let me decide?"

"Why? You wearing a body bug? You want the confession on tape?"

"Look, pal, lighten up on the outlaw bit and maybe we can cut some kind of deal."

There was a bit of roughness in his voice that should have warned me. Innes rarely showed emotion. That should have tipped me to something, but I was still fighting to control my rage over Fiora's stunt —words like "perfidy" and "treachery" rolled around on my tongue, leaving a very bad taste. It was the same for my mind. A bad taste.

"Maybe you should go back and check with the supervisor of supervisory special agents," I suggested to Innes, "just to refresh yourself on Bureau policy in such matters."

"Fiddler."

Fiora's single word was both a plea for my cooperation and an apology. I could also sense anger in her voice, and a whole lot more. I didn't look at her.

"Don't 'Fiddler' me. If anything goes sour, calling my name won't bring up the reinforcements. But you're going to need reinforcements, pretty lady. Things always go sour for civilians when you bring in guys like Innes."

"Grow up, Fiddler," Innes shot back. "This is the late twentieth century. You can't save the world by yourself."

"Fuck the world. I was just taking care of my own backyard."

Innes narrowed his eyes for an instant. "What were you going to do?"

"Dig a grave big enough for koi to swim in."

"Talk sense."

"I'm not the talkative one. She is. Talk to her."

"I already have. She said she didn't know what you were planning."

"She was right about that."

Innes look at me, waiting.

I looked back.

"Fiddler," Fiora said finally, "whether I did the right thing or the wrong thing by calling Mr. Innes, it can't be changed. We can't go back to where we were."

There was too much truth and no poetry in her words. I wondered if she knew how much, and how little.

"You wanted revenge on Volker," she said quickly. "Fine. You'll get it. Think about this: a featureless gray cell will be much harder for Volker to endure than the quick death you would give him. If you don't believe me, ask yourself which one you would prefer for yourself."

Innes' eyes widened fractionally. He turned to look at Fiora as though seeing her for the first time. He nodded slowly.

"So that's why you called me," Innes said. His mouth turned up slightly at the left corner. "I think I can guarantee a cell in Marion Federal Prison. That's where high-powered Soviet agents do their time when they get caught in the United States. Put simply, Marion is hell on earth."

For an instant I felt almost sorry for Volker, but only for an instant. He wouldn't be tortured or beaten or starved. He would simply be . . . bored. His talents, his charm, his instincts, all wasted. His mind occupied by nothing more clever than surviving just another day in the steel box that was both hell and paradise.

Boredom is not, however, as certain or as final as execution. When you're a corpse, there are no quiet international trades, no short walks across a bridge in Berlin.

Fiora was watching me. I could sense it even though I hadn't looked in her direction since I'd tried to head out the door of her office.

"There's just one snag," Innes said casually, watching me. "Before I can do any good, Volker has to be inside the U.S. How were you planning to get him north of the line?"

"I wasn't."

Innes' mouth kicked up again at the left corner. "Yeah, somehow I figured as much. One more shallow grave out in the desert of Baja California wouldn't be noticed, right?"

There was no point in answering, so I didn't.

"Ms. Flynn and I figured out a way to force Volker to come north," Innes continued, "but Volker is a very elusive man. If we waited for him just over the border, too much could go wrong. Spring Canyon is out of control. If we set a trap at the San Clemente checkpoint, he could evade it. Thousands of illegals do. Hundreds of thousands. If we set a trap at this end, he might sense it and go to ground. He has in the past."

I looked at the roughly circular scars on my hands and almost smiled. I knew where the conversation was going.

And I knew Fiora didn't.

"So you want me to sack Volker up south of the border and deliver him to you in L.A.," I said.

"Yes."

"No!" Fiora said harshly, rushing out from behind her desk to stand over Innes. "I don't want him anywhere near Volker! Why the hell do you think I called you? Volker is your problem, not Fiddler's! That's why we have laws and cops!"

Innes looked right past Fiora at me. "How about it, Fiddler? You catch him and I clean him. It's the best deal you can hope to cut."

Fiora went white but said nothing more. She simply watched me while I walked over to the leather couch where Innes had sat years before and listened to Fiora evade his questions about her twin brother. Sharp had been there, too, but he had been on the powder-blue love seat with me. A mismatch if ever there was one. Innes had the love seat now. He was welcome to it. Love was the furthest thing from my mind.

I looked at him. "Sold."

20

Usually when I'm angry, letting the Cobra loose on the road has a very soothing effect. Tonight wasn't usual. I was cold, not hot. I kept the big engine geared down and revved up anyway. Driving that way took all my attention, leaving none for the woman sitting within reach, her hair whipping around her pale face. Innes wasn't along, but he wasn't far away. He trusted me about as much as Fiora did.

Not one damn bit.

The Cobra howled up to the red line and hung there, filling the night with an eight-cylinder version of the primal scream. Eighty-five miles per hour, lights sliding by on either side in a ghostly stream. At one hundred the lights would be thicker, more substantial, and at one sixty they would be a solid wall separating me from the other, darker world.

Suddenly I remembered Volker driving the Cobra with a take-no-prisoners grin on his face as he felt the power of the car sweep through him. He had handled the Cobra as though born to it. At that moment I had wanted a second Cobra, and all of Nevada's emptiness stretching ahead of us. God's own race between Volker and me, with the Devil keeping score.

Things had been different then. I hadn't maimed Volker yet and Fiora had come to me for help, because she needed me and trusted me. I had done what I could, but it hadn't been enough. I thought she had forgiven me for not being able to save Danny. Obviously she hadn't.

It was the only way to make sure no one gets hurt this time but Volker!

The Jamboree exit came long before I was ready to surrender the streaming lights of the freeway. I backed off the accelerator, double-clutched and kept the revs up all the way across country to the coast.

At the corner of my vision, Fiora finger-combed her hair while the Cobra shot over the narrow bridge onto Balboa Island's self-consciously cute main street. She was wearing the army surplus fatigue jacket I keep in the Cobra's trunk for winter nights. She looked wan and frail beneath the cold streetlights. As I heard the adjectives in my mind, I stopped myself and almost laughed out loud. Wan, maybe. Frail? Not bloody likely. Like the peregrine falcon, Fiora's size begged the truth of her ferocity. She has a jugular instinct that surpasses anything I've managed to come up with in myself.

Traffic was backed up at a malfunctioning stoplight. I glanced in the mirror, as I'd done many times since we had left West Los Angeles. No single car had kept pace with the Cobra since Century City, but I knew the Feds were all around. There's a special squad in the Los Angeles field office that does nothing but trail people. One day it might be a Mafia capo from Vegas or Detroit, the next a suspected art forger delivering phony Miro plates to the printer, and the next a Czech businessman with a free-lance assignment from his country's intelligence service. But the FBI's S-squad, as it's called, is as good at covert surveillance as any group of agents in the world. If they want to follow you, they will—on foot, in cars, helicopters or hang gliders. Whatever gets the job done.

Innes had promised to stay well hidden in the underbrush once I left to go south after Volker. I put as much faith in that promise as I put in the three most common lies in the United States. The deal Innes and I had cut was simple: Fiora was to provide low-key entree to Mia Portman's house; I was to deliver Volker north of the line in any condition short of stone-cold dead; and Innes would take over from there.

In return, Innes would forget that I had been stepping on his toes; and he'd make sure the Soviets left Fiora, the Pacific Basin Fund and me alone after Volker was caught.

How Innes intended to call off the Soviets was never made clear, but I had no doubt that it would happen. Probably some FBI counter-spy would have a friendly chat with a trade councillor at the Soviet consulate in San Francisco. Eventually the word would filter back up the line toward Moscow Center: if anything happens to Fiora Flynn or Fiddler, you'll get more trouble than they're worth.

All very indirect but very efficient, in its own oblique way. That's how modern wars are fought. Obliquely. The century of total overt war is over. The nuclear sword that hangs over everyone's head makes for finesse, economy and deniability in great-power strife. A sidelong look or a whispered word can send a message that used to require full mobilization of the Seventh Fleet. Political/military exchanges take place in proxy guerrilla wars or civilian alley fights. The combatants may be client nations or trained agents or even unlucky laymen who get conscripted by crossfire.

Fiora had volunteered for her piece of the latest big-power action. I had been conscripted.

So had Mia Portman, although she didn't know it yet. She had been a bit surprised to receive a call from Fiora before we left L.A. At Fiora's insistence, the recent widow had agreed to a short business meeting tonight. That was why I was playing chauffeur to an ex-wife who disliked driving in the open Cobra at high speed through chilly nights. My conscience didn't bother me about Fiora's uncomfortable ride. Her choice. Her problem. I had told her to go with Innes.

From the looks of Mia Portman's home address, she wasn't hurting for her next million. The house, all seven thousand square feet of it, was on a point of land just across the channel from the Balboa Fun Zone. Property along the water was sold by the front-inch, and rich people lined up to buy it.

Teddy Portman had bought more than his share. There was a high, solid fence around his estate, complete with a wrought-iron gate to keep out the riffraff. The gate was opened by a man in what could have been a uniform. Fiora leaned out, murmured a few words, and we drove on by. Inside the fence everything was manicured with a perfection I hadn't seen since our visit to Vern Traven's digs in Napa Valley. I parked at the edge of the circular driveway, just behind a Rolls-Royce Silver Cloud and next to the departed Teddy's 560 Mercedes.

A few minutes passed before a late-model Plymouth came up the drive and pulled in beside me. To no one's surprise, the passenger was Innes. He hadn't trusted Mia to give in without a fight. In fact, he hadn't trusted her at all. Teddy's death had come at too propitious a time for the KGB. Suspicious man, Innes. Smart man, too. But then, he was paid to be.

Fiora got out, shed the oversize jacket onto the Cobra's seat and waited. I just sat where I was. This was her show, not mine.

The Plymouth's door thumped shut. Innes came and stood by the driver's side of the Cobra.

"After you, Fiddler."

I could have argued, but it wasn't worth it.

A maid answered the front door. There was no doubt about her uniform or her Cantonese accent. She barely came up to my elbow, but she was no child. We followed her down a marble-floored hallway to what looked like a miniature gymnasium. Mia Portman was facedown on a table and naked as a light bulb. All that kept her from smothering was the face-sized window that had been cut out of the padded table. A masseur as big as a mountain was kneading Mia's body into unlikely shapes. Nearby a manicurist waited, looking at her own nails with professional interest. They were as long as Spanish daggers and just a shade darker than fresh blood.

Mia groaned in pain or bliss.

Fiora walked up and stood beside Teddy's widow. "Hello, Mia. Sorry I'm late."

Mia didn't even lift her head. "Oh, hello, Fiora. Is it ten already? A little lower on the hip, Greg. That aerobics class was a killer."

"I realize that this is well past ordinary business hours, but—"

"You and Teddy kept unusual hours," Mia interrupted. "I know. Higher, Greg. Higher. Ahhh, that's good."

"Something as complex as the fund requires—"

"Harder. Harder, Greg. Yes, yes, that's perfect. Mmmmm."

It was a game. No matter how many times Fiora tried to bring up business, Mia ignored her in favor of instructions to her masseur.

"I have an offer for your PBF shares that you can't refuse," Fiora said.

The widow moved her hands until they entered the small square of visibility allowed to her beneath the massage table. I doubted that she knew Fiora had two men with her. I also doubted that Mia would particularly care.

"Susie, do you really think I should have stripes instead of stars on my nails this time?"

The manicurist stirred, popped her gum, and said, "Fer sure, ma'am."

Fiora looked over her shoulder at Innes. He went to the massage table, sat on his heels, and held his badge under Mia's recently sculpted nose.

"Michael Innes, supervisory special agent, Federal Bureau of Investigation."

The widow made a startled sound. Her head popped up out of the window. She looked right into Innes' medium gray eyes.

"What the hell are you doing here?" she demanded.

"Putting you under protective custody. Your household help, too," Innes added smoothly, giving the masseur a measuring look. "I wouldn't want them to be kidnapped and then used against you."

Mia goggled. "What?"

Innes repeated the whole thing, beginning with his name and rank. "We have reason to believe that you, as the major stockholder of the Pacific Basin Fund, are in personal danger from foreign agents who want to buy the fund."

"That's silly. If they could buy the fund, why would they steal it from me?"

I shoved my hands in my pockets to keep them out of trouble and walked over to look at the lights reflected in the bay. Mia had the IQ of a bottle of nail polish, and I had lost my patience for games.

"Besides, Richard is the one bidding on the fund, and he's one hundred percent American," Mia said. She looked past Innes to Fiora. "So if little Miss Brilliance here wants to carry on her affair with

Teddy's memory, she'll have to come up with more than thirty million to top Richard's offer. And I don't think she can do it!"

"Twenty-five," I said without turning around.

"What?"

"Dickie-bird offered you twenty-five million, not thirty."

"Who the hell are you?"

"The tooth fairy." I gave Innes a look. "Put the cuffs on her, will you? I've got places I'd rather be."

Innes ignored me. "Naturally, Mrs. Portman, we would prefer your willing cooperation, but the situation is quite urgent. If necessary, I am empowered to remove you from this house to a safe place. If, however, you cooperate, protective custody can be arranged in the comfort of your own home."

Reflected in the window I saw two women walking down the hallway. They both wore conservative suits and carried leather purses big enough to conceal pistols. The female of the FBI species. Maybe they would have better luck than Innes was having trying to explain what was at stake, but I doubted it. Mia hadn't had Benny sitting next to her on the way up from the border, telling her how the modern intelligence game was run.

In a word, money. The United States spent fifty million on a single surveillance satellite, knowing that it was only going to collect data for two weeks. At the same time, how do you put any pricetag on a single piece of information that gives you a significant edge against your opponent? And that was what the Pacific Basin Fund would provide for the Russians—a listening post that would collect invaluable data for years.

The way Benny outlined it, whoever controlled the fund would have access to the engineering infrastructure that would produce Star Wars. In the process of approving loans to companies working on government grants, Volker and the KGB would have an excuse to examine the books and plans of every American R&D firm that ever thought of borrowing expansion capital. One or two big fat loans, let them overextend themselves a bit, and Volker could probably start putting his own people on various company boards. Sooner or later someone would give away the game, of course. But in the meantime, the United States would lose technological bargaining chips at a startling rate.

I watched the talking reflections in the big windows and let the words go by me without real interest. I'd already heard the ones that mattered. *It's the only way to be sure no one gets hurt this time but Volker!*

Suddenly Mia got up off the table and strutted over to her robe like the Las Vegas showgirl she had once been. Whatever she paid her hired help to keep it trim, she got her money's worth. She looked better at forty than most women looked at twenty. The Mia who put on the robe, tied it and turned to face Innes was a different cat entirely from the one who had lain facedown baiting Fiora.

"Your badge is real and you're real and this is serious, isn't it?" Mia said to Innes.

"Yes."

"Well, shit," she said, exasperated. "My one chance to drill Miss Perfect over there a new asshole and the U.S. government won't let me."

"I'm afraid not."

"Well, shit," Mia repeated, then sighed. "The Russians really are trying to take over Teddy's fund?"

"They really are."

"Well . . . shit. That's Teddy's monument. I'm no financial whiz kid like that steel blond over there, but I'm plenty smart enough to know that Teddy was a genius. He gambled. He had vision and guts and cast-iron balls. If he'd lived, he'd have owned a first mortgage on the twenty-first century. Goddam baked brie, anyway."

I turned around and faced the room, liking Mia better with every word she spoke.

"What do I have to do?" she asked Innes.

"Convince Richard Toye that you won't sell your shares in the fund to him unless you personally meet and approve of his financial backer," Innes said.

"Why would I want to do that?"

Innes looked at Fiora.

"You want to be sure that Richard's moneymen want the same things from the fund that Teddy wanted—high risk, high return, high-tech investments," Fiora said.

Mia didn't look convinced.

Fiora put it in words Mia could related to. "You don't want Teddy's monument run by men with no balls."

"Damn right I don't."

"Short of putting your hand in a man's pants, how do you know that he has balls?" Fiora asked patiently.

"Some men do, some don't," Mia retorted. "A woman can tell at a glance."

"But first she has to meet the man, right?"

"Oh . . . right." Mia looked at Innes. "That's what you want?"

"Yes. More important, that's what *you* want. Now all you have to do is convince Richard Toye."

"No biggie," Mia said, shrugging. "Richard sings soprano."

She walked over to a phone that was done in the same scarlet as her nails and punched in a number. Richard must have been hovering over the phone, because it was answered immediately.

"Wonder Woman just called," Mia said into the phone.

I didn't know what Fiora had done to Mia, but there was no love lost between them.

"She's offering thirty."

Mia looked at her nails for a long twenty-count while Richard made noises. She put her hand over the receiver and called to the manicurist.

"Stripes."

Susie started pulling bits of plastic out of drawers in her manicure table.

"Look, Richard, I've been thinking about it," Mia said. "I still want to drill her a new asshole, but I want what Teddy wanted even more. Wonder Woman gives me a pain in the ass, but she's got more balls than most men. I don't know if your banker does. That's all Teddy cared about, you know. Balls and baked brie."

Mia's nails got another thorough inspection while Richard argued.

"Hey, I hear you," she said finally. "But you won't control Teddy's shares. Your banker will. I want to meet him. It won't take long. Five minutes, maybe ten." She clicked her plastic nails against the phone in an impatient rhythm. "Well, you'll just have to get him back here, won't you?" Pause. "Well, shit. Tell him he can get the fund for twenty-five million and a personal handshake in the next three days, or he can grab his ankles and kiss his lazy ass for practice." Pause. "Listen, honeybuns. I don't have to be reasonable. My marbles, my chalk, my rules. Got it? Good. Take it or leave it."

Mia hung up the phone and started counting on her beautifully finished nails. Before she got to ten, the phone rang. She smiled, picked it up, listened and said, "I'll be around home for the next three days." She hung up and turned to Innes, smiling like a cat with feathers between its teeth. "Like I said. No balls."

"He agreed?" asked Innes.

She nodded. "He'll call his banker tomorrow and set up a time for us to meet. Need anything else?"

"Not right now. Thank you, Mrs. Portman. We'll try to stay out of your way while we're here."

Mia shrugged. "Hey, I don't really mind. I get tired of solitaire about three in the morning. Haven't slept well since Teddy ate that last pound of brie, you know?"

Fiora hesitated, then walked over to Mia Portman. "I don't know what lies Richard told you, but I can guess. FYI, Teddy and I never slept together."

Mia gave her a cool look.

"It's true."

"Oh, I believe you," Mia said. "Teddy told me you said no."

"He never asked."

"You could have offered, you know," Mia said angrily, putting her fists on her hips. "You could have looked at him and seen more than a fat genius. He thought you walked on water, and you wouldn't even let down your hair enough to give him a quick feel. It's not like it was Teddy's fault you had some jealous stud for a live-in, is it?" She included me in her glare. "You ever heard of spreading it around?" Suddenly the anger ran out of her, leaving her looking very tired. "Oh, the hell with it. Where Teddy is now, nobody cares." She looked over at Susie. "You ready?"

Innes looked at me, then at Fiora. He jerked his head toward the door. I was tagged for chauffeur duty again.

The Cobra made it down the coast and the winding Crystal Cove road at just under the speed of sound. Instead of going to the garage, I stopped in the small parking lot.

"Stay here," I said.

Sand gritted between my boot leather and the walkway as I went to the garage. There was nothing inside but cars. I went back to the Cobra, drove it in and told Fiora to stay put. There was nothing but moonlight on the walkway to the cottage. Same for the house. Empty. I pulled open one of the kitchen drawers, the one where scissors and twine and other miscellaneous domestic junk collected. The Beretta I had given Fiora was there, right where she always left it, nestled in among the unused grocery coupons. A quick check showed me that the gun was clean enough, loaded, ready to go. I flipped the safety on again and walked down to the garage.

"Innes probably has a team watching the cottage, but carry this anyway," I said, picking up Fiora's hand and smacking the cold steel into her palm.

As I brushed past her on my way to the TII, she grabbed my arm with her free hand. There was a surprising amount of strength in those small fingers.

"Fiddler, please, let me explain."

"I've got good ears. I heard it the first time loud and clear, four by four, over and out. You don't trust me to keep you from getting hurt. I don't blame—"

"That's not what I—"

"—you for protecting your ass. But you can hardly expect me to—"

"—meant, and you know it! It was your ass I was trying—"

"—say thank you for your vote of no confidence, and you damn well—"

"—to protect! If Volker hurt you again because of me, I couldn't live with it! Are you listening?"

"—know it! You made your bed. Now you can lie in it—alone!"

	21	

S.S.D.D.

The van was gritty, dusty and dull-looking when Benny and I crossed the border into Mexico. After a sleepless night on Benny's couch, I had followed him down to the border, left the TII in one of the border parking lots and climbed in with Benny for the watch on the Che Guevara Battalion phone. We chose a different side street to park on this time—one where we could neither see Volker nor be seen by him.

The bugged phone started ringing at eight o'clock. Nobody was at the storefront to answer. The phone rang every ten minutes on the ten minutes until eleven ten. Then, at eleven-thirteen, the rhythmic popping of gum came over the phone bug as the woman settled in at her desk.

"Seven minutes more," muttered Benny.

"Yeah, old Dickie-bird must be wetting his pants by now."

Benny grunted.

At eleven-twenty the bugged phone rang.

"Bueno," answered the woman.

"I need to talk to him. It's urgent."

"He will call you at the usual number."

Benny looked a question at me. I nodded. The voice had definitely belonged to Toye. Benny's grin flashed whitely. I wondered if my answering smile was as feral as his.

There was the sound of a disconnect, followed by some squeaks and creaks as the secretary rearranged herself in the old chair. The dial clicked over numbers. At the other end a phone rang once. As before, whoever picked up the phone didn't speak. The secretary did.

"El cojo. Es muy importante."

She hung up. Benny and I settled in for another wait. Through the static of the FM radio tuned just below a major frequency came the sound of a door opening and closing. The storeroom bug was working well.

Volker was in a hurry. He appeared within half an hour of the secretary's call. Maybe his superiors were getting tired of handing over wads of U.S. dollars and getting mañana promises in return.

"You called?"

Volker's voice was very cool and very precise. It suggested that Richard Toye better have a good reason for sending up a flare.

"Wait. More slowly, please. You are not making sense."

I almost laughed out loud. Toye's job of translating Mia's demand into words Volker would understand wasn't an easy one.

Suddenly Volker's laughter came out of the FM speaker. It was impossible to hear that son of a bitch laugh without at least smiling yourself. Like Volker's voice, his laughter was flexible and inviting, telling you without words that he took a rare pleasure in sharing the company of such wise and witty people as yourself. Even knowing what Volker was capable of, I still felt the pull of his damned charm.

"Let me repeat what you have said. Mrs. Portman wants to meet me in person in order to determine if I have testicles?" Pause. "Ah yes, an idiom. She merely wishes to know if I am equal to the task of running her husband's fund as he would have if he had lived." Pause. "Three days?"

There was a long silence. I couldn't tell if Volker was listening or just clamming up to make Toye sweat.

"She cannot be persuaded that this is an unreasonable demand?"

It took Toye a long time to say what Mia had stated in six words: her marbles, her chalk, her rules.

"I will call you tomorrow. And Richard . . . if anything goes wrong with the purchase of the widow's shares at this point, you will be held personally responsible. My backers are losing patience. They are more kind than I. I have no patience left to lose."

Volker disconnected, dialed again and said, "One for Costa Mesa. Tonight." Pause. "No. Tonight." Pause. "Bueno."

The storeroom door opened, closed, and then nothing came through the bug except fading arrhythmic footsteps.

Benny looked at me. "Sounds like Volker has a long-standing arrangement with a smuggler."

"Yeah. His name is Hernández."

The neon sign on the front of Rickie's bar glowed blue even in daylight. Benny backed into the alley and parked. He looked at the stairway leading up to Rickie's second-floor office and then he looked over at me.

"I can still go up stairs," he said, "but I can't be fast or quiet about it."

"No problem," I said, pulling out the Detonics and checking its load. "Rickie and I are old friends." I shoved the pistol into the holster at the small of my back. "We're just going to talk some business."

"Talk fast. If you're not back in ten minutes, I'm going to fire an M-79 through the back window up there and go home."

I looked at my watch. "Ten minutes."

The back door to the office was open. Rickie was sitting with his eyes closed and his feet on his big desk, listening to music on a small stereo system. The music was a blend of rock, blues, Tex-Mex and mariachis—lots of electric guitar and percussion and one silly squeeze-box accordion. The singers spoke Spanish, but their sentences had English noun-verb constructions, muy típico border Spanglish.

It's heard a lot in the California barrios, too.

"Homesick?" I asked.

Rickie opened his eyes as he reached for his waistband. He froze when he saw the Detonics.

"You got something in mind or are you just playing gringo tourist?" he asked, leaning back in his chair again, his hands in plain sight.

"You want to make ten grand?"

Rickie sat and watched me with shrewd black eyes. The song ended, leaving the room in complete silence for three seconds. Then the musicians cranked it up again, sounding for all the world like an East L.A. baile band at a sock hop in the gym at Manual Arts High School.

"There's a bonus, if things work out," I continued. I walked over and sat down in the straight-backed chair in front of the desk. "How would you like to be able to go north and see Grandma Hernández once in a while without worrying about doing time on a manslaughter rap?"

Rickie watched me with his dark, hooded eyes while the vatos sang a chorus about Rosalie, except that her name was probably Rosa Lee.

"Grandma Hernández is dead," he said finally. "She died when I was three. She used to take me for doughnuts at some pinche little place over by City Terrace. It would scare me to death to do that today. I belong to White Fence, at least I used to. They don't own that turf no more." He shifted his weight slightly, but was careful not to move his hands. "Grandma Reyes is still alive. She lives on a lemon ranch up by Oxnard. I wouldn't mind seeing her. I was her favorite grandson. Nobody makes frijoles the way she does."

"You heard from your friends in Aztlán yet?"

"You get around, chico."

"Keep it in mind, Rickie baby. Tell me about the Aztlán passenger."

He shrugged. "What's to tell you? One more northbound mojado."

"Only he's not a mojado, is he? He's European, and he would be blond if he hadn't dyed his hair."

"So long as it don't glow in the dark, I don't care what color it is. Somebody has the fare, I'll move their freight."

Rickie gestured toward his suit coat pocket. I nodded. He dug out a cigarette and lit it, them smoked it halfway down in silence.

The music had picked up in tempo and volume. I recognized the group, now—Los Lobos. A California hybrid pony band, sired by Ry Cooder out of Flaco Jiménez, trained by Stevie Ray Vaughn and ridden by Paul Simon. Some call it amalgamation. Some call it mongrelization. It's the wave of the future in Southern California.

I like it.

"Ten grand, huh?" Rickie asked finally.

I checked my watch. Slightly more than five minutes before Benny started putting rocket grenades through the window.

"So what do I have to do for that kind of money—kill somebody?" Rickie asked.

"There's a man up north who's giving me a hard ride. He wants to talk to your Aztlán pollo. I've promised to make that possible."

Rickie moved his head and looked at me out of the corner of his eye. He didn't like the sound of what I'd said at all.

"The guy on my case isn't la Migra," I said. "He doesn't care how many mojados you've escorted into the Promised Land. He just wants to know more about Aztlán and this particular pollo. If you cooperate with he, he'll arrange a permiso for you. He'll even get you taken off the lookout list at the port of entry. If things work out really well, he might be able to convince the Immigration service to drop their indictment against you."

Watching me from the corner of this eye, Rickie said, "I'm not a snitch."

"Snitches talk to cops. You're talking to me. I'm not a cop."

I dug a bundle of bills from the pocket of my down vest and tossed the packet on the table. Fiora might have changed my plans, but she hadn't changed the amount I'd pulled out of banks to pay Rickie. The bundle of bills was heavy enough to make a satisfying thump as it hit the table.

Rickie looked from the bills to me.

"How will you move the Aztlán pollo?" I asked.

He shook his head. "Nothing about you adds up. Whose money is this? Yours, the CIA's or what?"

"I'm a free agent. The money is mine. I pulled it out of four banks yesterday afternoon."

"Why you want this pollo? He burn you on a deal?"

"Close enough. How about it, Rickie?" I looked at my watch. "You've got two minutes and two choices—yes or no. Maybe won't get it done."

"Ten grand, huh?" he asked, riffling the corner of the packet with his thumb.

"Count it on your own time."

"What do you want me to do?"

"Smuggle the load like always, but use my driver and van."

"That's all?"

"That's it. You instruct me on the route. I'll instruct the driver." He put out his cigarette. "No cops around the load."

"No cops."

"When do I go home?"

"Three days."

Actually, Suarez should have the permiso in his wallet in three hours, but I didn't want Rickie to think I was too eager.

Finally he nodded. "Deal."

"How are you going to make the move?"

"Like always," Rickie said, shrugging. "I just put the Aztlán pollo in with a bunch of Mexicans and maybe some Central Americans and shoot him over the line."

"He never goes alone?"

"It's safer to mix with a group. There are snitches on every street corner down here. They see you putting together a special load of one pollo and they call the Border Patrol right away. See, there's a bounty. Ten bucks a head for Mexicans, fifty a head for exotics."

"How do you cross the load?"

"Like everyone else—out over the Soccer Field and down into Spring Canyon. My guides usually start the load farther east, out near the airport, and walk them straight across the mesa and down to the edge of Chula Vista. We pick 'em up in vans and make the run north to Encinitas. If the checkpoint is down, we just keep going. If not, we stash the load in a house up there until the point shuts down and we can move again."

Rickie kept talking and I listened, realizing that smuggling hadn't changed much since Uncle Jake's day. Rickie was running a classic operation. It took the border one step at a time, bringing illegals across the international boundary in the rugged, brushy canyons between the ocean and Otay Mountain. Guided by Mexican smugglers who knew the worm-tangle of footpaths, groups of men would set out from Colonia Independencia in the dark. Using lights north of the border as their landmarks, the illegals would walk north four or five miles in rough open country before hiding in the brush close to prearranged pickup spots.

A smuggler's vehicle would pick up its designated load and head north to drop houses in northern San Diego County, where the illegals were held, sometimes in groups of a hundred or more, in vacant houses or rented motel rooms, sometimes even in the open air. The illegals would be kept under guard until the San Clemente checkpoint came down or until some alternative form of transport could be arranged. Either way, the Border Patrol was lucky to nail one in ten loads.

I intended to make sure that the unlucky one wouldn't be Volker's.

Quickly Rickie drew a map for me, showing routes his guides took out of Mexico and the pickup spots they used in the brushy canyons that intruded into National City's suburban housing tracts. He drew the map so easily, I wondered how many times he had done it, and how many polleros had looked over his shoulder while he drew.

"What happens if the Border Patrol gets them in here?" I asked, drawing my thumb down the swath of open country the groups had to cross to reach the pickup point.

"They spend a few yours in a Border Patrol cell and are shipped south again. The pollo you want has been north a lot. Regular commuter. He knows how to act."

As before, Volker had chosen to play a game of nerve as well as skill. Operating under loose cover in Tijuana was one thing, but walking into the anarchy of Spring Canyon dressed like a peasant from the Mexican interior took another magnitude of balls entirely.

"Do you stop anywhere along the way?" I asked.

"There's a drop house in an avocado grove near Fallbrook. It's real lonely. How about if you have the guide take your driver and the load there? You could grab the one you want and leave the rest of the pollos there. I'll have someone pick them up. That way the trip won't be a total loss for me."

"All right."

"But there's just one thing," Rickie said, lighting another cigarette. "When you kill him, make sure you do it off my turf. I don't care, one way or the other, so long as I don't know, one way or the other. It saves me having to go to confession on Sunday." Rickie gave me a cold smile.

"No problem." I showed him some teeth in return. "But there's just one more thing, chico. Don't stiff me on this one. I'd hate to make your poor old granny in Oxnard attend her favorite grandson's funeral."

22

César, the bodyguard with the bull neck and elegant hands, became my guide by default. On such short notice he was the only man in Rickie's organization who had the necessary permiso—a card issued by the United States that permitted the Mexican bearer to cross the border into the United States pretty much at will.

Rickie had summoned César from the bar while I went down the back stairs to put Benny at ease. César and I came in opposite doors to Rickie's office at the same time. César moved well, seeming no worse for the wear after his shocking experiences with the Crawlman, but he wasn't particularly happy to see me. He lifted his head and glared at me like I was a matador wearing a solid red suit.

Rickie smelled the resentment. He gave César a torrent of cold Spanish instructions, just to make sure that César's untutored grasp of English didn't get in the way of complete understanding. Then Rickie switched to English for my benefit and started all over again. I felt better about Rickie's desire to cooperate as it became apparent that the English version precisely matched the Spanish instructions.

"For this trip, you are César's boss," Rickie told me. "I tell him to do what you say just like you are me. He don't like that. I tell him he don't have to like it. He just have to do it. He agrees. He is a very good guide."

César nodded to me. *"A sus órdenes, señor."*

You bet. Just as long as I didn't turn my back.

"Since you're at my service," I said, "let's stick to English."

"Sí, Yes. What do I do?"

"Follow me," I said, heading for the back stairs again. "I'll be in touch real soon, Rickie."

I put César in Benny's van. We crossed into San Ysidro well ahead of the international commuting crush. I retrieved the TII and pulled off the road at a service station to use the phone.

Matt Suarez wasn't in his office, but he must have been in radio contact. The Calexico Customs dispatcher who answered the phone took my number and told me to wait. Two minutes later the pay phone in front of me rang.

"How quick can you get to San Diego?" I asked.

"If I had a good enough reason, I could get one of our pilots to fly me over after dinner."

"How does the man who hired the Cuban assassin strike you as a reason?"

"I'll be at Brown Field in ninety minutes. You want me to bring anything? Or anybody?"

"It's a B.Y.O. ammo party," I said. "But leave Dana home. It's going to be a night when less is better, and he's too big and too tired to move fast anymore. Oh yeah, one more thing. I need a permiso."

"What for?"

"A Mexican who is going to do you and me a very big favor. Unfortunately, he's a smuggler who's on the INS shit list."

Suarez was silent for a few moments. "That may take a while."

"Just so you're at Brown Field no more than an hour after dark. Otherwise I'll go hunting alone."

"You sure about the man who hired Aaron's assassin?"

"Dead sure."

"I'll be there."

I left the TII in a McDonald's parking lot and climbed into Benny's van so that César could show us the stops along the underground railway from Tijuana. The hidey-hole in the brush at the edge of National City was ingenious. A thick clump of acacia concealed the stub end of a storm-sewer drain that ran back into a subdivision of town houses a quarter mile away. A trickle of swampy water ran down the bottom of the three-foot-high pipe. Half the state of Oaxaca could hide in it.

"La Migra don't check this place," César said proudly. "They are lazy. My poor country cousins hide in there all night long, if they have need, like pollos hiding from a hawk."

"Poor country cousins is about right," I snorted. "I'd be poor, too, if I had to pay three hundred bucks for the right to ride from Tijuana to Los Angeles in the back of a produce truck."

César didn't like the implication that he might be exploiting his own kind. He gave me the taco-with-claws look again. "Señor Rickie, he is great man, the same like Pancho Villa," César said coldly. "In the barrio Señor Rickie is hero. When he go to cantina, he no buy no drink for himself. Pollos line up to honor him."

"The smuggler as revolutionary leader," I said. "Uncle Jake would have loved it, if he hadn't died laughing first."

"Who is this Uncle Jake?" César demanded. "I don't hear of him."

"Don't worry, he's not planning on hustling your pollos."

César started to lean on me, then apparently remembered his instructions. He gave me his best killer look and settled into the back of the van. He didn't say anything until we reached the Fallbrook drop house at the end of a little road off Highway 78. The building was an abandoned mission-style stucco farmhouse with several adjacent outbuildings. The land was mostly avocado and orange groves and scattered brush.

The farmhouse was left over from another era. Today Fallbrook is populated mainly by airline pilots and artists and writers, people with enough money and freedom to live at the fringe of the megalopolis that the Gold Coast is rapidly becoming. All around us on the steep hillsides were beautiful split-level homes. None of the houses was closer than a half mile, which meant that the farmhouse and outbuildings had the kind of privacy smugglers crave.

When César and I got out of the van, the air was cool, crisp, hinting at the cold night to come. From across the valley came the mechanical rumble of a wind machine being tested by a farmer worried about the possibility of frost that night. If the temperature dropped below freezing, wind machines all over the valley would growl into life, defending the alligator pears and lemons and oranges from a premature and unprofitable death by freezing.

César stood alone in the still air while I checked the house and barn. Eighty years ago, Rickie's drop house had been someone's handsome home. Beneath the scars made by careless feet, the wood flooring was beautifully grained and carefully laid. The cracked and chipped tiles around the fireplace had been decorated and set by hand. One of the original beveled-glass windows was cracked but otherwise intact, with the faint rippling that only came from age. The rest of the windows were a shambles. The glass was fragmented and dirty. Rusty screens hung in tatters. Curtains had been reduced by sun and time to a few rotten patches hanging from bent brass rods.

The barn was down at the heels, too, but it was in better shape than the house. There was a new padlock on the barn's big sliding door. I got the key from César and opened the lock, pushing the door aside. Even in the cool air, the smell of human excrement was like a blow. That alone told me how closely the pollos had been held by their smugglers; no human being lives in an open sewer by choice. Necessity, however, is different.

Alien smugglers have their own necessities as well. They go to great lengths to control their clients in transit, since human contraband tends to get restless and forgetful about paying once the journey is complete. Drop houses along the smuggling route usually are medium-security affairs. Once the immigrants reach the north end of the underground railway in East Los Angeles or Santa Ana or Fresno, the control becomes much more ruthless. People are held under lock and key until someone pays off the remaining fare.

Not surprisingly, most of the drop houses get pretty unpleasant after a few thousand illegals pass through them, waiting to be ransomed by a relative or a middleman for some big employer. This particular drop house was carpeted with trash. Discarded fast-food containers and drink cups were scattered around. There were several charred spots on the dirt floor where illegals had built fires to say warm while they waited to run the last of the gauntlet into Los Angeles.

I flipped on a wall switch. Nothing happened. Either the naked bulb overhead was burned out or the electricity had been shut off. I tugged the barn door closed behind me and went over to join César. The fresh air tasted unbelievably sweet.

"No electricity?" I asked César.

He shrugged. "For why we need light?"

That was a question I wasn't about to answer. I had tangled with Volker once before in the dark. That had been enough. Somehow I didn't think César would have a lot of sympathy for my problem.

The hum of Benny's wheelchair approached from behind us. Normally he went on hand power, but he had wired in a battery for this occasion. It's damned hard to shoot and push tires at the same time.

"I don't like hunting rattlesnakes in the dark," I said to Benny when we were far enough away that César couldn't hear. "But since Volker's been through the pipeline a time or three, I don't want to make him goosey by adding lights and changing the routine."

"What about the new van and driver?"

"I don't think that's a problem. Rickie has a stable of drivers and load cars, and most of the vehicles have American plates. He keeps switching people and cars around so that they won't be recognized by snitches or border patrolmen. I doubt if Volker has ever come north with the same vehicle or driver twice."

Idly Benny combed his heavy whiskers with one hand. "You'd have the edge on Volker if he came from light into dark. So I'll just pull up beside the barn, kill the headlights, and turn on the van's interior lights. That will ruin his night vision. You should be able to walk up and cut him out of the herd before he has a clue."

I thought it over for all of two seconds. "I like it. He killed my night vision the last time we met."

"So long as that's all that gets killed this time."

"Yeah. Innes would be purely pissed off if we delivered a corpse."

Benny gave me a look that told me he hadn't been worried about Volker's health. Then Benny turned the chair and guided it back toward César, letting the heavy battery pack do the work.

"Getting lazy in your old age?" I chided.

"Let's put it this way, boyo. People see a cripple coming and they don't worry." He smiled. "Nice thing, peace of mind. Bloody useful."

I smiled. "So long as no one sees the butt of that Hi-Power sticking out."

"I'll have a blanket tonight." Benny looked at the barn, then at me. "Watch César. He'd sooner kill you than look at you."

A Piper Catalina pivoted into the hard white floodlights in front of Brown Field's jury-rigged airport services office on top of Otay Mesa. I flashed the headlights of the TII. Thirty feet away, the side door on the blue and white Piper popped open and Matt Suarez stepped out into the prop wash, holding his hat firmly on his head. With his free hand he hefted out a kit bag that sagged heavily. He handled it with a lean, whiplike strength that reminded me of Sharp; desert men don't carry extra weight.

The instant Suarez stepped lightly off the wing, the pilot reached over, secured the door and gunned smartly out into the darkness. I got out and opened the TII's trunk. The air was clean and chill. A small wind stirred across the top of the mesa. Off to the south, three quarters of a mile distant and just across the line, the mesa continued on into Mexico. The Mexicans, too, had taken advantage of the table-flat top of the mesa to build a landing field. The runway lights of Tijuana International Airport shone white and red and blue in the cold air. The full moon was just rising behind Otay Mountain, flooding the land with a silver brilliance that pushed dense shadows out of trees and rocks alike.

"Shooter's moon," Suarez said, following my glance.

For an instance it was as though Sharp had spoken. Shooter's moon. Hunter's moon. Predator's moon. Just enough light for an experienced rifleman. Just enough light to kill.

"Uncle Jake hated this kind of moon," I said. "Sharp nailed him on a night just like this."

The kit bag Suarez had brought settled into the trunk with a muffled metallic clanking that suggested farm tools or firearms. A name was stenciled on the bag: SHARP.

I turned and looked at Suarez as though I hadn't really seen him before. In many ways, the important ways, I hadn't.

"Aaron had a good Mossberg nine-shot," Suarez said when I looked at the bag again. "It was in the trunk of his car along with some other things."

"Was he wearing his Model 59 when he died?"

Suarez' face didn't change expression as he peeled back his short Levi riding jacket and pulled the handsome firearm out of a leather loop on his belt. He hesitated, then handed the pistol to me.

Beneath the shooter's moon, the weapon gleamed like running water. Sharp's dress-up gun was a Smith & Wesson Model 59, silver-plated and engraved, a presentation-quality nine-millimeter with fancy pearl grips and a forty-point diamond set in the front sight blade. The intricate scrollwork on the slide had been copied from the design on a sword Sharp had once seen in the Metropolitan Museum in New York. Like the sword, the gun was beautifully made, perfectly balanced, potentially lethal . . . and a work of art.

"Sharp always used to say he didn't dare wear this piece in Mexico," I remembered. "He was afraid some cholo cowboy was going to try to kill him and take it away."

"Afraid? He was afraid of nothing!"

Suarez' thin, handsome face was a study in black planes and silver light that heightened the bone structure beneath. I had seen a face very like it once before, under a different shooter's moon.

"Sharp wasn't afraid of dying. He just didn't like killing on his days off," I said, handing the gun back to Suarez. "How about you? Do you wear that piece down into Mexico's cholo bars?"

"I was born down there. Remember?"

"If I forgot, you'd remind me, wouldn't you?"

Suarez gave me a long, dark look. "I still don't know why he liked you."

"I don't know that he did," I said, understanding this time that Suarez was thinking of Sharp, not Lighter.

"He did," Suarez said, easing the gleaming silver piece back into its loop. "Aaron liked the fact that you would kill or get killed to save a woman who wasn't even legally yours. He did the same thing once."

"Your mother?"

Suarez turned away without answering.

Benny and César were waiting in the parking lot at the seafood restaurant on C Street in Chula. Benny handed me a box the size of an unabridged dictionary and almost as heavy. It was a cellular phone with a power pack, the civilian's answer to the age-old military problem of instant mobile communications.

"I got one for the van, too," Benny said. "Normally it takes a week to get numbers assigned from Pacific Telephone, but Radio Shack had five on repossession. You can call me anytime you want, all night long. Just remember that whatever you say goes out in the clear to anyone with a receiver."

"What about it, César? Do your checkpoint scouts use radios?" I asked, not wanting to introduce anything that might make Volker uneasy.

"*Sí. ¿Cómo se dice?*—channel nine."

"Citizen's band?"

"*Sí.*"

I put the phone pack into the trunk of the TII, which was beginning to look like the equipment locker of a special weapons team. When Benny added the night vision glasses and an extra set of batteries, the resemblance was complete.

I introduced Suarez and César by first names only. They measured one another for a few moments, each trying to place the other in the hierarchy of border cops and robbers. Then they nodded formally without shaking hands.

"We're all on the same side, this time," I told Suarez. "Next time through there are no guarantees."

Suarez smiled thinly.

César squinted up at the moon through one slitted eye. "She is too much bright, ver' bad for us, but a man must do his job, no?"

Nobody argued. We all knew that the moon would be higher, brighter and more dangerous three hours from now, when Spring Canyon's nightly game of Red Rover would begin in deadly earnest.

23

It was twenty-six minutes until midnight. Streaks of high cirrus gleamed beside the full moon. The ground was rugged and dry, churned to powder in placed by hundreds of thousands of feet. As I followed Suarez over the edge of Otay Mesa and into the black shadows of Spring Canyon, I wondered if all the rich folks of the Gold Coast knew what their cheap labor went through just to get to work. No wonder it was so hard to get reliable help—it was a hell of a commute.

Off to the west, toward the ocean and the I-5 checkpoint, a shot rang out and then echoed in the cold air. The report was flat, tinny, the sound of a small-caliber weapon. It could have been a homicide in progress or a drunk celebrating his saint's birthday. There was no way for us to tell.

Suarez and I froze in place for a moment, waiting for return fire. All we heard was a coyote barking, twice, sharp and biting. Then he cut loose with a long, keening howl, celebrating the cold wind and the hunter's moon balanced high overhead. Like the shot, the coyote's call went unanswered.

In the moonlight Spring Canyon seemed empty, deserted, utter lifeless. Off to the west, on the flat ground called the Soccer Field, few campfires flickered where mojados warmed themselves one last time by a Mexican fire and drank one last Styrofoam cup full of oily, weak instant coffee laced with tequila as fortification against the trip.

Someday Spring Canyon will be as famous as Ellis Island, but while Ellis Island is yesterday—*Birth of a Nation* and *Going My Way*—Spring Canyon is rock-video modern. Spring Canyon is today. It stars Ozzie Osbourne biting off chicken heads, with Mother Teresa as the love interest and Mad Max as choreographer. Spring Canyon makes the East Bronx look like downtown Spencer in Iowa. The only place I can think of that's as treacherous as Spring Canyon is Beirut, where the violence is also free-form and almost casual. But there are no sides in Spring Canyon, no alliances, no religious schisms, no plans for a new and better society. It's every gunslinger for himself, and let the wild dogs eat the leftovers.

In the moon-washed darkness, the canyon looked like it went on forever. I had to keep reminding myself that the place wasn't much more than a half mile wide and maybe a hundred fifty feet deep. It wasn't even much of a canyon, more a network of interconnected gullies that were scored by countless well-beaten trails. But no matter how much I reminded myself of Spring Canyon's true dimensions, the primitive part of my mind recognized the canyon for what it was—a dark, effectively boundless hunting ground.

I wondered what Volker was thinking now as he hunkered down somewhere in Colonia Independencia. He was probably replaying the trail in his mind, remembering how it had been the times before when he had dropped down over the canyon's south lip through one of the cactus-lined finger canyons. From there he and the other pollos would follow their guide across the flat canyon floor to any one of a dozen escape routes that clawed up onto Otay Mesa with its barley fields and row crops and tall eucalyptus windbreaks.

Was Volker out there on Spring Canyon's opposite rim even now, waiting in silence as Suarez and I were waiting, listening with his breath held for more shots to be fired?

After a few more minutes of silence, Suarez resumed the descent into the canyon. I applauded his caution. It we got in trouble down e, it would be our problem. The Border Patrol worked the canyon's fringes from on top of Otay Mesa, but the floor of the canyon self had been pretty much ceded to Mexico or anyone else who wanted it badly enough to fight for it every night. Suarez had told me that the San Diego Police Department ran a task force into Spring Canyon's netherworld from time to time, using well-trained, heavily armed officers disguised as illegals. The result was the highest incidence of officer-involved shootings in the free world.

Most crime in the canyon never gets reported. As Suarez put it, would you report a crime if the price of making that report—deportation—was worse than the heaviest sentence your assailant would ever receive?

It was eerie to descend the trail and know that in huts, hovels and houses from Argentina to China to the Punjab, thousands of would-be immigrants were reading letters from cousins who had made it, who had passed successfully through Spring Canyon to the Promised Land beyond, their way marked by the greenish light of the Border Patrol's night-scope on Mojado Lookout, just as their European predecessors had used the greenish light in Lady Liberty's torch as a beacon.

The trail continued to drop steeply, but was otherwise easy enough for a man wearing rough-country hiking shoes. I pitied the mojados who took on Spring Canyon barefoot or wearing sandals made of rope and a chunk of tire tread. Suarez and I were much better equipped. In fact, we made quite a pair—me with a cellular phone in one hand and a shotgun in the other, and Suarez with the night glasses and Sharp's Mossberg.

We had just reached the flats at the bottom of the canyon when Suarez held up his hand and stopped cold. Crackling sounds in the brush off to the left signaled the flight of some creature. An animal broke cover and sprinted into the moonlight.

"Mule deer," Suarez said very softly, letting out a breath. "Wish to hell you had let me check with San Diego PD. Then I'd know where their task force is. I'd hate to run into those high-tech cowboys with a twelve-gauge in my hands. They shoot first and discuss rights with the next of kin."

"After you checked with San Diego PD," I said softly, "then you take the Border Patrol's temperature. They, of course, want to check with your boss at Customs to make sure all the proper forms h[...] been filed, and then your boss would call you and ask what the h[...] you plan on doing with a civilian down in no-man's-land, and the[...] we'd be up to our nuts in an intragovernmental pissing contest the[...] likes of which you haven't seen since Congress started asking Ollie North where he bought his groceries."

"Listen, Ace," Suarez hissed. "This may be a lark to you, but my badge is on the line!"

"So is my ass. If you're worried about getting the first barrel of double-aught, I'll be glad to take the lead."

Suarez ground that between his teeth for a moment before he spat into the moonlight. Then he adjusted his jacket against the surprising cold, looked around and gestured curtly for me to walk in front of him.

As I passed him, he said, "FYI, in an ambush the man in back usually gets picked off first."

"FYI," I said flatly, "if I didn't think you could cut it, I'd have come alone."

He hesitated in exactly the same way he had before he showed me Sharp's gun. Then he nodded slightly, another gesture I remembered from another time, another shooter's moon. I wondered if my subconscious mind had picked up on those ghostly resonances long before the conscious part of my brain had, and if that was why I'd known that Suarez would be a good partner for a man caught between moonlight and midnight in Spring Canyon.

I hoped Suarez was at least half the tiger his daddy had been.

On Spring Canyon's floor I stayed with the widest of the multiple branching trails and watched the dark pools of nearby shadow for movement. The canyon walls sheltered us from the northwest wind, but cold air slid down the slopes and gathered like water in depressions on the canyon floor. Walking past the mouth of a ravine and feeling the sudden chill rolling down was like a premonition of death. Whoever said that hell was red and hot had never been in Spring Canyon during a winter night.

We walked for ten minutes before I caught a hint of movement on an adjacent trail. Silhouetted against the lighter canyon floor ahead, a large group of men was walking single file. As I watched, the leading

of the group stepped into thick shadow and disappeared. Suarez
I were also in shadow. We froze and stayed that way while about
rty men came closer to us through the darkness.

Suddenly the first man emerged into less dense shadows between
two clumps of brush. The trail forked. He stopped and looked over his
shoulder. From back in the line came a whisper instructing him to take
the right-hand trail. As usual, the guide was well hidden in case the
group was discovered by the Border Patrol. Mojados got a free ride
home from la Migra. Smugglers got a hard time.

I hoped the smuggler wasn't some Tijuana cowboy with a loaded
gun and an urgent concern about the state of his testicles.

The group was almost on top of us before the lead man spotted me.
He could see that I carried something in my hands, but the flat black
cammie shotgun could have been a club for all anyone could tell in the
darkness.

"Pase, señor," I said softly.

The lead man didn't move. Somewhere back in the line, a man
cursed him for being the son of a whore. The second man in line
shoved the lead man and got him walking again. There were forty-
three men in the group. Forty-two of them shuffled past in utter
silence, leaving behind the smell of cigarette smoke and nervous
sweat. The last man was shaking. His teeth chattered audibly, uncon-
trollably, and he clutched a rosary in his hand.

After that encounter, Suarez and I saw no one else on the canyon
bottom. We had begun the climb back up toward the south lip of
Spring Canyon when a flicker of movement on the rim caught my eye.
Without turning around, I held out my hand. Suarez put the night
glasses squarely in my palm. I waited while the gyro spooled up to a
faint whistling squeal, then lifted the glasses and focused on the trail
ahead.

The glasses showed me a landscape in negative form, like a strip of
developed photographic film. Light forms became dark in the shimmering greenish vapors, and dark became light. It took me a few
moments to orient myself to the new reality. Then I saw three men
gathered beneath a ragged eucalyptus. The men were standing casually, waiting rather than walking, relaxed rather than apprehensive.
One of the men struck a match to light a cigarette. The tiny flame

burned blackly in the glasses. Although the men were more than hundred yards from us, I could almost hear them chatting quietly a. they passed the cigarette around. Mota, marijuana. It helps to kill the time in hell's anteroom.

"Bandits," I said softly to Suarez.

He pulled back the cuff of his jacket and told me what the glowing hands of his watch showed. "Five minutes to midnight."

"If Rickie's good to his word, the group I want should be moving out in five minutes," I said, staring through the glasses again. "They'll be at the lip five minutes later. These pendejos are going to give our group a bad time."

"And Aaron said you were inventive," Suarez muttered derisively.

"There are three ways we can go," I said very quietly, still watching through the glasses. "I'll talk slow so I won't get too far ahead of you."

"I'm pretty smart—for a Mexican—if that's what you mean," he shot back, his voice a harsh whisper.

"Do us both a favor, Suarez. Give it a rest."

"*Tu madre,*" he replied without heat, brushing past me and heading up the trail.

We both knew we had to get rid of the bandits at the lip of the canyon. The rest was just talk. Fifty yards short of the lip, the path widened out into a jeep trail. I stashed the phone pack and the heavy glasses, touched Suarez' arm, pointed at myself and gestured toward a side trail that bent off to the left. Then I gave him two fingers and a sweep of the wristwatch dial, meaning I wanted two minutes. He nodded and made a sign that he would move straight up the trail.

Walking carefully, I eased off onto the side trail, trying to make as little noise as possible. The wind was blowing on the south rim of the canyon. The dry rustling sound of eucalyptus leaves and the spiky whispering of branches in the brush covered any noises I made. I was in position up on the rim fifty yards east of the main path with thirty seconds to spare. A eucalyptus tree rose like a ragged black torch in the moonlight, marking the spot where bandits waited in ambush. Shotgun at port arms, I moved toward them.

The bandits were twenty yards away before I saw one of them move. A cigarette arced to the ground and was instantly extinguished. One

the men made a kissing noise with his lips, the sound a Mexican
ses to catch a waiter's attention. Then he pointed down the trail in
the direction of Suarez' approach. They were close enough that I
could hear a hoarse, faintly stoned whisper. They spoke in border
Spanish, a language invented by and for no-man's-land.

"Un hombre, un guía."

They had decided that Suarez must be a guide returning from a run
with his pockets full of money. One of the men stepped out onto the
path. A knife gleamed in his hand.

"Buenas noches, cabrón," he chuckled coarsely. *"Es un noche profitable?"*

Suarez was as cold as the knife. He walked up the trail another six
steps and stopped, his arm at his side, holding the Mossberg by its
pistol grip.

"Out of the way, asshole," Suarez snarled.

The other two bandits quickly moved out into the open, trying to
intimidate Suarez with numbers. The second bandit reached for his
waistband, the gesture of a man drawing a gun. Suarez brought the
shotgun up. I knew there was a round in the chamber because I had
seen him load it when we left the car. He wasted the shell by racking
the gun as he leveled it.

He wasn't completely Sharp's son. Sharp would have fired and
dumped the man right there, no warning and no regrets.

Even so, the racking of a pump shotgun had a chilling effect on the
bandits. There was no mistaking that sound. I wasted a shell of my
own, racking the shotgun I held. When the three bandits spun toward
me in surprise, I had the gun at my shoulder.

"Manos arriba," Suarez barked, reminding the bandits of his presence.

He was thirty-five feet away from them. With the short-barreled
Mossberg shotgun, the buckshot would spread immediately into a
wide pattern. He could have hit all three men with one shot. They
knew it as well as he did.

The bandits were outgunned and caught on the triangular point of
a perfect crossfire. But something got the better of their judgment—
either machismo or marijuana. The taller of the three must already
have had his gun out, because he leaped to the left, crouched and fired

with one motion. The report told me he wasn't firing a pinche caliber. The slug zipped past my ear like an angry hummingbird.

I was too busy moving to take careful aim, but there are nine slug in a load of buckshot, so it's hard to miss entirely. The slugs fell short, fanning out as they skipped off the ground. The man who had flashed the knife went down with a high yelp. The bandit who had reached for his waistband grunted and lurched, but came up with his gun. He was closest to the trail, so he fired in Suarez' direction, three snap shots from a .22, the muzzle flash a thin flame that lanced away from his hand.

Instead of a fourth shot, there was a snapping metallic sound, like a cheap semiautomatic pistol jamming. The gunman's curse was subsumed by the double blast of Suarez' shotgun, followed by the odd whine of slugs ricocheting off rocky ground. The heavy reports of the twelve-gauge echoed through the depths of Spring Canyon. When the sounds died away, there was silence but for the scrabbling noises of three men dashing off into the cover of night. Suarez held his fire for the same reason that he had fired into the dirt twice; he was no more interested in cold-blooded executions than I was.

I ran to the trailhead. Suarez walked toward me, the riot gun held loosely in one hand, looking for all the world like he had been hunting quail rather than men.

"You okay?" I asked.

He grunted and then turned to examine the spot where the bandits had made their five-second stand. Moonlight glinted on the dropped knife and shone more dully on what looked like a piece of discarded metal pipe. It turned out to be a homemade single-shot zip gun—a pistol barrel tied down on a crudely carved handgrip with steel strapping material that had been salvaged from a packing crate. The firing pin was a roofing nail snapped home by a pair of heavy rubber bands. The tube was wide enough to take a .45 slug.

A Saturday night special, a knife and a zip gun. You can always tell a workman by his tools. Crude killers, but killers all the same.

There was a heavy smear of dark black color on a flat rock where the man with the knife had gone down. The smear was wet and came off on my fingers.

Don't lick they clean," Suarez said. "Lots of these border bandits
hypes, so some of them have AIDS."

"You're a real ray of sunshine," I muttered, wiping the blood spoor
on my jeans. "C'mon. Let's get the hell off the trail."

24

Rickie must have gotten good terms from either God or the Devil. Whichever patron, the bastard sure got all the breaks he needed as a smuggler. A heavy cirrus layer veiled the moon at the stroke of midnight, cutting the ambient light level by half. If I hadn't had the night glasses, I would have missed the group of men who appeared silently at the edge of Colonia Independencia and started across the open field in single file, heading for the trail Suarez and I had just cleared of bandits.

There were twelve pollos. They moved in obedient single file with no talking back and forth. Their features were unrecognizable even with the glasses, but Volker's faint rolling gait made him easy for me to find. He was second from last in line and had no trouble at all keeping up with the more able-bodied pollos. In fact, there was an odd grace in his movements that was almost eerie.

Suarez was waiting for me below the lip of the canyon. We had to stay ahead of the group without giving ourselves away, which meant moving quickly. I picked up the glasses and the cellular phone and joined Suarez. The two of us jogged down the trail to the canyon floor and hid in the dense shadow beneath a sycamore. From there I watched the trailhead behind us.

After a few minutes the guide shepherding Volker's group appeared and stood alone at the edge of the canyon, looking for bandits or border patrols. Moving only his head, he checked and rechecked the route. Suddenly he turned and made a sharp signal with his arm before he went toward the eucalyptus tree and dropped down behind a boulder.

Instants later the hard drone of the Border Patrol's Hughes 500C came in from the west. Some patrol unit on the north rim must have heard the recent gunfight and called for aerial reconnaissance. The chopper came in at three hundred feet and made one quick pass over the area. When that drew no fire, the pilot dropped a hundred feet and made another pass, this time perched on a moving column of hard white illumination from the chopper's searchlight. The pilot worked the canyon like a bird of prey, moving quickly in one direction, spinning and doubling back, cruising all the likely places. The third time through, he came in about thirty feet off the deck, as though hoping to startle his quarry into flight with the shrill roar of his turbine.

Nothing broke cover.

I swung the night glasses back up to the trailhead. The guide was sitting casually on his heels behind the rock, waiting for the helicopter to go away. It would take more than a few feints from a flying machine to raise that man's pulse.

The chopper roared past us once more, its high-pitched, throbbing sound so loud and hard, you could have walked on it. Suarez and I watched while the aircraft worked east for a quarter of a mile, then wheeled and came back toward us very fast. The blades made a stuttering sound as they changed pitch and slowed. The harsh spotlight mounted between his skids lanced into a patch of scrub, turning the chaparral a blinding milk white.

Suddenly the spotlight snapped off and the helicopter leaped into the night as though freed from a leash. The aircraft climbed steeply and roared off toward I-5 at top speed, making me wonder if the pilot had just gotten a hot call.

Suarez touched my shoulder and murmured, "They're moving."

The guide got everyone back on the trail quickly, no false moves, everything by the numbers. He had his chickens rounded up and headed down into the canyon before their ears had stopped pounding from the chopper's roar. It was enough to make me suspect that the guide had anticipated the flying bloodhound being yanked off onto another scent.

"I'll bet a gang of Tijuana street kids just stormed the fence on the levee, right in full view of a border patrolman," I suggested softly. "Rickie's operation is the kind that would run a diversion, just to hold down the costs."

"The kids will get rounded up quick enough, but they'll be home by morning," Suarez said, his voice almost too faint for me to hear. "A free Border Patrol meal and five thousand pesos from el jefe. Pretty good wages for Tijuana."

Silently we watched while Volker's group descended into the canyon. When the men disappeared behind a hognose, we left our cover and trotted ahead along the trail. Halfway up the north canyon face, I spotted a stand of scrub blue oaks that had knitted themselves into a cleft. I pointed toward it. Suarez nodded. By the time the group appeared again on the flat canyon floor, we were hidden in the oak thicket, waiting and watching.

The veil of cirrus moved on, letting the moon's hard silver brilliance pour over the canyon floor once again. Volker's group was caught in the open. At the guide's urging, the pollos broke into a trot. Their soft, hurried footfalls drifted up to the scrub oaks. Soon the men appeared, climbing up toward us, coming closer with each step.

For the second time in thirty-six hours, I sat with a gun in my hands and watched Volker approach. It was harder this time because I knew that he had again managed to pull me and Fiora apart. Finally I put down the night glasses so I wouldn't have to see how close Volker was, how easy it would be to kill him.

Suarez took the glasses from me and held them to his eyes. "Which one?" he hissed softly.

The urgent edge to his voice reminded me that he had a personal interest in Volker's life and death.

"Second from last," I said so softly that I wasn't sure that Suarez had heard. "The one with the odd kick to his gallop."

Yet once Volker had run like a god, his head up, his pale, angel-fine hair lifting on the wind, running me into the ground and never breaking a sweat.

Suarez focused on the rear of the column. For a long time he watched, saying nothing. The group was close enough now for me to see the men without the aid of night glasses. Even at a trot Volker had no trouble keeping up with the rest.

Suarez watched the group intently. As the men passed, he twisted and half rose to follow them with the glasses. His movements threatened to reveal our position. I grabbed his arm to remind him that there was more in Spring Canyon tonight than Sharp's killer. Suarez flinched away from my hand and drew a hissing breath between his teeth. My fingers came away wet and darkly smudged with blood.

We sat silently until the sound of Volker's group faded away. Then I showed Suarez my hand.

"How bad?" I demanded.

"Messy but no big deal."

"Bullet still in?"

Suarez shook his head.

"Move your fingers."

He stared at me, then held his hand in front of my face and moved his fingers. They all worked. I peeled down his jacket. The wound was across his biceps. Blood oozed steadily but not dangerously. The bandanna around his neck was clean enough for what had to be done.

While I worked, Suarez gritted his teeth and looked back toward Mexico, studying the south edge of Spring Canyon and beyond, toward the glittering lights of Tijuana. When I finished, I looked up at Suarez. Beneath the chill illumination of the shooter's moon, his face wore an expression that was angry and hard and utterly cold. His resemblance to Aaron Sharp was uncanny, making me wonder how I had missed it during the full light of day.

The cold welled up around us again as the canyon floor filled with an invisible flood of sinking air. Suarez shivered a little when I helped him back into his jacket. The silver butt of Sharp's Smith & Wesson gleamed against his body like ice. Suarez saw me looking at the gun.

"It was about the only thing of value he had," Suarez said quietly.

"He had you. The last names are confusing, though."

Suarez hesitated, then sighed. "It's no secret. I just don't make a big deal out of it. Neither did he. My mother was married to a man who went north during the Bracero Program and never came back. Later on she met Aaron. She was crazy about him, but she wouldn't marry him because she was already married. A few years ago Mama found out that her husband had died six months after he'd left her. By then, Mama was used to the way things were, and so was Aaron. So they never got around to marrying. But he was more of a father than most boys get. He took care of his own."

"Is that why you're in Customs?"

Suarez shook his head. "I knew if I went into the Border Patrol and started chasing wets, there would be a day when I got up and looked in the mirror and saw another goddam Mexican heading north." He smiled wryly. "It was the right choice. Dana's a good friend. I don't like leaving him out of this. But it's probably just as well that I did. He'd have tried for that cojo, right here and now. There's plenty of room in this canyon for one more shallow grave."

Suarez' voice was flat, neutral, yet somehow reproachful. He wanted to know why I hadn't dumped Volker when I'd had the best chance any man could ask for.

"Oh, I wanted to, but somebody tied my hands," I said, hoping my voice didn't sound as bitter as I felt. It did, though. Suarez' head came up and he looked at me like I was a stranger.

"Who?"

"Sharp ever tell you about the woman whose life he saved?"

"You mean your wife?"

"Ex-wife."

"That's not what Aaron thought. He said you two were married, with or without the paper."

As Mia would say, *Well, shit.*

"Fiora called in the FBI," I said flatly. "They've been wanting to have a chat with Volker for a long, long time. If I don't bring him in alive, there are a lot of old ashes they could rake through, and some new ones as well. Sooner or later they'd burn my ass."

"Volker? I've heard that name before. Who is he?"

"The man with the limp."

"Why does the FBI care who killed Aaron?"

"They don't. Volker's a Soviet intelligence officer."

There was a silence, then a hissed curse. "Aaron never told me about that part of it."

"He didn't care. To him, Volker was just one more smuggler in the cross hairs."

I wiped my hands on my jeans, hung the night glasses around my neck, slung the shotgun over my shoulder and picked up the cellular phone. Suarez stood up, moving carefully. I watched him.

"Why don't you wait here for me?" I said.

He gave me a look Sharp would have been proud of. I shrugged and said no more. I'd seen men go over a lot harder country with wounds that were worse. If Suarez thought he was up for it, I'd be the last one to say no. It was damned nice not having to watch my back.

We went up the trail slowly, making sure we didn't overrun Volker's group. Just below the north rim of Spring Canyon we stopped so I could do a quick sweep of the flat mesa top with the glasses. I caught a glimpse of the group going to ground in a small gully halfway across a field of barley stubble. I passed over the group and went looking for whatever had sent them into hiding.

Two hundred yards to the east, rolling silently along a dirt field road, was a Border Patrol van with its lights off. To the west I could see the headlights of another vehicle prowling on one of the side roads that came off the four-lane highway across the mesa.

"Bad news," I said quietly. "Volker's group is caught between two patrols. The pollos are facedown in a little gully on top of the mesa."

"The Border Patrol is using seismic sensors on some of these trails," Suarez said quietly. "It's Vietnam-era stuff that monitors footfalls. Twelve men probably sounded like a herd of elephants, so the dispatcher ran a couple of units out here to check. There's been a lot of foot traffic through here tonight."

I eased back below the lip of the canyon and snapped on the cellular phone. Benny was out there in the van somewhere, close enough to hear me but far enough away not to attract any unwanted attention. After midnight, all vans in the vicinity of Otay Mesa got a second and a third look from the Border Patrol.

Benny answered on the first ring.

"You okay?" he demanded. "It sounded like another Tet Offensive down there."

"We're okay, but Rickie's group has stepped into caca up to their lips. They're pinned down in the middle of barley stubble with a couple of patrol units looking for them. Where are you right now?"

"César's been showing me the sights of East Tijuana," Benny said. "We're just leaving the Otay port of entry."

I looked to the east. In the far distance there was a lone pair of headlights leaving the floodlit port. "Flash your lights."

The headlights went out, then came back on.

"I can see you," I said. "Shut them off again and make a run down the highway as fast as that crate can go. Make it look like you're trying to slide through to I-5 in the dark with half the state of Oaxaca in the back of your van."

The headlights vanished. I brought up the night glasses. Benny was driving a Dodge with a turboed V-8, nothing ultra-high-tech by modern standards, but it can go like hell in a straight line. Two miles away and closing fast.

"Not too fast," I said into the phone. "They have to see you."

"If they don't see me, they'll hear me," retorted Benny.

He was right. In the background I heard the turbo spooling up and the motor taking on that eager, howling sound as it began to really open up. The sound vanished when Benny dumped the phone back in its cradle. I didn't blame him; he needed his hands for driving.

Suarez and I waited in the cold wind for another thirty seconds before we would hear the muted growl of the Dodge. The sound got louder as the dark van popped over a small rise and came screaming down the road at what looked to be a hundred miles an hour. I hoped there were no loose pebbles on the hardtop. If Benny hit one at that speed, he'd probably attain low earth orbit. Very low earth orbit. Like about three feet.

For a few bad moments it appeared that the two patrols poking around the barley field were going to miss Benny despite the van's noise. The driver of one patrol vehicle was probing the dark land with a hand-held spotlight while the other vehicle, a Jeep, was bouncing along a rutted field road, trailing a faint plume of dust in the moonlight. Just when it looked like Benny would scream by unnoticed, a third unit appeared. That Border Patrol vehicle was just turning into the field when Benny appeared out of the night like a black rocket. He shot past at warp speed.

The cop's reaction was predictable. The sedan's tires barked on the pavement as the driver jammed on his brakes. He was stationary just long enough to yell an alarm on the radio. Suddenly the unit's light bar flashed and danced in the darkness. The border cop executed a rapid three-point turn on the narrow road. Even so, by the time he got straightened around, the van was half a mile away and howling. Tires squalled as the sedan took off, but Benny was still pulling away.

The other two patrol vehicles hesitated, reluctant to give up the prey they scented in the field of barley stubble. In the end, they followed the sure bet. A cop can no more resist a code-three pursuit than a dog can resist a bitch in heat. It has to do with the same kinds of hormones, I suspect.

Suarez and I watched the two remaining vehicles wheel around and take off across the rutted field, headlights bouncing in the dark and light bars flashing in full mating display. God bless testosterone. I looked over at Suarez. He shook his head and gestured with his chin toward a line of trees on the other side of the highway and a quarter mile away.

"I thought I saw something move over there a minute ago," he said.

The greenish wash of the night glasses was disorienting for a moment. Then I recognized the snout of a Border Patrol sedan poking out from behind the picket line of eucalyptus trees.

"Nice catch," I said to Suarez as I scanned the row for other watchers. There were none. "I guess that one has chased too many wild geese to get all hot about one more."

"Border patrolmen play the same game every night," Suarez said. "That old boy's just a little more inventive than most. Good for him."

"Like hell it is. He'll get his head blown off if he tries to take Volker. He's come too far to go quietly."

"I just said I liked the patrolman's style. I didn't say it was going to get him any gold stars. Lead, maybe."

With that, Suarez lifted the Mossberg and let fly at the patrol car.

He worked the slide with his injured arm, racking another shell into the chamber, and fired again before I could yank him down behind the cover of the canyon rim.

Too late. A few of the nearly spent slugs slapped metallically on the front end of the Border Patrol vehicle, followed by the sharp, bright sound of a shattering headlamp. Into the silence came the noise of an engine starting up. I didn't need a crystal ball to know that the patrolman would be headed our way, and madder than hell.

"You crazy son of a bitch!" I whispered fiercely.

Suarez hissed through clenched teeth, lowered his gun and began shoving shells in. "If I were you, I'd beat feet into that clump of brush over there," he said, jerking his chin toward the edge of the barley field thirty yards away, where rabbit brush grew thickly at the end of an irrigation ditch.

"What about you?"

"I'll decoy. No patrolman can resist a drunken Mexican."

"Where should I pick you up?"

"Nowhere. I'm going to do what Pancho Villa did—shoot and run south." Suarez thumped my shoulder in silent farewell. *"Adios, amigo.* Call me if Volker ever gets loose again. I'd sure like to send Aaron a playmate."

Suarez turned and jogged off down the trail toward the canyon floor. As I scrambled for the rabbit brush, the opening chorus of "La Bamba" floated up from the dark canyon below, sung by the clear, unschooled tenor of Aaron Sharp's son.

25

The Border Patrol sedan came sliding to a stop in the dust beside the north end of the Spring Canyon trailhead. I was flat on my belly in the brush twenty yards away, glad as hell that the snakes were all in hibernation. There was a chaotic babble of radio traffic and then two slamming doors.

The raucous strains of "La Bamba" wafted up over the edge of the canyon, followed by a few shrill yips.

"Lay-in Four to Brown Field, we're ten ninety-seven at the head of Dillon Canyon. We've got a drunken Mexican with a shotgun. Be advised that a Border Patrol unit has been fired on. Broken glass and some chipped paint. No injuries. We're going down into the canyon after him. Send Foxtrot for air support."

It was all very precise. If you listened only to the tone of voice, you would have thought the agent was reporting a flat tire. He and his partner were fast as well as efficient. They were already on the trail toward the bottom of the canyon when the dispatcher responded.

"Ten-four, Lay-in Four. All mesa units are tied up in a pursuit on the one seventeen, and Foxtrot One is ten ninety-seven on the West Side. We'll get you some help as soon as we can. ETA ten minutes."

"Ten-four," the agent replied. This time there was emotion in his voice. Disgust.

I peered through the brush at the agents, who were far enough down the trail that I could only see them from the waist up. One man had a radio set and a heavy Kelite flashlight. The other carried a short-barreled riot gun at port arms.

"Ten minutes," the gunner grumbled. "We've got a clown with a shotgun blowing holes in units, and we can't get help for ten minutes. Talk about pissing into the wind."

So quit grumbling and get on with it, pal. Things are tough all over.

No one moved.

For a few long minutes I had visions of the two of them standing there waiting for help until the area was crawling with patrol agents. The dozen aliens waiting in the gully in the middle of the field must have been sweating bullets. The patrolmen were less than fifty yards away, and the moon made the pale stubble gleam.

Suarez yodeled something unintelligible from the bottom of the canyon and followed it with another Mossberg salute. The nine buck-shot slugs sighed as they passed overhead, too high to do damage but low enough to be heard. The two patrol agents ducked involuntarily. So did I.

"That does it," snarled the gunner.

He threw his weapon to his shoulder, fired, pumped, fired again. His partner pulled out his sidearm and joined in the volley with three rounds from a .357 magnum.

"Hey, pendejo," the gunner shouted. "You like that?"

The canyon was deathly silent for a moment. Then came another round of thunder from the Mossberg. The sound of the shot over-whelmed the first part of Suarez' curse, but the last part got the job done.

". . . k you in your mother's ass!"

The slurred words were followed by four more Mossberg salutes, buckshot raining down like steel hail.

Suarez must have been running low on shells and on blood by now, but not on balls. There were a few more choice insults, then the sound of somebody racking and racking an empty shotgun. The two Border Patrol agents took the suggestion that the drunken Mexican had run out of ammunition. They charged down the trail. I waited until the sound of their footfalls faded away before I crept out onto the mesa.

The gully was empty.

Rickie's guide had balls, too. He had moved his group across the open field the moment the patrol agents began looking for the elusive Matthew Suarez.

Through the glasses I barely caught a glimpse of the last men in the group as they disappeared behind the tree line where the patrol agents had been hiding. The pollos were running fast, headed for the far side of the mesa, perhaps five hundred yards from the culvert pickup point. I didn't see Volker's uneven gait. Nor was there anything out in the field. If anyone had been left behind, he wasn't moving.

The radio inside the patrol car was turned up loud enough that I could hear reports of action from all along the front. The cops were about to be overrun, but they were taking it with grace. They had had a lot of practice at being trampled into the ground along the line. It had been happening every night for the past decade and was likely to continue every night for the next decade as well.

Suddenly a transmission came from the canyon below. "Lay-in Four. Any update on Foxtrot?" The agent's words were breathy and broken, as though he were jogging and talking at the same time.

"Negative, Lay-in Four. He's still tied up."

"Lay-in Four. Tell him to forget it unless he's here in the next few minutes. This little peckerwood's real quick for a drunk. He's already made the south wall. In another five minutes he'll be through the fence."

The agent's voice was harsh with adrenaline and anger. Getting shot at will do that to you.

"Ten-four, Lay-in; will advise."

The two agents in the canyon sounded as though they might be losing their taste for the chase, so I vanished into the night in the direction of Brown Field. The TII was a half mile away, and I had to get north to the Fallbrook safe house before Benny and César arrived with a vanload of pollos.

The shotgun on the sling kept clipping me behind the ear as I jogged along, and the phone pack slapped me in the thigh a time or ten. I skirted the edge of the ragged mesa top, keeping to cover as much as I could, but there were still open spaces to cross. One of them was a hundred yards short of the car. I slowed to a walk and checked the area through the night glasses.

I was repaid for my trouble: a Border Patrol Jeep was parked in a crease along the edge of the mesa.

These guys were shrewd, setting traps within traps within traps. I went down flat at the edge of the barley stubble. I stayed that way for five minutes, waiting for the ambush unit to move. As I waited I began to appreciate Rickie's skill even more—he lost only one in ten loads.

In the fitful wind, the sweat trickling down the skin inside my wool shirt felt like a cool finger probing for the right spot to put in a knife. During the moments when I wasn't admiring the cleverness of the smugglers and the persistence of the cops, I was trying to come up with a lie that might work if the border patrolman turned on his spotlight and pinned me in the stubble like a moth on a collection card. The shotgun and the pistol and the night glasses were easy enough to explain: I'm hunting quail, right?

The cellular telephone taxed even my imagination.

From the crease came the faint babble of a patrol radio. The cop might well have been asleep, but there was no way to be sure, short of standing up and yodeling. Finally shivering set in. It was move or freeze, so I rolled over and elbow-crawled for the brush along the canyon's edge. The rough stubble raised hell with the wool shirt and down vest, but it got the blood moving again.

Two minutes later I found a narrow game trail through the brush. Duck walking is good for the thighs, but I hadn't been doing enough of it. Fifty yards into the brush I got a cramp that made me groan. I sat down on the trail, straightened the leg and tried to knead the knot out of the muscle. The whole time I rubbed and prodded there was this clock running in my head, telling me that I was getting farther and farther behind Volker's load.

After more duck walking than I care to recall, the trail broke around to the right and passed behind the crease where the patrol car was hidden. I straightened up a little and moved at a quicker pace, trying to keep the brush from scraping against the plastic phone pack or clawing the shotgun off my shoulder. I was twenty minutes behind schedule when I finally climbed back onto the mesa, well past the ambush point, and broke into a jog again on a field road.

The TII's engine made about as much noise as the battery pack on the night glasses. I'd already disconnected the car's taillights, and the bulb in the dome light was in the glove box. I drove out of the shelter of the tool shed and headed straight across a plowed field toward the highway. A layer of cloud slid over the moon. The tires spun in the frosty grass on the embankment beside the highway, but momentum carried the little car up onto the gravel shoulder.

Once on the blacktop, I quit screwing around. The gas pedal went to the fire wall and stayed there, taking the RPMs right up against the redline. The tires barked as I shifted into second, then barked again when I hit third. The speedometer read seventy when I grabbed fourth, turned on the lights and started downhill off the mesa and back into civilization. The sweeping right-hand bend onto Interstate 5 can be made at eighty, but I don't recommend it. Michelin MXLs sometimes pop off their rims under that kind of lateral stress.

In order to punch through to Benny, I had to hold the battery pack of the cellular phone on my lap, roll down the window, hang the antenna out and dial—all while I was merging with northbound I-5 traffic. A Von's grocery truck in the number four lane almost got a new tail ornament before I completed a connection with Benny.

"This is the Kookaburra Express, come back," Benny said, sounding like a trucker on the CB.

"What's going on?"

"Ten-four, good buddy," he drawled. "We made our pickup, and now we are definitely northbound, fer sure, fer sure."

"Everybody?" I knew Volker couldn't hear the conversation, but I was somehow reluctant to use his name.

"Ten-four the everybody. We're about ten minutes from home."

"Bad news, pal. I'm at least fifteen minutes behind you. Why don't you take the scenic route?"

There was a pause. At first I chalked it up to the distraction of traffic. Then I began to wonder.

"You still with me?" I said.

The pause lengthened.

Finally Benny said, "Yeah, you're coming in four by four. Can you hear me?"

"You having phone trouble?" I asked.

"That's the idea," he said. "We may have to go to another channel, mate. I'm getting a blast from the past."

The connection went hollow for a moment. I heard a voice say something. It sounded like César. Then there was a sudden electronic snap and the connection went dead.

Swearing, I punched redial and got a busy signal. I dialed again and got the same signal. I slowed to eighty because traffic was getting thicker around the National City off ramp. When I dialed again, I got the busy signal again. And again. Finally I tossed the phone pack aside and floored the accelerator again. So much for the miracles of modern communication.

I went thirty miles, freeway and country highway, at an average speed of ninety, and not one cop. The ratio of highway patrolmen to speeders is even less than that of border patrolmen to illegals. The moon was sliding downhill when I double-clutched into second and made a controlled skid onto Gird Road. Then I killed the lights and coasted along softly, looking for landmarks. Finally I spotted a dirt road going off to the left toward a willow thicket that marked the course of a tributary of the San Luis Rey River. Across an open field three Washingtonia palms on top of a small rise were silhouetted against the moon-washed sky.

I turned onto the dirt road. All around me the narrow little valley was quiet, deeply sunk in shadow. The farm Rickie used as a drop house was a quarter mile away. I stopped long enough to use the night glasses. They took a lot of time to spool up to power; the batteries were running down.

There was no sign of Benny's van in the farmyard. There was no movement except the wind machines stirring the cold air above the groves that bordered the dirt road and the farmyard. I turned off the road and drove between rows of bushy navel orange trees, hoping that the throaty purr of the wind machines would cover any sounds my car made. When the TII was hidden from sight, I parked, checked the load in the shotgun, slung it, grabbed the night glasses and took off across country toward the drop house.

The farmhouse with its line of palm trees was on a little rise surrounded by low-lying citrus groves. At a hundred yards, the place still appeared deserted. One possibility was that Benny had managed to stall long enough to get behind me. The other possibilities weren't nearly so appealing. Just to be on the safe side of all possibilities, I stuck to cover as I trotted toward the house.

A thick tangle of pomegranate brush formed a hedge at one side of the yard. The breeze had dropped, but the wind machines stirred the air enough to make the dry, round pomegranate husks clatter hollowly against their stems. I listened for three minutes and heard nothing but the wind.

Cautiously I stepped out into the open and trotted across what had once been a handsome lawn but now was a tangle of Johnson grass and tumbleweed. I circled behind the barn at a respectful distance, trying to think like a coyote in Kwame's backyard. There was a sour smell in the air that reminded me of the barn's major purpose these days—a holding cell for tired, apprehensive people.

The batteries in the night glasses were fading fast. There was just enough juice left to give me a fast look at the setup. Something was out of place, but I couldn't figure out what. While the batteries died I swept the area again. Nothing jumped out at me, yet the skin on the back of my neck felt tight. The primitive part of my brain was trying to lift a ruff against the unknown.

I put aside the useless glasses but made no move toward the barn. In my mind I walked through the place as I had seen it once before. I got as far as the front door of the barn and remembered the padlock. César had given me the key and I had returned it when I was done. I'd closed the barn door, locked it, and left. But now there was no padlock. So far as I knew, César had the only key.

It was beginning to look like César didn't take orders worth a damn.

The north end of the barn had no windows. Keeping in the cover of the orange grove, I worked around to the north side before I approached the barn. My route took me within ten yards of the front of the abandoned house. As I slipped by the front picture window, I heard a faint scraping sound—metal on metal, like a pistol sliding over a belt buckle as the weapon was being pulled out of a man's waistband. Even as I spun around, I heard the distinctive metal click of a pistol being cocked.

César was a stubborn man. He had bought himself another single-action Colt, an old-fashioned gun that had to be cocked by hand before it would fire the first round. Modern semiautomatics can be cocked and fired with a single pull of the trigger. The result is a time savings of perhaps a quarter second. That was about how long it took me to turn and fire from the hip with the shotgun.

In the burst of light from the muzzle blast I saw César standing directly behind the smashed farmhouse window. I jacked another round into the twelve-gauge and fired again, shifting a few inches to chew up Volker or anyone else who might have been hiding in the house with César. Some of the pellets buried themselves in the wooden frame of the window. Most of them found a much softer resting place.

César got off one shot as he pitched forward through the empty window frame and fell heavily into a flower bed that was overgrown with weeds. His shot ripped through the side of my down vest and skimmed past my ribs. Not a hit, really. More like a red-hot kiss.

I dove for the cover of a palm trunk at the side of the yard and racked the shotgun again.

"No, no, no! No shoot! No shoot!"

That wasn't Volker. Volker didn't beg. Perhaps he was behind me somewhere in the dark or hiding out in the house . . .

There was a flicker of movement in the empty window. A form appeared with arms upraised.

"Don' shoot, señor, please. I am the guide, Manuel. I no have gun. I am shooted already."

Not seriously, from the sound of it. I eased around to the other side of the palm tree and listened, but heard nothing more.

"I go out, *sí?* No shoot. No shoot!"

"All right. Come out."

As soon as I spoke I dove for the shelter of the next palm tree. No shots ripped through the darkness. Perhaps César had been the only one with a gun.

A small man stepped off the porch and into the open. His hands were up and empty.

"Keep walking toward me," I called, and shifted position again.

When Manuel came close enough that I could see his hands were shaking, I grabbed him. We hit the ground behind the palm tree, with him on the bottom. I flipped him over, laid the shotgun muzzle under his chin and pushed hard.

"Who's with you?" I asked in a low voice.

"N-no one."

"The pollos—where are they?"

"*Allá.*"

He gestured toward the barn.

"Is El Cojo with them?" I asked.

"He go in the van. *¿Dos cojos, sí?*"

Benny's paralysis was more serious than a stiff knee, but I didn't argue Manuel's description. I looked down into his wide, frightened eyes. He looked back at me as sweat ran down onto the shotgun barrel digging into the soft skin beneath his chin. Underneath his light-weight jacket, blood oozed, making a dark patch on his left shoulder. He was shivering with cold and fear and shock. I frisked him, found only a pocketknife and a rattail comb, and threw them both into the darkness beyond the palms.

The dark splotch on Manuel's jacket was spreading, but slowly. He wouldn't bleed to death right away.

"Up," I ordered, standing and dragging him with me.

He moaned through his crooked teeth, swayed, but managed to stand upright.

"Go to the barn. Tell the pollos to come out one at a time, hands above their heads, then to lie facedown in the yard and don't move. *¿Me entiende?*"

"*Sí.*"

"I'll be nearby. Anybody goes sideways and you get it first."

I shoved him into the open with the barrel of the shotgun before I retreated to the shadows and paralleled him to the barn. I propped the flashlight so that everyone who came out would have to pass through the hard white beam. Then I took up a position to the side, where I could see the pool of light and the doorway.

The pollos emerged into the flashlight beam one at a time, silent and shivering with cold, their empty hands held high. Some of the men smiled uncertainly; others stared into the light beam like jacklit deer.

"Facedown and spread 'em," I said to the wounded guide.

He knelt, spread out and groaned. I frisked the other ten men, found nothing dangerous, and concentrated on the barn. The biggest danger came going through the door, so I went in fast and low. After that it was easy.

Nobody was home.

I went back outside, laid the shotgun muzzle against a pollo's graying hair and asked in harsh border Spanish about the man with the limp. His story matched the guide's. Volker had gone in the van. Benny was driving.

Manuel nodded and gave me a look of relief. "I tol' you, man. Los cojos, they go. Now help me, man. I need a doctor. I bleed. The bullet, it hurts. You gotta help me."

"I don't have to do a damn thing, chico. I can let you bleed to death right here. Now tell me what happened. Why did los cojos leave?"

"The pollo, the one with the limp, you understand?"

"Yeah."

"He have ver' big hurry to go Santa Ana. So he take out his . . . his anteojitos."

"What?"

"The little other eyes, verdad? He take out the brown so that the blue show. He look Anglo, sí? No have worry about la Migra no more."

"Okay," I said. "He took out his brown contacts so he'd look Anglo. Did he act like he knew the driver?"

"¿Quién sabe? He no have the name of the driver. He just put his ver' nice gun in the face of the driver, and tell him go Santa Ana. The drop house, you unnerstand. It is there," Manuel said, moaning the last word. "I hurt, man."

"So you say." I got up, put the muzzle of the shotgun against the base of Manuel's neck and said, "Okay, chico. Here's the big one. Where is the drop house?"

Manual trembled. "In Santa Ana?"

"*Sí.*"

"I don' know."

I moved the muzzle to his left shoulder blade and leaned. Hard.

Manual screamed. "I don' know, man! I never go north of San Clemente in my life!"

26

A few minutes after I turned onto Highway 78, the San Diego County Fire Department paramedics passed me rolling Code Three toward Gird Road. A green and white San Diego County Sheriff's Department sedan with flashing light bar loped along a mile behind, following up on the anonymous cellular phone call reporting a man shot and a gunfight still in progress. The latter was a slight exaggeration that would attract every cop and highway patrolman in north San Diego County, leaving the road open for some serious speeding.

I didn't want to put my second call out in the clear, so when I spotted a pay phone in an Oceanside gas station, I pulled in. Rickie must have been jumpy. He answered it himself on the first ring.

"César thought he was bulletproof. He was wrong. How about you, Rickie?"

Rickie dragged on his cigarette. I could hear the faint inhalation and then the breathy sigh as he blew smoke.

"He's dead?"

"Like a stone."

"Too bad. I hoped he was smarter or quicker, but I'm not surprised.

He was getting sloppy. But I tell you straight, I didn't put him up to it. I told him he couldn't take you. I told him he shouldn't even try. He didn't believe me. What about you, man? You believe me?"

The silence hung between us for a full ten seconds while I listened to Rickie smoke and breathe.

"I don't want to go to war, man. I'm getting too old for that shit," he added matter-of-factly.

"It's called a midlife crisis," I said. "You'll survive yours if you give me directions to your drop house in Santa Ana."

"I thought you weren't going to bust my operation."

"Your drop house or your balls. Take your pick."

He took another drag, sighed something that sounded like "shit," and said, "I been using that one too long anyway."

He gave me an address that put the drop house in the southwest corner of Santa Ana, just north of the Costa Mesa Freeway and close to John Wayne Airport.

"What's it look like?" I asked.

"A little truck farm down by that big shopping center. What do they call it—South Coast Plaza?"

"Yeah."

"My uncle owns the farm. He's un gallero. He raises fighting chickens."

"Is that where you always take El Cojo?"

"That's where they all go. We put the ones that don't pay in a garage until somebody buys them out, but El Cojo always pays in advance."

"Where does he go from there?"

"¿Quién sabe? He pays, he goes."

"Does somebody pick him up?"

"César said El Cojo keeps some different clothes there. He changes and walks off toward the big buildings."

Apparently Volker had it down to a science. He went into the mojado pipeline as a sweaty illegal from Michoacán and emerged at the other end as a well-dressed business commuter with a Hartmann two-suiter in one hand and a leather briefcase in the other, ready for a round of meetings. Volker was probably one of the few men in the world who could have made that act work, but I had no doubt of its plausibility in his hands. He made you yearn to believe everything he said in that black-magic voice of his.

"Who's at the drop house?" I asked.

"Just my uncle, Ernie Estrella. He'll be getting up pretty soon now. He has to feed the fighting cocks very early ever since they built those houses next to his farm. If the neighbors bitch about the noise, he'll have to get rid of the chickens."

"Call him," I said. "Tell him I'm coming. Tell him I don't like funerals, but I'd rather go to his than mine. And one more thing . . ."

In the silence I heard Rickie take several quick hits on his cigarette. He was more nervous than his voice had revealed.

"I'm north of the border right now," I said, "so I'm talking like a nice Anglo boy. But if anything goes wrong, I'm coming back to the other side of the line, and I won't be talking at all."

I hung up and got back on the road.

Interstate 5 is never empty, but after 1 A.M., traffic thins out a lot and goes like hell on wheels. I hooked up the taillights, took the TII up to ninety and held it there, fog lights and high beams blazing. Nobody got in my way, and a few people passed me. The long open stretch through Camp Pendleton is as close as the United States comes to the autobahn.

Even though Benny's van has a distinctive rear profile, I almost overran it just north of Las Pulgas Road. Benny was dragging anchor in the slow lane, looking like a man coming back from a long weekend of partying.

I dropped back and fell in behind a northbound dual trailer rig that had been painted with a leering portrait of a blue-eyed Navajo. Then I killed the brights and fog lights and dogged it for a half mile before pulling into the number two lane again. To anyone who had been watching his mirrors, I would look like a different automobile altogether. I passed the truck and pushed on at a respectable clip, finally falling in about fifty yards behind Benny's van, the way travelers often do, unconsciously seeking the company of another car.

Through the back window of the van, two heads were outlined against the flare of southbound headlights. Benny was still wearing his cabbage-leaf hat. Once in a while he gestured to emphasize whatever he was saying. He was probably keeping Volker at bay by talking Aussie/New Zealand politics and playing dumb. I eased off on the gas and drifted back another hundred yards, waiting to see what developed at the San Clemente Border Patrol checkpoint.

When the flashing amber warning lights came into view a mile south of the checkpoint, Volker slipped out of his seat and into the back of the van. Even with blue eyes, he still looked enough like a mojado in his rumpled clothes that he wasn't going to parade his act in front of professional skeptics who wore uniforms and watched traffic ooze by the portable stop signs. Volker's head vanished, telling me that he was hunkered down in the back. For the moment Benny was alone in the cab.

I waited until we were half a mile from the gate, rolling along at thirty-five and slowing with every yard of forward progress. I pulled into the next lane and moved up until the hood of the TII was even with Benny's door.

Benny must have already known I was there. He may have recognized the driving lights and the 2002 profile in his rearview mirror. He glanced toward me once, the way any driver glances over at a car pulling in alongside him. Then he looked straight ahead, paying no attention to me. Simultaneously, he reached up with his left hand and pushed his index finger into his ear, like it itched. It was a nonchalant gesture, but unmistakable to a man expecting a hidden message. For good measure, Benny gave his earlobe a tug as well.

Listen!

Swell. To what?

Shielded from Volker's view, Benny's left hand showed me two groups of three fingers, then a closed fist, then three quick groups of three, then a closed fist, then a circle made by thumb and forefinger followed by a closed fist. The entire series of gestures took about five seconds. Then, for the benefit of his slow-witted friend—me—Benny repeated the whole thing again after first glancing in his rearview mirror to make sure Volker was out of sight.

Six, break, nine, break, zero.

I had been paying so much attention to my own signals that I had missed Benny's. *A blast from the past.* Those had been Benny's words just before the cellular phone link went out, probably because it had been sabotaged by César. Six nine zero, 690, the dial position for XTRA, the oldies but goodies station Benny had used to cover the signal of his eavesdropping transmitter in Tijuana.

God bless technology, particularly black technology. Benny must have put one of his remaining ersatz ballpoint pens into service as backup communications for the northbound ride.

I gave Benny a left blinker/right blinker acknowledgment and dropped back several car lengths. When I turned on the radio, 690 on the AM dial gave me nothing but Joni Mitchell. I switched to the FM band and tuned in XTRA-FM, the short-range sister station. There, just beneath the rapidly fading FM signal, was the hollow crackling of a nearby poor-quality transmitter.

At first there was no sound but the hiss of the carrier wave itself. Then Benny started whistling "God Save the Queen," as though he were nervous. Not bloody likely. Benny has the nerves of a ferrocon-crete statue.

"You out of sight back there, mate?" he asked. "We're coming up to the checkpoint now, and I don't want the green shirts to spot you as we roll by. And God save us, mate, keep the bleeding gun out of sight!"

The transmitter picked up a response too muffled for me to under-stand.

Quite a crowd had gathered at the checkpoint. That's why the damn thing is there. It is an immutable fact of California geography that traffic headed north from the San Diego/Tijuana border area has virtually no choice but to use Interstate 5. There is an inland route, Interstate 15, which has its own checkpoint, but with the exception of a backcountry road called De Luz Canyon Fire Truck Trail, you can't get here from there except by I-5. Geography has created a natural bottleneck, the kind that lends itself to inspection and control by bureaucracy.

The inspection occurs just south of the bulbous concrete breasts that house the San Onofre nuclear power plant. Freeway traffic is funneled from four to two lanes and gradually forced to slow as it approaches the checkpoint. This isn't like Checkpoint Charlie in the Berlin Wall; the exigencies of California's freeway traffic wouldn't tolerate a full stop and a careful examination of papers. The San

Clemente checkpoint is little more than a stop sign on a pedestal between the two lanes. A uniformed Border Patrol agent in his straight-brimmed Smokey the Bear hat stands behind the stop sign and watches vehicles. Same as any attentive border guard anywhere, he's interested in one thing—eye contact and a guilty conscience. Meet his gaze and he'll likely wave you through. Refuse to make eye contact, or look at him a bit too eagerly, as though you're trying to prove what an agreeable, upstanding citizen you are, and he'll wave you over to secondary inspection for a closer look.

Benny passed the eye contact test without a pause. I was next in line. I didn't even rate a second glance. The joys of a bulletproof conscience. Benny's van was fifty yards ahead and accelerating into the night by the time I passed the checkpoint. The TII climbed sedately through the gears, but I was making up ground on the van just the same.

"Stay put another few minutes back there, mate," Benny called to Volker. "Sometimes those bloody bastards keep another copper in a car up the road, just to play with your mind. A few hundred yards up the road should do it."

Right you are, Benny. Just as soon as I can.

While Volker kept his head down, I passed the van and ranged ahead into the night, becoming just another anonymous pair of red taillights on the freeway.

"Okay, mate. That should do 'er," Benny said after a while.

Scrabbling sounds came from the radio speaker as Volker emerged from his hiding place.

"You did that very well," Volker said.

I nearly jumped out of my skin. The clarity of the transmission was such that Volker could have been in the car with me.

"Lots of practice, mate. That and the fact that those two-legged bastards look at the wheelchair card in the windshield and think a cripple isn't good for anything but the dole."

There was enough bitterness in Benny's voice to be quite convincing. Not surprising. He was telling the truth.

"Is that why you became a smuggler?"

Volker's voice set the two halves of my mind at war with each other. One half insisted that anything so warm, so mellifluous, so goddam *charming* as that voice couldn't belong to a man without real emotions, a stone killer. The other half of my mind screamed back that some very beautiful things were also very deadly—things like ceremonial swords, presentation pistols and Volker.

"Bloody right," Benny said. "Up theirs all the way to Adam's own apple. Besides, the pay is better than I'd get making bleeding brooms or selling bleeding light bulbs over the bleeding phone."

Volker's warm laugh made the skin on my neck ripple even as I fought against the impulse to laugh with him.

"You are very wise, my friend. An injury is the same as any other aspect of a man; it can be used to make him weak or it can be used to make him strong. Each man makes his own choice."

There was silence, then Benny said, "If you don't mind me saying so, mate, you're not like the lot I'm used to hauling. Seems like a bloke with your style could go first-class, and bugger the limp."

"Thus speaks a man with no legs." Volker laughed softly. "The world sees only the limp, my friend, not the good leg. Each time El Cojo moves, he must prove his worth all over again."

Benny laughed, too. It wasn't a pleasant sound.

"Yeah, well, you know what they say, mate. Life's a bitch and then you die."

Volker's laughter expanded, filling the night with warmth and color. I prayed that Benny had listened to me when I talked about Volker's lethal charm.

There was silence for a few minutes, than someone yawned.

"Say, mate, you never got around to telling me where we're going."

"That is correct."

"Well, it's going to make it bloody hard for me to take you there."

"When the time comes, you will receive instructions."

"What's the big—"

"Until then, please be quiet," Volker interrupted. "I have much about which to think."

"But—"

"Please, my friend," Volker interrupted again. "No more talking."

"Whatever you say, mate. Mum's the word, just so I get my pay and my pistol back on the other end."

Volker's request for silence had been so gently spoken that had

Benny not reminded me—and himself—of the true situation, it would have been easy to believe they were just two men temporarily bound together by a common destination and making polite conversation from time to time.

But conversation time had just ended. My hanging around wouldn't help either one of us now. I knew all I was going to about Benny's situation. I pulled over into the number one lane right on somebody's bumper and flicked the high beams up and down twice. It's a common highway signal that translates as *Get your slow ass out of the fast lane. Please.*

It can also mean *Message received.*

The car in front of me pulled over into the number two lane. The TII sped past, heading up the freeway at eighty. Like Volker, I had some thinking to do.

Somehow, between here and Santa Ana, I had to figure out a way of nailing Volker that didn't get Benny killed.

27

Although Ernie Estrella's small ranch fell within the moon-shadow of the Center for the Performing Arts, Rickie Hernández' uncle was no part of the center's high-tech polished red granite arches. Ernie Estrella was a loner and a gallero, a throwback to Californio days, when the closest law was God and He could be bought off with a few laps around a rosary.

Estrella's house was a one-story bungalow with a slightly sloping roof and a spacious screened front porch whose design predated electric fans and air-conditioning. Behind the house were several unpainted outbuildings—a barn and machine sheds—remnants of Santa Ana's agricultural salad days. The ranchito itself was just off one of the old-time country roads that had metamorphosed into an urban thoroughfare. On either side of the wide road Estrella's row crops grew; on all sides of the ranchito were condos, industrial parks and multistory corporate headquarters.

When I drove up the rutted dirt farm road and parked in the driveway, Estrella walked into the glare of the headlights and stood quietly, letting me give him a good once-over. He was an unshaven

Chicano with the watery eyes and stooped posture of a man who had spent too long squinting against the sun while holding the working end of a short-handled hoe. He wore baggy trousers and a heavy wool jacket. His feet were covered with bedroom slippers so floppy that he had to shuffle to keep them on his feet.

He made no objection when I took a fast reconnoiter of the house. The place was like its tenant—well past middle age, rumpled around the edges and empty of secrets.

"Is there some place to hide the car?" I asked when Estrella and I were back outside.

He looked around the farmyard. "Ain't nothing in the shed there," he said, nodding toward a lean-to that was attached to the hip-roofed barn. "Just go around behind and park it. Nobody can see from out here."

When I got back from moving the TII, Estrella was standing exactly where I had left him. Beyond his house and crops, rising out of the plowed fields like a floodlit mirage, was the Center for the Performing Arts. A thousand yards and damn near as many years away.

A cock crowed from one of the farm buildings, calling to the dawn that waited somewhere beyond the black curve of the earth.

"Where do you keep the pollos?"

"The cocks?"

"No, the mojados."

"Oh. Them." He looked toward the barn.

"Show me."

I let him go first into the barn. He flipped a light switch just inside the doorway. I looked over his shoulder. The interior illumination had an odd pattern, creating a harsh light in the center and dense blackness everywhere else. It was obvious that the lights had been put in well after the barn had been built, probably about the same time that the inside of the barn had been gutted, leaving an open area surrounded by makeshift bleachers. The roughly circular floor of the arena—for that was what the barn had become—was surrounded by a knee-high wall of boards topped by two feet of chicken wire. The floor of the arena was hard-packed dirt mottled by dark stains. The place smelled of chicken shit and blood.

There's no fat lady to sing the finale of a cockfight. It doesn't end until at least one of the contestants bleeds to death for the gratification of the hard-betting crowd.

"What else is in here?" I asked.

Estrella shuffled across the empty ring, found another light switch and turned it on, revealing that one side of the barn was lined with a double rank of twelve cages, each the size of Kwame's kennel and carpeted with fresh, bright straw. There was just enough room between the barn wall and the back of the cages for a man to walk. Although the contents of the cages represented a lot of money, the doors were secured by no more than a slender wooden peg. Only an idiot would try to handle a fighting cock that wasn't his.

And that was what each cage held—a thigh-high, muscular rooster that had been born, bred and trained to wear four-inch razor-steel spurs over his own natural leg armament, the better to spread his opponent's guts over the arena's hard-packed dirt floor. The cocks were without their man-made scimitars at the moment, but the ones nature had provided were tough and sharp enough to rip through a man's flesh all the way to the bone.

The brightly colored roosters stirred and stared balefully through their wire cages, blinded by the sudden arrival of light. One of the roosters recovered very quickly. He was in the cage closest to the front door of the barn. When he stood up and shook out his feathers, he looked huge. As we walked closer he paced his cage with long-legged strides. He was the color of garnets or of oxygen-depleted blood, and his feathers glistened sleekly with each motion he made. He flexed his neck ruff into fullness and glared at us before he resumed pacing, moving as though he walked on steel springs, watching us with eyes as black as Apache tears.

"*Buenos días, Rápido,*" Estrella cooed, walking toward the front door of the barn. He knelt by the cage. "*¿Cómo estás?*"

The rooster flexed his whole body as he turned his head from side to side, looking for the feathered opponent he had been born and raised to kill. There was nothing for the bird to see. The cages were blind on all sides but the front, to prevent the cocks from working themselves into a frenzy over neighbors who could not be reached.

"Rápido is the champion of Delhi," Estrella murmured. "Never defeated, never cut. Thirty-four fights. One more and he can retire and make little hens happy at ten dollars a throw. Half the mojados in Southern California have a hen they want him to breed."

"If he doesn't end up as one more stain on the arena floor at the end of his thirty-fifth fight."

Estrella looked startled, as though the thought had never occurred to him.

"Where do you put the mojados?" I asked.

"In there." He gestured toward the ring. "They get one call to their people, tell them how much money to bring. When César gets paid, they leave, but not until then."

Just like a night in the Santa Ana PD's drunk tank.

"César won't be around anymore. He lost his last fight. Where does El Cojo keep his clothes?"

Estrella gave me a quick sideways look of surprise but asked no questions about César's last fight or anything else. He led me to a small anteroom that once had been a high-sided stock stall. The luggage in the enclosure wasn't Hartmann, but it was fine leather. Inside the garment bag hung two wool suits, their thin chalk stripes perfectly matched on pockets and seams. The labels were from a Los Angeles tailor who specialized in movie stars and Iranians. Everything Volker would need to complete his metamorphosis was waiting for him here—shoes, shirts, ties, even a heavy pair of gold cuff links made from Krugerrands.

It made me wonder how many investments like Pacific Basin Fund Volker might be "managing" in Johannesburg.

"Does he change in here?" I asked.

Estrella nodded.

"Then what does he do?"

"He goes to one of the big buildings."

"Which one?"

Estrella shrugged. "I don't ask. I don't care. It's better that way."

"Yeah, I can see how it would be. Are the barn lights on when you expect a load?"

"No."

"Then turn them off."

We went through the barn together, turning off lights. The rustling sounds from the cages diminished as the barn became dark once more.

"You have a car?" I asked.

"*Sí.*"

"Get in it and drive. Don't come back until daybreak. *¿Me entiende?*"

He didn't like it, but it was plenty clear. I watched while he climbed into an ancient Chevy truck and drove away, keeping his lights off until he turned onto the paved street. I went back to the TII and turned on the radio, listening to the scratchy, barely audible FM signal from XTRA in Tijuana. There was no point in making plans until I knew if Volker thought of Benny as a hostage or a chauffeur to be released or killed as soon as he turned off the engine in front of the barn.

If Volker intended to turn Benny loose, the only plan I needed was a way to catch Volker without killing him. If he killed Benny before I could stop him, there was no need for an elaborate plan, either; Volker would die the instant he walked through the barn door. That left the hostage possibility to plan for. I was praying that Volker, my dark reflection in life's mirror, would see Benny as a hostage. It was what I would do in Volker's shoes, not knowing for sure what was happening, but sensing it all coming apart around me. A hostage could be very handy for times like that.

So I sat in the TII and listened to old songs Jake had loved, and I tried not to think of how a reflection in a mirror is not the same as reality.

The stars behind Modjeska Peak had just begun to fade beneath the onset of dawn when I heard the first faint scratching of a transmitter riding the edge of a blast from the past.

". . . here and then take a left to the . . ."

Volker's supple voice sounded as though he were issuing instructions from the bottom of a well.

"What's the address, mate? Just give me the bleeding address."

Benny's tone was flat, almost bored. He was still trying to give me the edge, in case I was nearby and needed it.

"In a moment," said Volker, his tone just as calm but far more resonant.

Their voices quickly became clearer. I hesitated, then punched the number Innes had given me into the cellular phone. A man answered instantly. In the background a woman asked a question. It sounded like Fiora.

"Meet me under the firebird in twenty minutes."

Before he could say anything, I pulled the plug. Volker's voice drifted out of the radio toward me.

"Turn to the right here and then drive straight ahead until I tell you to turn again."

Memories turned queasily in my brain. Pain is the best teacher, and the last time I'd been close to Volker, I'd learned things about pain I would have preferred not to know. Ever. His voice had been the same that night with me as it was now with Benny. Calm, solicitous, attentive, gentle. And then Volker had slammed the top of the packing crate down on my hands, punching nails through flesh and bone, pinning me in place.

I grabbed the shotgun out of the backseat and stuffed a handful of shells into the pocket of my vest. The Detonics, loaded with Benny's untraceable ball shot, was already in the holster in the small of my back. I jammed Jake's Model 1911 into my belt. With Volker there was no such thing as overkill.

The sky in the east became the iridescent rosy gray of a mourning dove's breast.

Across the open field a pair of headlights swept down the paved road. The profile was right for Benny's van. When the headlights were three blocks away, I went through the side door into the barn. It took me twenty seconds to get into place beside the front door and behind a head-high stack of bagged chicken feed. Less than a foot away from me, cages of fighting cocks were arrayed in a ragged line down the side of the barn. In the closest cage Rápido sensed my presence and stirred restively, expecting some action. He would have to wait his turn.

The barn wall was old, uninsulated and full of small cracks. One of them gave me a good view of the farmyard and the van rattling up the rutted driveway. I looked away from the headlights and racked a shell into the shotgun's chamber just as the first red light of dawn stained the eastern sky.

Morning, Jake. How'd you sleep? Have you seen Sharp yet? Say hello for me. If I had my way, I'd be sending an enemy to keep him company, just like they used to do a long, long time ago.

Inches away from my thigh, Rápido called to the dawn with a harsh, rising cry.

The van stopped two feet beyond the barn door, so close that I couldn't get a clear view of the action, much less a clean shot. The driver's door opened and something hit the ground, hard. I saw just enough to realize that it was Benny.

"Do not move while I climb out."

"Fuck you, Jack. I'd rather die out here than in there."

"But I won't kill you," Volker said calmly. "Not quite. I will simply take from you the ability to use your arms and your tongue and leave you to live the rest of your life as an agile brain trapped inside a dead man's body."

Gentle, melodic, paternal, Lucifer's angelic voice before the Fall. And after, too.

Don't move, Benny. Let me take care of it. God, let me.

"Now crawl into the barn. While you crawl, pray very hard that no one is waiting inside. No matter what happens to me, I will manage one shot. If you are lucky, you will die. If not . . ."

Benny was in no position to argue Volker's conclusion. Neither was I.

Watching Benny slither out of the surf as bright as a penny coming from a washing machine is one thing. Watching him drag himself across the ground toward the door of the barn under Volker's gun is quite another. I was hit by a wave of adrenaline that made time stop, sound stop, breathing stop, everything dead but my finger on the trigger . . . squeezing. Things got very far away for a few instants, so far away I didn't think I was going to come back in time.

All that stopped me from killing Volker was the dawn light shining on his gun. Its barrel was pointed at the back of Benny's head. Volker was very close to Benny, all but stepping on his legs. Volker couldn't miss at that range even if I blew him out of his shoes.

Unless you are very good or very lucky with a head shot, it takes an instant to die. That's long enough to pull a trigger. A sawed-off shotgun is the wrong weapon for finesse, and I wasn't feeling lucky. Besides, there was still time to do it another way.

Very carefully I eased off the shotgun's trigger. Down at the end of the row a cock called. He was answered by a ragged chorus from the other birds. Volker didn't even look up from his prisoner. He had been in the barn enough times to know what the roosters sounded like.

But had he ever seen them outside their cages?

I duck-walked through the darkness between the barn wall and the cages, reaching over from behind and pulling wooden pegs as I went. The sounds I made were covered by the increasing shrillness of the cocks. Dawn was seeping through the thin-walled barn, the birds were hungry, and a stranger was messing with their cages.

The door of the barn swung open. Volker ordered Benny inside. In the center of the row of cages, I crouched in darkness and checked the safety on the shotgun by touch. Still off. The old scars on my hands ached in the early morning cold and damp. I wondered how Volker's arm felt. I slid the shotgun between two cages and took aim once more. My finger curled on the trigger, waiting, waiting, waiting for the stupid cocks to realize they were free.

Just as Benny pulled himself through the door, Rápido stepped out of his cage, strutting his stuff, his feathers burning red-black in a shaft of dawn light. The cry that cock gave was as savage as anything I've ever heard.

The other roosters went berserk. They hit their cage doors clawing and screaming. Feathered shapes exploded out into the barn. Benny moved so fast I almost shot him by mistake. He levered up and around with one hand and flung a fistful of dirt into Volker's face with the other. An instant later Benny brought the edge of his hand against Volker's knee—or what would have been Volker's knee if he hadn't moved suddenly, protecting his eyes and keeping Benny in his sights at the same time. Benny's chop missed the hinge point of Volker's knee, but it landed midway up his thigh. The heavy blow staggered Volker. His pistol moved fractionally off target. Before he could regain his balance I was over the cages and had the barrel of the shotgun screwed underneath his chin.

"Hello, Volker."

He froze. He had already measured the angles, computed the velocities, added in the reflexes. He knew he was dead.

"Fiddler." Volker smiled. "Someday you will disappoint me."

28

"Don't bet your life on it." I eased the pistol from his fingers. "You all right, Benny?"

He grunted and rolled aside, uneasily watching the cocks' sudden, ferocious battles. "I'm fine," he said. "Don't dump the wanker on my account."

Volker and I looked at each other, ignoring the bursts of sound and fury as cocks fought throughout the barn, bloodlust burning in their black eyes. If the roosters had worn steel spurs, the fights would have been over in thirty seconds. Reduced to natural weapons, the cockfights were less bloody and far less lethal. Even so, losers were already bailing out into the darkness to hide and victors were screaming savagely to the other victors, their next opponents.

Still watching Volker, I handed his gun down to Benny. He took it with the same startling speed he had used when turning on Volker. With the quick, sure motions of a gunsmith, Benny checked the load in the chamber and the rounds in the clip. Volker's eyes narrowed with surprise and sudden respect.

"Yeah," I said. "You made the same mistake with Benny that peo make with you. You judged him by his legs."

Volker looked at me and smiled ruefully, as though my continue hostility saddened him.

"Facedown and spread 'em, Volker. Hands out where I can see them. Do it slow."

With a kind of ruined grace that made pity move in me despite everything, Volker complied, first kneeling stiffly and then lying down as though to embrace the hard dirt floor.

"Arms out all the way," I said curtly.

"You might as well ask me to fly. My right arm is quite dead. It is an old injury." He laughed quietly and looked toward me. "Self-inflicted, you might say."

"Shut up."

From the corner of my eye I saw Benny looking at me narrowly, wondering if I was fully in control. Volker didn't wonder. He knew. His low laughter was more savage than the triumphant screams of the last of the fighting cocks. I looked down the barrel of the shotgun at the dark head only a few feet away. Volker's dyed hair was the same color as the bloodstained dirt. The shotgun's muzzle fit very neatly against the occipital bone at the back of his head. The trigger was smooth and hard against my index finger.

After too long a time I bent down and frisked Volker with great care. He had a hideout gun in his belt and a knife positioned for a left-hand pull. His ID was as phony as the color of his hair, but far more carefully done. Keeping him pinned to the floor with the muzzle of the shotgun, I pulled a pair of handcuffs from the back pocket of my jeans and pushed the bracelets through the ratchets.

"Put your hands behind your back, wrists together."

Volker brought his left wrist behind his back and managed to jerk his body so that his right wrist inched closer to his legs. I couldn't bear watching and remembering the extraordinary grace of the gymnast Volker had once been. I shifted the gun and grabbed his right wrist, trying to turn the arm and fold it backward. The skin of his hand felt cool and dry. Volker clenched his teeth and moaned involuntarily when I tried to force the arm back past his hip. Beneath his rough ket the limb moved as a single piece, yet it was curiously resilient, though carved from balsa.

I wished to hell I could despise Volker. It would have allowed me to enjoy the situation more.

"Shit," I hissed, shifting the gun.

I grabbed Volker's left ankle and cuffed it to his left wrist. While I tested the bonds, Rápido screamed his final victory to the rising sun. He strutted in front of the cocks that were still caged, crowing and driving them into a frenzy. I hoped his bloodlust had been slaked, because if he came in our direction, I would have to shoot him.

"It would have been easier if you'd died the other time, Volker," I said, ratcheting down the bracelets a few more clicks. "You've caused me a lot of grief."

"I might say the same of you," Volker pointed out, his flexible voice containing both amusement and camaraderie. "I cannot say I am sorry for the inconvenience I have caused you. You know me well enough to realize that sorrow is not something I understand very well. Yet if it is any comfort, I honestly can say I never inflicted any pain on you or on Fiora unless it was necessary."

Hearing Volker say Fiora's name did nothing to improve my temper. "Tell it to Aaron Sharp when you meet him in hell."

"Sharp? Oh, the Customs agent I used to draw you down to Mexico."

Something about my expression must have changed, because Volker looked at me curiously.

"If you feel that way, why didn't you kill me a moment ago?"

"I'm not the guy calling the shots this time. If I were, it would have taken only one. What Fiora has in mind is more sophisticated."

"Fiora!"

I'd finally managed to surprise Volker. I took a certain mean satisfaction in it, the kind of pleasure a reflection might feel if it reached out and tweaked the guy on the other side of the mirror.

"Yeah. Fiora. You have a positive genius for getting between me and that woman, Volker. Someday it will get you killed. But not today."

The fountain beside the entrance of the Center for the Perform.
Arts made a pleasant rushing sound that was at odds with reali
which was neither pleasant nor quick-moving at the moment. Th
light behind the twin peaks of Saddleback gave the falconlike metal
sculpture in the arch of the music center a sanguine aura, suffusing
the bird shape with malevolence. The hue reminded me of the garnet-
colored cock that had finally fought as God had meant him to—at
dawn, unarmed, outside the bright lights and restraints of the cock-
fighting ring.

I envied Rápido at that moment as much as I've envied anything in a
long time.

Detonics in hand, I leaned against the van's front right fender. The
gun was pointed at a spot just to the left of the bridge of Volker's nose,
so he could look at the muzzle without straining. If the view bothered
him, he didn't show it. His expression was both serene and alert. He
stood quietly, one handcuff through the door handle and the other
around his left wrist. Except for the stiffness of his right knee, he
looked very much at ease. It irritated me.

"Who kneecapped you?" I asked.

"I injured my knee running cross-country in the dark after you
knifed me," Volker said matter-of-factly. "I had to stay in the brush
for several days in order to evade Aaron Sharp. Then I walked four
miles. By the time I got medical aid, irreversible damage had been
done to the knee."

Volker turned and looked at the polished granite gleaming redly in
the dawn. "I saw *West Side Story* here. The acoustics are better than in
the Chandler Pavilion." He laughed that magical laugh. "But then, I
am sure you know that already. You are a remarkable judge of pitch,
clarity and tone. Do your scarred hands prevent you from playing the
violin as well as you once did?"

"Belt up," Benny said from the driver's seat. "Fiddler doesn't want
to discuss acoustics with you."

Volker smiled. "Then why are we at the Center for the Performing
Arts?"

"So that he can turn you over to Fiora and go home and get some
sleep."

Volker's eyes flashed gas blue in the light as he turned and looked at

"Fiora is a woman of formidable passion. I doubt that she has given the circumstances of her twin's death."

"Don't worry," I said. "I'm the one she hasn't forgiven for Danny's death."

"Ah. Then I am a peace offering to your former wife and my former lover. . . ."

"Tell you what, Fiddler," Benny said casually, "I'll kill him for you. That way Fiora won't have to worry about the state of your soul, and you won't have broken your deal with the Fan-Belt Inspectors."

"Don't tempt me."

"It's an open-ended offer. This wanker's got too many lives. He makes me believe in wooden stakes and exorcism."

I smiled slightly, but without amusement. Volker's charm was a weapon. In another era he would have been a messiah. Or he would have been burned on a warlock's pyre.

"You're third in line," I said to Benny.

"Who is second?" Volker asked.

"Me."

His thin, dark eyebrows lifted. "Then who is first? Fiora?"

"A guy called Innes."

"Innes?" Volker said sharply. "Is that Michael Innes, FBI counterintelligence?"

"You've got good sources," I said.

"But of course. I am a Soviet intelligence officer. The counterintelligence division of your FBI has been after me since well before Danny's unfortunate death." Volker looked at me intently. "Recently I thought they were getting rather close, so I was forced to accelerate my plans for acquiring the Pacific Basin Fund."

"By killing Portman," Benny said without rancor. "How did you get the stuff into him, anyway?"

"Richard was certain he could handle Mia if the obese Mr. Portman would simply vanish," Volker murmured, obliquely agreeing with Benny even as he appeared to ignore him. "After Mr. Portman's timely death, all that remained was to remove Fiora from the fund. She would not sell and she proved far too intelligent to outmaneuver."

"So you decided to kill her," I said flatly.

"She left us no choice. We have spent years and millions of infiltrating the Fund. But there was no point in trying to kill her you were alive." Volker's tone was matter-of-fact, oddly soothing, he explained why three people had been slated for execution. "No matter how accidental her death was made to appear, you would not have buried her and walked away. Eventually you would have unraveled the trail back to the Fund."

The fingers of my left hand had begun to ache from gripping the Detonics. My reasons for sparing Volker no longer seemed persuasive. I wanted very badly to remove him from my life.

And then I saw Volker watching me with his vivid blue eyes and knew he was hoping for just that response from me. He knew that talking casually about Fiora's death would move me more deeply than anything else he could do to me.

"Why didn't you just send your sniper north?" I asked, easing my grip on the Detonics.

"You were being watched by the FBI. Ah, you did not know that, did you?" Volker smiled gently, as though he had just given me a gift—or received one from me.

Suddenly a car came racing up the Center's front drive. I didn't have to turn around to know who it was; the sound of Fiora's BMW 635 in full cry is distinctive. I waited to hear other cars. Only the noise of the BMW coming to a hot-tire stop penetrated the fountain's idiot pleasantries.

A car door slammed and Fiora came toward us, moving fast. She was dressed in black 501 Levi's, a black turtleneck and a black down vest. The pockets of the vest bulged with her fists. I didn't have to ask how she had slept; the somber clothing accentuated the dark circles under her eyes.

Her glance went over me like hands, taking my temperature, looking for signs of new damage, finding it.

She turned and looked at Volker.

"Where's Innes?" I asked.

"He's a cautious driver," she said, not looking away from Volker.

"Hello, Fiora," said Volker. "You are still beautiful. Are you also still blaming Fiddler for being a better man than your twin brother?"

The words were so gently spoken and so shrewdly cruel, I could

believe what I had heard. Fiora had no such trouble. She
a closer to Volker as he calmly continued his onslaught on her
e of mind.

It was not Fiddler's fault that Danny died," Volker murmured. "It
as not even mine. It was yours. Danny died because you were so
much better than he could ever be, and he knew it. You knew it, too,
and you hated it."

Volker's flexible voice mourned over past hatreds and mistakes like
a cello superbly played, softly, and his audience leaned closer in order
to hear each beautiful, rending note, ignoring the noise of cars driving
closer, stopping.

"Sometimes you even hated Fiddler, did you not? How foolish for
such an intelligent woman. It was yourself whom you should have
hated. You were far more cruel to your twin than a bullet. You brought
Danny down by millimeters, the death of ten thousand loving cuts,
draining his self-confidence away drop by drop. Such a sweet child to
die so slowly."

Fiora jerked forward, rage and grief burning in her eyes as she
struggled to free her hands from the vest's deep pockets. I saw a flash
of black metal and understood too late.

"Fiora! *No!*"

I lunged forward, but Volker's reflexes had always been better than
mine. For an instant Fiora had been within Volker's reach. That was
all he needed, all he had ever needed. His injured arm swept out in a
low arc, scooping Fiora close. His good left hand closed around her
right wrist. She made a high sound of pain and fury, but he was
stronger than she was, quicker, far more cruel. The Beretta was
wrenched from her grasp and slammed up against her temple.
Stunned, she stopped fighting. He held her hard against his chest with
his right arm, using her as a shield against my gun. The Beretta's
muzzle was jammed beneath her chin.

In Volker's injuries, as in his emotions, the reality was far different
from the expectations he aroused in the people around him. If
Volker's arm was badly crippled, I was Danny Flynn.

"No one move or Fiora dies," Volker said. "I have excellent periph-
eral vision. For Fiora's sake, I hope that your deceptively crippled
friend believes me."

Volker didn't raise his voice. He didn't have to. Command presence isn't a matter of yelling.

Benny froze. Had he been as agile as a cat, he still would have been helpless. The angles were all wrong—too much metal and glass between him and his target.

It was little better for me. Volker had made of Fiora a shield of living flesh and blood. He was too large to conceal himself entirely behind her, but everything vital was hidden.

"Put your pistol on the pavement, Fiddler."

I looked down the barrel of the Detonics and saw only Fiora's honey-blond hair. Then she shook her head as though coming out of a daze and I saw Volker's right eye. I moved the muzzle of the Detonics slightly.

He measured the angle of the shot. "Even if you kill me, she will die," he said calmly.

I shook my head slowly. "Your brain will be jelly before your trigger finger can twitch."

"Perhaps. Perhaps not. You love her too much to risk that."

"You're behind the times. I don't have a damn thing to lose. Fiora turned me over to the FBI just like she did you. She doesn't love me, Volker."

Fiora made a broken sound that I ignored. I didn't want to hear her message any more than I wanted to hear the message from my memory, the screaming reminder that my pistol was loaded with ball slugs that made the Detonics slightly less accurate than a slingshot. I didn't have time for doubts. Not now. Not with Volker's gas-blue eyes burning, measuring the steadiness of my hand and my intention.

More cars screeched to a halt, but no one came running up. I didn't need to turn around to know that Innes and his men had taken up firing stances behind their car doors.

"FBI! Drop your guns!"

The words meant no more to me than the babble of water.

"Three seconds," I said to Volker. "One."

Motionless, he watched me.

"Two."

"But you love her!"

"Th—"

With feline quickness, Volker bent and skidded the Beretta across the pavement toward me, beyond Fiora's reach. Then he straightened, ran his fingertips over the bruise the gun had left on her temple and smiled with something close to sadness as he slowly released her.

"If you really wanted to kill me, you should not have wasted time removing the gun from your pocket," Volker said gently. "Men have died for less. Even worse, they have lived."

Fiora shook her head slowly, denying things she did not yet even understand.

Volker touched a flying strand of her hair before he dropped his hand and looked up at me. "We are more alike than we were the last time we met."

And he smiled.

EPILOGUE

The wind off the desert was cool and dry. It stirred the delicate leaves of the pepper trees lining the street in front of the First Pentecostal Church of Holtville. Beneath the trees Aaron Sharp's funeral cortege formed. The line was a mixture of bobtail Mexican diesels, a Ford Ranchero, three Chevrolet pickups and a Mercedes-Benz. The Mercedes had belonged to an unlucky dope smuggler and was now being driven by the lucky regional commissioner of Customs.

At the rear of the procession was a dark blue Shelby Cobra. I was in the rear because I wanted to be. I was alone in the Cobra for the same reason.

About halfway out of town another car fell in behind me. It was a government-style sedan that looked vaguely familiar. As the cortege turned a corner, I checked in the rearview mirror and saw a cellular telephone antenna in the middle of the sedan's trunk deck. It reminded me of another sedan and another cellular phone and the man who had watched me from the highway through powerful binoculars.

The FBI was watching you. Ah, you didn't know that, did you?
I knew it now.

Seems like I learn a lot of things that way. Too damn late.

There were three men in the car. When the cortege halted inside the cemetery, I got a good view of the driver behind me. He looked very much like the man who had watched the cottage while I dug a hole deep enough for a grave. Next to the driver sat Supervisory Special FBI Agent Michael Innes. I couldn't see the agent in back until we all got out and began walking toward the grave site on the other side of a small rise.

Heat and cold and blowing sand raise hell with headstones in the desert, but there hadn't been enough time yet for the stone on Sharp's grave to weather into round-edged history. The polished black granite was from a quarry in Montana not far from my childhood home. Below Aaron Sharp's name and the dates of his birth and his death were three words: *Feo, Fuerte y Formal.* The epitaph was older than the cemetery, older than the town, older than the West that Sharp had been born too late to tame.

"You bought the headstone. What do the words mean?" Innes asked.

I turned to face him, wondering what else he knew about the private things in my life. And why he knew them.

Just beyond Innes stood the other two agents. One of them was definitely the man who had watched me from the highway. The other was also familiar. I had seen him once before, in Dana Lighter's office, telling Dana that the FBI wasn't going to move their crime lab to Mexico for the sake of a dead Customs agent.

"It translates as ugly, strong and dignified," I said.

"Two out of three isn't bad."

I didn't ask which two. There were other questions to be answered, more urgent ones. "Does the man in the dark glasses belong to you?"

Innes nodded.

"Is he the one who pimped Sharp into going south on the midnight raid that got him killed?"

There was a long silence.

"You were setting fires everywhere you could," I said, "from the obvious bug in Volker's Aztlán office to whispering in Sharp's ear about the one that got away. Then, after Sharp bought it, you left a message on my phone."

Silently Innes watched while the pallbearers slowly approached the open grave thirty feet down the rise. I watched as well. Matt Suarez walked at the head of the coffin. He moved easily, showing no sign of injury.

A fine-boned Mexicana in a black shawl and black dress moved slowly behind the pallbearers. Her face was lined by grief and yet oddly serene. She looked often toward Matt Suarez. Perhaps she was taking comfort in watching her tall son, or perhaps she simply was relieved that she no longer had to lie awake nights waiting to find out if the man she loved had been killed.

Was that how Fiora would feel?

"Volker was beyond FBI jurisdiction in Mexico," Innes said finally.

"Tell it to the judge."

"I did. But by the time we got our hands on Portman's body, the KGB's trademark heart attack drug had dissipated. There was no case."

Machinery whined softly as the casket was lowered into the grave.

"What about Richard Toye?" I asked. "Busting his candy ass shouldn't have been a problem for you."

"There's no law against ambition, greed or stupidity," Innes said. "Toye's cleaner than you, so far as the statutes are concerned."

Innes' voice was like his eyes, like his clothes, like his coloring. Utterly neutral, utterly deceptive. He had emotions, but he had them on a very short leash.

"Is that why you were watching me?" I asked. "You thought I was dirty?"

"We were watching Ms. Flynn. We knew that Volker would have to take her out if he wanted to control the Pacific Basin Fund. When she moved in with you, we watched you as well." Innes looked at the crowd gathered around the grave. "Where is she?"

"Wherever I'm not."

He looked sideways at me. "Your choice, not hers."

I'm not as good as Innes at concealing. He saw my surprise.

"Haven't you figured it out yet?" he asked. "She drove at ninety miles an hour through six red lights and God knows how many stop signs for the express purpose of killing Volker. When I asked her why, she said, 'Not for the past. For the future.' " Innes turned and looked at me with eyes the color of desert rain. "An unusual woman, your former wife."

Without waiting for an answer, he turned and walked down to the people gathered around the minister, pausing only long enough to gather a handful of dirt from the graveside mound. The other two agents followed him, leaving me alone on the small rise.

Mrs. Suarez stepped up to the grave. Her graying hair was nearly hidden beneath the shawl, just as her fine-boned, slender body was nearly hidden beneath black mourning clothes. She stood there for a moment, holding on to the tall son who was an echo of the lean, tough man she had loved and lost.

I've been to too many funerals. I should be used to them. I'm not. Each time the ritual catches me as though I've never before seen the tears or heard the words of people caught between the past they shared with the dead and the future they would not be able to share.

Ashes to ashes, dust to dust.

A woman's hand opens, letting dry earth rain down onto varnished pine.

Whosoever believeth in me . . .

That's always the problem, isn't it? What to believe.

Jake had believed in the next load. Sharp had believed in a shooter's moon. Fiora had believed that Volker would kill me. Volker had believed that I was becoming more like him. They had all been right, and they had all been wrong.

And me?

I believe that yesterday always comes, bringing with it the wreckage of the past, leaving you standing by an open grave with a fistful of dirt and a gutful of regrets, waiting for tomorrow and another chance. □